LOLA CARLYLE's 12-STEP ROMANCE

LOLA CARLYLE'S 12-STEP ROMANCE

Danielle Younge-Ullman

Entangled Publishing, LLC
2614 South Timberline Road
Suite 109
Fort Collins, CO 80525

Entangled Teen is an imprint of Entangled Publishing, LLC.

Visit our website at www.entangledpublishing.com.

Edited by Stacy Abrams
Cover design by Alexandra Shostak
Cover Photograph (c) Aleshyn Andrei/Shutterstock
Interior design by Jeremy Howland

Print ISBN 978-1-62266-785-7
Ebook ISBN 978-1-63375-001-2

Manufactured in the United States of America

First Edition May 2015

10 9 8 7 6 5 4 3 2 1

This book is dedicated to my grandmother, Edna Saville, aka Fast Eddy. She will be ninety-nine fabulous years old when this book comes out, and still ready to dance, swim, roll around on the floor with my kids, enjoy a glass of champagne, and deliver a few zingers while she's at it. There is more than a little bit of Eddy in Lola, and vice versa. I love her madly.

CHAPTER ONE

"You could bounce a quarter off my butt cheeks."

Crap. Sydney. I shouldn't have picked up.

"I'm serious," Sydney continues. "The combo of yoga and surfing—it's like magic. Not to mention, I have a real tan. I've never looked hotter."

"If you do say so yourself," I mutter in a low voice, so as not to disturb my mother or the zillions of tiny, disgusting fish currently nibbling on the dead skin of her feet.

"Yes, I do say so. There's nothing wrong with a healthy self-esteem, Lola. That's something else I've learned."

Right. As if Sydney has ever been lacking in self-esteem. Modesty, yes, self-*awareness*, maybe, but self-esteem, no.

"Also, two words: *spa food*," she says, and rambles on about vegan pizza, free-range carrots, yada yada, happily oblivious of my hurl-worthy situation and deliberately ignoring the fact that we haven't spoken for two months.

"Anyway, this is way less boring than spending the summer in L.A.," she says.

"And the city is a safer, saner place."

"Ohhh, bitchy. It's okay, I know you're just jealous. But with a few minor adjustments to your daily routine and some work on your parentals, you, too, could find yourself booked on this fabulous vacation."

"Vacation, huh? Love the euphemism."

"No, listen, rehab is the new 'vacation.' Everyone's going these days."

"Not if they have no addictions."

"Sure they do. People go for just about anything. Gambling, internet addiction, eating disorders, cutting, prescription drugs. They go to convince their spouses they'll stop boning other people—the list goes on. For you, you'd just need to go to some clubs, come home stinking of booze and pot, and/or get photographed wearing no underwear…"

"That is an officially terrible idea, Syd."

"But your mom would die if you did that. She'd pack you off in two seconds."

"I don't think so." I glance over at Mom, who is covered in mud up to her neck, while her feet sit in the mini fish tank. I'm here to protect her from the (supposed) hordes of paparazzi that might barge past reception and up the celeb elevator for the sole purpose of photographing her.

"Or ask your dad. Doesn't he say yes to everything?"

"He's not involved enough to be saying yes much." I lower my voice further as a precaution, even though Mom's wearing organic beeswax earplugs.

"Don't be such a baby. He buys you some great stuff and he doesn't cramp your style. He lets you be yourself."

He certainly does.

"So?"

"Sure," I say, not even trying to sound like I mean it, then breathe through my mouth while I switch out the cucumber slices on Mom's eyes. "When do we get to the part where you apologize for stealing my boyfriend?"

"Oh Lola, you have to get over that. I mean, I *told* you I was going to steal him. And I didn't *keep* him. I dumped him after two days, practically on your behalf."

"On my behalf?"

"I have no guilt about it. I did you a favor."

I nearly choke at this, and Mom makes a hushing sound, somehow without moving her face, which is smothered in a mask that is supposed to contain (I wish I were kidding) *real gold*.

"A favor, huh?" I say to Sydney.

"I'm serious. How much do you want a guy if he's so easily stolen? It was a test of character, and he failed. And come on, was he not the worst kisser?"

Up floats the unpleasant memory of Trevor's limp, over-moist smooches, and despite my best efforts to stay mad, a bubble of laughter escapes from me.

"Besides, if he'd been loyal, you'd have been stuck with him and his smooshy kisses. You'd have stayed with him out of pity, with the exact thing you wanted to dump him for—the bad kissing—simultaneously being the reason you felt you had to stay."

"That makes no sense."

"Don't tell *me*."

"But…" I trail off because in a twisted sort of way, she's right.

"Whereas my approach is much more direct. I told him. I said, 'Trevor, you can't kiss worth shit. You're like a dying frog.'"

"You did not!"

"I did. And again? A favor. I even tried to give him some pointers, like how to firm his lips up a bit and how *licking them first* is not working."

"Oh God."

"I *know*. Also, I told him not to lunge in so fast," she adds.

"Oh, I know! It's like you're standing there innocently and then all of a sudden he, like, lands on your face."

"Like a big, juicy bug splatting on your windshield on the highway!"

"*Eeeewwww!*"

"*Lola!*" It's Mom, pulling out an earplug and risking a crack in the gold by speaking.

"Oops. Hang on," I say to Sydney and put my hand over the phone. "I'll be off soon, Mom."

"Have some respect," she says, like it's a funeral instead of a pedicure.

"I just need a minute."

"Fine, go outside then, and send the girl—I need her anyway. But watch the door for me, and don't let anyone else in."

"Sure. But if the paparazzi get up here, I think they'll storm Anne Hathaway's room first," I say, and then head to the hallway, gesture to the tiny aesthetician hovering there, and flop down on a hemp cushioned bamboo bench.

I'm all for a bit of personal upkeep, but my mother always goes for the most bizarre treatments—cactus massages, masks with bird droppings or snail slime, ass facials—the list is mortifying, as is the job of accompanying her.

"Sorry, Syd," I say. "Mother-Daughter Day."

"Oh joy."

"Yeah. Quality time." I roll my eyes. "Now, where were we?"

"Trevor's lips as squished bug."

I snort.

"So I offered him some tutorials, but seeing as I'd just dumped him and wounded his ego, he turned me down. I was like, 'Dude, it's not like I said you have a small penis. This is fixable.' But he stomped off in a total huff. Men are such wusses. Wait. He doesn't, does he?"

"He doesn't what?"

"Have a small—"

"Oh! No. I mean, I don't know because I didn't— Oh my God." I look up and down the cork-floored, over-scented hallway and hiss, "I am not talking to you about this."

"Ah," Sydney intones, "because we must not discuss the Private Details of the Sacred Pen—"

"Stop. You're just trying to distract me and make me forget I'm mad."

Sydney sighs. "Okay, Lo, how about this: I promise I won't do it again. Even if you pick the worst possible guy."

"What about the best possible guy?"

"That assumes you know the difference."

"This from the girl who made out with Willie the War-bler?"

Sydney makes a gurgling, gagging kind of sound. "All right. I promise I won't hook up with any more boyfriends of yours, even if it's for your own good. Are we over it?"

"Can I have your Louboutin clutch?"

"Which one?"

"The hot pink."

"Come on, you could totally get your dad to buy you that."

Right. Mom deposits a portion of the child support directly to my bank account, and if you expand your definition of "truth" just a little, then Dad *does* buy me a lot of stuff.

"That's not the point, Sydney. I want *you* to give me something—to make up for my pain and suffering, and as a future deterrent."

"You drive a hard bargain. I haven't even been seen with that bag. But *then* you'll be over it?"

"Think so."

"Jeez, you should've just told me that in the first place. I'd have bought you a bag before I stole him and we could've saved ourselves all this drama. Done."

"Fine. Okay." Bag for boyfriend. More than fair, consid-ering the boyfriend in question, considering she probably did save me weeks of pity-dating before I could bring my-self to break up with him, and considering she never apolo-gizes for anything, ever.

"So, when you get here—"

"Oh, now I'm coming?"

"Just make sure you don't tell them you know me. I think they frown on friends being in rehab together, and it might cause them to suspect you're not legit. We'll just pretend to have an instant bond when we meet. And then you can unplug, get fit, learn to surf, detox on all levels. I mean, you should see my skin!"

I laugh and shake my head. I've missed her. Even living in L.A., I don't know anyone so entertaining, so hilarious, so full of every kind of trouble. I don't know anyone who relishes her own shallowness, *nourishes* her own shallowness, quite like Sydney. Nothing can quell Sydney or bring her down.

Although, given that she's in rehab, perhaps something *has* brought her down...

"Seriously, you doing all right?" I ask.

"Me? Please, I'm fine," she says. "I still haven't gotten to the main reason I called. You haven't heard the best part."

"Mm."

"Aren't you going to ask me the best part?"

"Nah." She'll tell me anyway.

"You'll never guess who's here..."

"Probably not."

"Only your dad's protégé and your star crush, the smoking hot, gorgeous cutie pie... *Wade Miller*."

My heart lurches and I'm breathless, and then, as I get past hearing the name and what she's saying sinks in, I feel sick and a little bit panicked.

"No," I say, "not Wade."

"Yes, Wade."

"Someone else with a similar name, maybe."

"Wade Miller, star of *Drift*. That's what I overheard. He just checked in."

"Did you… Is he okay? Does it sound serious? Sydney, Wade is— Well, first of all let me remind you he is not a star crush. I *know* him. But that's the thing: Wade is sweet. And grounded. This should not be happening."

"*Was* sweet. *Was* grounded. You haven't seen him in ages—how do you know? Mind you, he could be here for Snapchat addiction or something."

"But what did they say he was—"

"Oh, sorry Lo, I have to go."

"But—"

"Think about my idea," she says, suddenly whispering. "Imagine, you'd be here together for weeks, you and Wade. You'd essentially be spending your summer with him. And there's me, of course. I'm lots of fun."

"But Sydney—"

"I'll call you tomorrow."

Without even saying good-bye, she's gone, leaving me sitting in the spa hallway, staring at my phone, looking for answers it can't give me.

Wade Miller, rehab.
    Wade Miller, drugs.
Wade Miller, trouble.

While watching Mom try on dresses at every store in the Grove, I find a lot about Wade via Google. Most of it's rumor, none of it confirms he's at Sunrise Rehabilitation Center, and there's nothing recent from his PR team. Not that I don't trust Sydney, but I don't 100 percent trust her. Or, I do trust her—but what I trust her for is to look out for number one—ie, herself. Which means I have to do the same.

Not that I am actually considering faking my way into rehab.

Although…I come across Sunrise in my Googling too, and it does look more like a spa than anything else, and people do come out of rehab looking refreshed and happy and like all their problems have been solved.

As the search goes on, I find some photos where, admittedly, Wade looks drunk, and some where he has that pale, sweaty, possibly high look. But getting drunk or high a couple of times isn't exactly a big deal, in Hollywood or anywhere else for that matter, and it doesn't mean he's addicted to anything.

He can't be.

And it isn't because I've had a thing for him since I was thirteen and saw him standing outside his trailer on the set of one of my dad's films—a zombie musical—or because we got to be really good friends and he became my first and only (unconfessed and unrequited) love. I mean, I realize no one's perfect.

It's because Wade is better than that. He wasn't some entitled asshole and he wasn't desperately insecure either; he was a hardworking guy, a nice guy, a good person, and talented.

And because my dad saw something in him and took a big chance casting him, and when it looked like he was about to crash and burn out of pure lack of experience, I helped him. Rescued him, sort of. When my dad found out who was responsible for the major turnaround, he was so proud of me, and working on that film was the best time ever. The happiest time. The last time Dad was proud of me, I think. Definitely the last time I was happy.

So Wade can't be an addict because he was at the center of all of that, and his skyrocketing career has been the only good thing salvaged from it.

He can't be an addict because, aside from my having a secret-but-furious crush on him, he was my friend—a real one—in a place where a lot of the friends aren't real.

And he can't be an addict because if Hollywood has destroyed him, I am more than partially responsible. I am in the direct line of responsibility.

Not that I could do anything about it.

Even if I did somehow get into Sunrise…

Chapter Two

"Shall we grab some dinner — me, you, and your phone?" Mom says once she's done shopping. "Sushi?"

"My phone is a vegetarian," I say, and she rolls her eyes. "Besides, I thought we were going to shop for me."

"You? Oh honey, I'm exhausted."

"Me, too," I say, knowing better than to pick fights with her but unable to help myself this time. I'm upset — upset about Wade, and upset because all this thinking about Wade has made me think about all the other stuff, including how shitty these mother-daughter days really are. "I'm also exhausted. But in my case it's not from spa treatments or choosing new clothes, it's from boredom and disappointment."

Mom swivels, making sure no one is watching or listening to us, her strawberry-blond hair lifting and settling so perfectly she could be in a shampoo commercial. Her smile stays in place as she hisses, "You're exhausted from staring into a small rectangular screen all day. And don't even talk to me about disappointment. For goodness' sake, you're one of the most fortunate —"

"Blah, blah, blah…" I say, starting to walk away from her.

She catches up, heels clicking along beside me.

"We shopped for me because I have events to attend, multiple events. And everywhere I go I have to be ready to get photographed."

She is right about that part. The crazed, tabloid-frenzied, paparazzi-induced hiding-in-the-house days that followed my parents' scandalous breakup are long over, but she still gets papped. They got some photos back then that were pretty bad, and Mom hasn't been the same since — it's hard to explain, but the attention was somehow both violating and the tiniest bit addictive.

Addictive and even comforting, because as a star of a not-critically-acclaimed, guilty-pleasure nighttime soap opera, she knows her job could disappear very easily. Years ago there was an Emmy, but she was younger then. Now she needs continual reassurance that she is still "someone," and paparazzi are good for that.

So, along with most of Hollywood, she hates them and yet dresses for them and acts as if they are lurking about somewhere at all times, which makes public outings and communications during public outings part of a giant performance. It's very meta.

"You, on the other hand," she continues, "have nothing to do but loaf around on the beach all summer. You don't even have to save for college."

"So maybe I need bathing suits," I say. "And loafing-around clothing. Maybe as my mother you might have noticed I've grown out of most of my sandals. Not to mention you stole my Ray-Bans."

"Those Ray-Bans make you look fat," she says.

"What?"

"It's true. They make your cheeks look puffy."

"And my ass, too, no doubt," I say, almost spitting out the words. "Sunglasses have a way of doing that."

"If your mother can't tell you the truth, who can?"

"The truth according to you is that I should be anorexic. Maybe we should all start doing coke for breakfast. Would that make you happy?"

"I just want you to realize that a healthy weight—"

"I *am* a healthy weight. I'm shorter than you and I have hips and boobs, which, in real life as opposed to television, look just fine. And so what if I were fat?"

"Then you'd have a very difficult future ahead of you," she says, with such a convincing worried-mama face that I almost believe her concern is real.

"Let's not pretend you give a crap about my future, Mom. You just don't want me to have a Kardashian ass."

"God, no," she says. "Certainly not unless you were taller."

"You are such a freak show."

"Stop it," she snaps. "Quit sniveling and go shop."

"Wow, this gets warmer and cozier by the minute," I say, taking long strides and making her hustle on those stilettos. "Girl time. Yay."

"You have five minutes," she says. "I'll wait here on the bench."

"What—you don't want to do fatness patrol on my choices?"

"Four minutes and thirty seconds…"

"Perfect," I say. She thinks the short time frame will deter me, but damn if I'm not going to get something out of this mother-daughter fiasco. I hold out my hand for her credit card. She passes it to me and then crosses her arms over her chest.

"That bench makes *you* look fat," I say, and witness her momentary look of panic before I storm away.

Ten minutes later, I return. In the bags I'm carrying are:

-Three bathing suits, one particularly awesome with bottoms that look like lace shorts

-An oversize tee with kittens on it (Mom is allergic)

-A pair of sequined leggings

-A pair of round-eyed Miu Miu sunglasses

-Two new pairs of Ray-Ban Wayfarers, the same kind I had before. From now on I'm calling them my "Ray-Ban Fat-Asses."

And I'm going to wear them a lot.

Mom stands up. "Happy now?" she says, and links her arm in mine like we weren't just ready to kill each other a few minutes ago.

"Ecstatic."

"Fabulous."

"I love these days we spend together," she says, and sort of leans into me like we're going to cuddle, and suddenly I *am* happy. For real. Because she's my mom and I love her and, okay, we're both a little bit crazy.

It's a wonder I'm *not* an addict, come to think of it.

That night I try texting Sydney, then calling her on the number she dialed me from, but she doesn't respond to the text and the phone goes through to the main voicemail for Sunrise. No chance I'm leaving her a message there.

I Google Wade again, this time under News, but there's still nothing.

As I think about this, not seeing anything posted about him being in rehab is worse than if it were all over the internet. Because if, say, he isn't an addict but just did something stupid and/or got into some trouble, his PR team might send him for a bit of rehab just to quell the concern and clean up his image. We love to forgive people who admit they've messed up and get help publicly. Rehab is a weird kind of substitute for church, or jail in these cases, from a public perspective—go in, suffer, repent, return forgiven.

Silence and secrecy on the part of Wade's people is worse. It could mean real trouble, not just mischief. It could mean he's a serious mess—bad enough that they think he's fragile and wouldn't be able to handle it if the news got out, bad enough that they need to cover it up lest it damage his career.

Either way, he's not on a good path, if it's true that he's at Sunrise.

I put a Google alert on his name, leave my phone beside the pillow, and lie down.

But I can't sleep, and soon I'm sitting back up, phone in hand, fingers hovering over the keypad, ready to call my dad. He'd know if there was anything going on. He's worked with Wade a couple of times since the zombie movie, and he's connected, and he would care. I know he would care.

He probably cares about Wade more than he does about me.

Which is why...he does not want to hear from me, especially at two thirty in the morning, and why I must not call or text him at two thirty in the morning—it would only confirm all his worst ideas about me.

Come to think of it, my dad would be the person most likely to believe I need to be in rehab, if I did it. He is one of the few people who've seen me drunk.

It wasn't a good night. And taking a limo up into the hills to stand stinking drunk at the base of Dad's driveway, then raging and crying into his security monitor, which I know records everything, wasn't very smart. It definitely wasn't the way to make up after the epic fight we'd had a few weeks before, as his terse email demonstrated the next day. That night is one of the reasons I don't drink much— mine are not inhibitions that should be let loose.

So Dad would probably be delighted and relieved if I checked into rehab. And then he'd be able to blame all our problems on my being an addict, like he blamed their marriage falling apart on my mom. He might even decide to speak to me.

Right.

God, I hope he deleted that video.

But it's no good thinking about any of that. Usually I don't, but this thing with Wade has me all messed up, and that makes me vulnerable to thinking about all the shit I can't do anything about and that I usually keep successfully at bay.

I put the phone back down and roll to look at the ceiling, where there are still glow-in-the-dark stars from when I was a kid. It's not that I'm one of those girls still living in my little-girl princess bedroom—we redecorated—it's just that I wanted to keep the stars. I'd have liked to keep a lot of things—my dreams, my intact family, even some of my illusions.

I roll into the kitchen just as "the moms"—my mom and her now-infamous, ass-kicking stuntwoman/ex–porn star partner, Elise—are sitting down with their disgusting-looking breakfast smoothies.

"You guys hear anything about Wade Miller lately?" I ask, trying to sound casual.

Elise shakes her head, her long black ponytail swishing from side to side.

Mom says, "Who?" even though it's nearly impossible for anyone not to know who he is in this town, which means she's either willfully blocked all knowledge of him out of her mind because of his association with my dad or is pretending not to know of him for the same reason, or because his show is far more successful than hers and she's jealous, or all of the above. Or she is getting old. Perish the thought.

"Hot young actor, does film and TV?"

She shrugs.

"Worked with Dad? And me? We had him at the house, for God's sake. He was my friend. Come on, don't do this."

"Your friend? Where is he now, then?"

Another sensitive spot—the division of friends, the taking of sides, post divorce. Mom, being the more obviously guilty party, didn't come out well, and it didn't help that Dad was/is higher up the food chain than she was. So it hurt her social life and her career. Which means she's still pissed, years later.

"He's a little busy, starring in *Drift*."

"Oh," she says now with a sniff, "that little turd."

"Nice," I say.

"Well, is he still your friend?"

"That isn't anybody's fault," I say pointedly.

Actually, it could be said it was her fault, since her affair with Elise broke three days before the premiere of the zombie movie. It had been eight months since production wrapped, and I hadn't seen him since. But to my relief and delight, puberty had finally gone to work on me, changing me from an awkward, short, flat-chested, no-hipped, brace-faced kid into a full-fledged teen. A girl. I had boobs, curves, I'd grown taller, and I'd even convinced my orthodontist to accelerate my treatment (painful!) so I could have my braces off in time for the event. In preparation for seeing Wade again and hoping to show him once and for all that I wasn't a child anymore, I'd paid Sydney's big sister for flirting lessons, learned how to apply makeup, and bought a gorgeous crystal-beaded dress, in which I looked very grown-up. I hoped it was enough to make Wade look at me in a new light.

But I never got to the premiere, because I was stuck inside my paparazzi-surrounded house with my crying, raging, lunatic family. Wade and I texted for a while, but I could tell he still thought of me as a kid and was just being nice, and I didn't like anybody feeling sorry for me.

"Well," Mom says, "I haven't heard anything about him lately, no."

"Why?" Elise says. "I mean, why do you ask?"

"Oh," I say, shrugging. "I was just wondering."

Even saying something here at home about how he might be partying too much could be the inadvertent cause of a rumor, if Elise or Mom repeats my line of questioning to the wrong person. And I won't be the cause of that.

Sydney doesn't call. I spend two days worrying and obsessing—frankly, I have nothing else to do, as I am stranded, carless, and with no summer plans of any kind. Despite my telling them none of my friends would be around (every other seventeen-year-old I know is off working as a counselor at camp, or in Europe, or in rehab, apparently), Mom and Elise thought it would be healthy for me to be "unscheduled" for all of July and August.

"You have your whole life to be zooming around—take one last summer to be a kid."

"I haven't been a kid in a long time," I pointed out. "I'm, like, only a year away from being an official adult."

"Exactly," Elise said. "I can't tell you what I'd give for a whole summer of nowhere to be and nothing to do. And when I was seventeen? I had to spend my summers working in my dad's store. Whereas you have the chance to be free."

Free. Sure. Awesome.

I read a bit, but I'm too distracted to stick with it. Then I try on all my new bathing suits with various combinations of sunglasses, and imagine what I would wear in rehab with Wade. Then I go online and order a bunch of clothes—casual—from Free People and Forever 21 and Topshop. Then I check my phone a million times. Then I Google Wade again. In the process of Googling him, I've seen a lot of pictures, which means, damn, how can I stop thinking about him? He has only gotten hotter over the past four years. It's ridiculous how hot he is.

And it's horrifying thinking of him in the grips of addiction because that gets ugly, fast. People get dead fast.

No, no, no, no, no.

It could be "not serious" and his team still might be keeping quiet. It's not impossible. It could be he's just tired, overwhelmed, needs a break, but doesn't want to talk about it to the world. Sunrise sounds like it could be that kind of place.

Sydney still doesn't call.

I still don't call my dad, though I am constantly on the brink of doing so.

I finally put my phone down and go for a walk, and as I'm walking, I imagine the things I might say to Wade if I saw him. About the pitfalls of fame, about staying human, about remembering the craft and remembering where you come from and staying true to that, about never being desperate but never being a dick either, about not drinking your own Kool-Aid—or drinking just enough of it to remain confident but not enough to become an asshole, about staying in the driver's seat of your career, keeping people you trust around you, people who will tell you the truth even if you don't like it, people who aren't with you for all the shitty reasons.

I would tell him the truth.

And if he happened to then fall madly in love with me? What would be wrong with that? I'm not trying to be an actress and I don't have any illusions about fame. I don't need his money. I'm not addicted to anything you can't buy at Starbucks, so I can't lead him into any of that kind of trouble. I know him—I know the real him.

Those people at Sunrise don't know him at all.

And if I don't go...he could fall in love with someone else while he's there—Sydney, for example—or someone who's totally dangerous and inappropriate and would be bad for him.

Although Sydney promised...

And I am not going, not thinking of going in a serious

way…

Okay, I am seriously *imagining* going, but that's not the same thing as planning on it.

When I get home, the message icon is blinking on my phone.

"Shit!"

Of course it is, and of course the message is from Sydney.

"Damn it, Lola, pick up!" she hisses. "I've only got a minute and I'm not supposed to be on the phone right now anyway. Okay. You have to come. I'm going to harass you about it because I don't want to do this by myself—I mean it's awesome, but I miss you. I need a true friend here, and you're the only one I have. Oh, and I saw your boy in the flesh, so if you come, that'll be an added benefit. Mind you, he looks like shit—pale and kinda sweaty, and skinny— so I'm not sure if you're still gonna dig him. But imagine the walks on the beach, lying together by the pool, catching up on old times with him…it could be good.

"Anyway, I was thinking, stick with something simple— just alcohol. 'Cause all the other stuff has side effects you'd have to know about and symptoms and signs and withdrawals you can't fake. Alcohol has withdrawals too, but only if you've been hitting it really hard for a really long time. Otherwise you're only looking at, say, three days of feeling hung over. The thing you need to say when you come in is you feel out of control. That's partly true, right?

I mean, you are a crazy-ass bitch when you drink. So. 'Out of control'—that's the buzz phrase you need. And…as for your parents, same thing, really. Do some research, but the thing is, they'll be way too freaked not to send you if you just tell them, or show them, that you're having a problem. Uh…at the same time, if it's your mom, you might try a bit of reverse psychology—I know she's tricky. Trust me, this will make for a seriously memorable summer, Lo. It's a six-week program, so you'd better hurry. Don't call me back on this line, by the way. Shit…gotta go."

I play the message over three times, hearing "he looks like shit—pale and kind of sweaty, and skinny" the loudest.

Then I go to my laptop and into my photos and scroll back a few years to the pictures of us on set. I took a ton of pictures of him—hanging out in his trailer, goofing around with the background performers (does he still do that?), hanging out by the craft table, under the lights and cameras. I also took a few of him and my dad, and there are some selfies of the two of us with half our faces cut off. And then there's the one with Wade, my dad, and me at the wrap party. Dad is in the middle, with an arm around each of us. I look hideous of course—short and scrawny with braces and atrocious hair—but we're all beaming, happy, envisioning only good things in our futures.

Over the happy images, I keep getting flashes, visions of the kinds of headlines, the photos you see when one of these talented young actors is found dead—in a hotel room, on a bathroom floor—and the pain of it is sharp and real. It could happen to Wade. That could be his future.

Gazing at his bright, hopeful, open face on my computer screen, I suddenly know what's in my future.

Maybe I'm crazy, but sometimes you get a gut feeling, a sense of a path opening up in front of you and the certainty that you need to take that path.

I have that sense now, and I see the path.

The path leads to rehab.

CHAPTER THREE

dab tequila behind my ears, then dribble some down the front of my T-shirt.

It's a bit gross and not super honest, I realize, but I'll get over the guilt.

The stars have lined up to give me this chance, and I am *meant to go*. There's just that irritating lack-of-addiction problem to conquer, and the fact is, I don't have time to get addicted for real.

Hence I am dousing myself with tequila and staging my own intervention.

It might seem a little extreme, but I'm running out of time, and my more subtle attempts have not been successful. For example: To start, I was extra moody and bitchy and combative, but apparently that wasn't, um, enough of a change from normal. Then I poured myself a huge glass of wine at dinner and guzzled it right in front of them. Then I carried a bottle of vodka in my purse and let it clank around and peek out of the top at strategic moments.

When none of this raised so much as a perfectly sculpted eyebrow, I siphoned off most of the hard alcohol in the house and replaced it with water, figuring Mom, at least, would notice the difference in her predinner martini.

But no.

So I emptied the vodka, rum, and tequila completely and left the bottles in strategic places—the jasmine plants outside the front door, beside the path to the beach, under my bed, et cetera, thinking they'd see or that at least I'd get ratted out by Ida, the cleaning lady.

No dice.

Finally I texted some people from school whom I don't particularly like or even hang out with (because they are anarchist stoners whose major effort at style involves overapplication of kohl eyeliner) and dressed up like them (eww) and went to two of their supposedly wild parties, both of which turned out to be excruciatingly boring, especially considering they're supposed to be rebels. The first time, I came home reeking of booze and pot, but no one was up to see me arrive—a flaw in the plan I should have foreseen—so I threw myself on the couch and slept there until morning. Mom found me, frowned, told me the couch wasn't for sleeping on, and gave me shit about getting my kohl eyeliner on the beige fabric, and said she hoped I wouldn't go out in public again until I was over this particular style evolution.

After the second party, I didn't come home until the next

day. I walked in, figuring I'd find them there, all panicked and calling the police, but I didn't hear anything. So. Fine. It was the weekend; maybe they were sleeping in. I could just sneak into my room and go to bed, but the entire effort would have been wasted.

Instead I re-created a moment of stumbling in so I could find out where I'd have landed, and then gently face-planted between the foyer and the great room, making sure for my own sake to land my upper body on the rug.

I was there so long I actually did fall asleep, but when I woke up, nothing had happened and no one was around. I got up, investigated, and discovered I'd been alone in the house all along—they'd left a note in the kitchen saying they were going to the Farmers Market, and to enjoy my sleep-in.

They were either much denser than I thought, or they figured I was going through a phase that they should simply ignore.

Or they didn't care.

Fast-forward to now. A Friday night. I am sitting at my 1940s mirrored deco vanity supposedly once owned by Ava Gardner (my mom is a sucker for these kinds of pieces—they make her feel more famous by association) using tequila as perfume.

I choke some of the burning stuff down my throat—do not ask me to eat the worm; what is *wrong* with people?—pour some on my shirt, and then rub my made-up eyes until they're itchy and red. Finally I purposely neglect to brush my teeth and go to bed in my clothes.

It's hard work, becoming a drunk. It's exhausting.

But surely it will all be worth it, and I know I'll have a chance to rest up once I get to Sunrise. And who knows, the whole thing might set off an unprecedented show of parental concern, affection, consternation, guilt-driven buying of designer shoes, et cetera.

At best I will soon be poolside in Malibu with beautiful Wade Miller pouring his heart out to me, while bouncing quarters off my butt cheeks, of course.

Morning comes and I feel disgusting and smelly enough to pull it off.

I tiptoe out of my room and down the hallway of my wing of the house, then peek around the corner. Elise is there in the kitchen, gazing out at the ocean and making coffee in the French press, which means Mom is still in bed.

Perfect.

I slip behind the kitchen, down the opposite hallway, and pause outside the bedroom door to think a bunch of sad thoughts and drum up some tears, but despite my belief in method acting, my genuine sadness about a lot of things, and inherited talent for melodrama, I'm nervous and they won't come.

Fine. *Try acting*, as the saying goes. I take a deep breath and jam a thumb in each eye, which freaking *hurts*, and enter the room with a stifled sob.

"M-Mom?"

She moans.

"Mom. I—I need you."

Her striking green eyes open, just a slit.

"It's early, Lola. You know I don't do 'need' until I've had my coffee."

She doesn't really do "need" at all, I'm starting to realize, but I refrain from pointing that out. She's going to do it today.

"BUT I—I—I *REALLY* NEED YOU!" I wail, and throw myself onto the bed.

"Oh my! Uh…"

"PLEASE…I don't want to go to Dad about this but I—I…"

She sits bolt upright. If she had any idea the state of things between Dad and me, she'd know I was bluffing, but I haven't told her about our falling-out. I haven't told anyone. Plus, she hates hearing anything about him, so she doesn't ask.

"Lola, calm down. Please just calm down."

I channel inconsolable, then topple myself onto her lap, making sure to breathe in her face on the way.

She flinches. "My God, Lola, you…you smell! And once again, you look disgusting."

"I—I—I know," I say, with a long moan.

"Okay, okay," she says and pats feebly at my back.

"I've hit…I've hit *rock bottom*, Mom."

"Rock bottom?"

"I can't hide it anymore. I've been…I mean I have a…a…"

"Yes…?"

"I've been drinking," I say, looking her full in the eyes. "I'm so ashamed but…I've been drinking and I think…I think I have a *problem*."

(I *have* been drinking and I *do* have a problem. Just not a *drinking problem*.)

"A problem?" She lets out a great sigh. "Oh, Lola."

"I'm s-so s-sorry. It's…I can't control it, I feel like I can't control it. I'm so scared, Mom."

"Shh, I'm sure it's not so bad," she says. "It's not like you're Lindsay Lohan."

"Oh, but I could be! I just know I'm going to end up one of those stereotypical Hollywood kids who're getting busted and photographed stumbling out of clubs without their underwear at three in the morning," I say, and see her growing pale. "Mom, I don't want to do that to you; I don't want to do that to your career. I know it would reflect badly on you, but I can't stop. I've tried and I can't…" I say, and then throw myself back down on the bed and sob convulsively.

It's an awesome performance, if I do say so myself.

Mom gets up, paces to her mirror and back, and shushes me a few times.

"We'll have to get you some help," she says. "Please calm down, Lola. We'll get you some help. You can…see a counselor and perhaps join AA."

I keep my face down to hide my frustrated expression, and wail, "Not AA!"

"You've asked for my help, and I'm going to help you. But you'll have to do as I say."

"I'll try," I say, ready to roll out the reverse psychology. "But please…whatever you do, don't…don't…"

"Don't what?"

"Please don't send me to rehab."

Three days later, I'm on my way to Southern California's hottest rehab facility for teenage addicts and delinquents.

I love it when I get my way.

Mom and Elise have been super sweet and very attentive while I stayed in bed faking my physical withdrawal. There have been cold cloths for my forehead, plates of fruit and buttered toast with the crusts cut off, gourmet caramel, hot chocolate with marshmallows—quite a pleasant change from the benign neglect I'm accustomed to.

Sydney called again once before I staged the intervention, so she knew I was trying to make it happen. She said Wade was looking better, but she didn't seem to have been making any effort to get to know him, so she didn't have any real details. Perhaps I should be grateful for that, actually. Anyway, she hasn't called since then, so she has no idea I've finally succeeded. Possibly she's too busy doing yoga and getting massages, and/or has given up on my coming.

All that lying around in bed gave me plenty of time to think about how to deal with Wade when I first see him, and also about what to pack. My stuff from Forever 21, et cetera, conveniently arrived yesterday, and it's all perfect rehab-wear—casual, stylish, a little bohemian, and slightly subdued. Well, subdued for me. I'm calling the look "rehab chic." After this, I might start a line of clothing—it's a pretty good niche market and I don't think anyone else is doing it.

I've also packed my never-used yoga mat and Lululemon ensembles, all my new bathing suits plus another bikini, the Fat-Ass Ray-Bans, the Miu Mius, lots of sunscreen, and dark chocolate. I've got Pink's "Sober" and Eminem's *Recovery* on my phone and I've memorized the alcoholic's prayer. ("The courage to change the things I can." I'm coming, Wade.)

So. Rehab.

As we get closer, I feel a teeny, tiny bit guilty and nervous about the whole thing.

But it's been a lot of work getting this far, and it would be a shame to waste it, not to mention I'd rather eat mud than confess to Mom and Elise, not to mention they would never understand about Wade and my gut feeling that I am meant to do this.

Rehab it is. I am committed.

We arrive at the tall iron gates of the Spanish Colonial–style mansion and find an interesting surprise: paparazzi. Only two, but they are unmistakable with their camera equipment and in-your-face-ness.

Elise, riding shotgun, turns to look at my mother.

"Jules, darlin'…?"

"Mm?" Mom says as she pulls up next to the intercom.

"Who's there?" asks a voice.

"Jules Carlyle with daughter, Lola," Mom says in her lilting TV voice and then tucks a perfectly blown-out strand of strawberry-blond hair behind her ear and glances at the two guys who've walked up beside us to snap pictures through the open window. If I didn't know better, I'd think she was posing.

"We'll buzz you in right now," says the voice through the intercom.

I wait for her to tell them we have company, to ask them to send security to get rid of them, but all she does is roll up her window and drive through when the gates open, which means the vultures walk right in with us.

"Ah, Mom…?"

"Oh, Jules." Elise is frowning. "You didn't."

She did—tip off the photographers herself, that is—I know she did. A bit sad from a mother-daughter perspective, not to mention a personal history perspective, but I guess I shouldn't be surprised. I fake my way into rehab; my mom calls the paps to document my arrival. Welcome to show business.

"Rehab costs money," Mom says with a shrug. "And I make money being famous."

"You make money being an actor," Elise says.

"Same thing. I stay famous, I stay employed."

"Excuse me," I say from the backseat. "I'm a tad traumatized here already without having to worry about this moment being posted on TMZ."

"Sorry, dear," Mom says.

Oh man. Suddenly the trouble I could be in if I get caught is bigger and more public than I bargained for. Maybe I *should* have gotten addicted for real.

"You could have warned me at least," I say. "I'd have prepared myself better, worn more makeup."

"This is not about you," Mom says.

"Uh, hello? I'm the one going to rehab."

"Listen, Miss Alcoholic—your father isn't exactly paying enough to keep us in the beach house or you in your three-hundred-dollar jeans. I'm the one."

"Oh my God, Mom, please, not the beach-house-expensive-jeans speech. It's not my fault people only send free stuff to you and Elise."

"Nothing is free, Lola. Keep that in mind. And listen, I've been killed and brought back to life three times already. How many more lives do you think the network will give me? I'm old. I'm old and therefore I need publicity. Just be happy we're interesting enough for them to send anyone. As it is, there are just two of them. I'm almost insulted."

Mom is only thirty-five, actually, but it's a cruel, precarious business she's in, and she knows it. We all know it.

"Fine," I say.

"Now," she says, putting the car into park, "keep your mouth closed, try not to trip, and don't start sweating or you'll look shiny."

"Thanks a lot."

"And for heaven's sake, take off those sunglasses."

It's steaming hot out, but I do my best not to sweat and at the same time to look the typical chastened celebuspawn (entitled yet insecure, stylish yet lazy, glamorous, desperate, bored, damaged, possibly dumb but more likely underachieving) as we get out of the car. Elise pulls my two large suitcases out of the trunk and Mom stands in a protective pose, her arm over my shoulders and the "good" side of her face tilted perfectly so the photographers can get their shots and shout questions they know we won't answer.

"Please, please," she says, voice suddenly husky, "some privacy for our family during this difficult time."

Click, snap, click…

I stand there, stomach churning with nerves, imagining the photo—Mom standing willowy and tragic, me next to her, not willowy, probably not tragic enough for her standards, but with the exact same coloring—pale skin, strawberry blond hair, green eyes. I hate it. And I wonder what Dad will think when he sees this. Because he will see it.

Finally we start to move toward the large arched doorway at the front of the mansion. On the threshold, Mom pauses again. Bulbs are flashing, there are tears in her eyes, and from somewhere in her handbag, she whips out a soft, fuzzy thing and presses it into my arms.

I look down. Oh, please. It's a pink teddy bear.

I never liked bears and I'm not into pink.

Not to mention, I am seventeen, not seven.

Imagine how this could mess me up if I really *were* an alcoholic.

Inside, the air is cool with a hint of lavender and I hear the tinkling of falling water. We are in a beautiful two-story circular foyer with marble floors and columns, double spiral staircases with wrought iron banisters, an inlaid Spanish tile fountain, and one of those giant circular iron chandeliers—the kind you might imagine Zorro (or Wade, or Wade as Zorro—he would be very cute in the cape and mask and even the mustache) swinging from in the middle of a dramatic rescue.

Cape or no cape, every cell in my body is aware I might see him at any moment, and I am filled with a mix of excitement and worry.

"Here," I say to Mom, and hand the teddy bear back to her.

She takes it without comment and puts it back in her purse.

Suddenly a gorgeous man with coffee-colored skin and perfectly coiffed black hair appears in front of us, teeth blazing.

"Welcome. I am Dr. Valente Koch, program director for the Sunrise Center."

The three of us say hello, and then Dr. Koch does a bunch of deep-voiced hand-kissing and looking fascinated while both my mom and Elise blush, giggle, and generally fall all over themselves, making me want to remind them that, hello? They are supposed to be lesbians.

The next thing I know, we're following Dr. Koch down a hallway and into a large room.

"My study," he says with a faux-humble wave.

The study is resplendent in gold and iron statuary and draped in silk. Behind an antique desk that looks like it doesn't see much action in the way of real work is a gallery of framed photos, all of Koch with his arm slung over the shoulders of various celebrities.

Aha.

"Please, sit," he says, and ushers us over to a brown leather swallower of a couch in front of a massive fireplace. "I would offer you ladies a drink, but under the circumstances…"

My mom actually laughs.

He slides onto a throne-like chair across from us, careful not to crease his pants.

"I wanted to reassure you that you are safe inside these walls, Miss Carlyle. And of course, I will be taking a particular interest in your case."

"Why a particular interest?"

"We are known for our excellent program, of course. Our philosophy of healing the soul and body simultaneously through physical therapies and creative outlets is groundbreaking. However"—he gives me a knowing look—"we are also experts at treating a category of people who have… unique needs."

Interesting. My needs are definitely unique, but probably not in the way he means.

"That's very reassuring to me as a mother, Dr. Koch," Mom says, launching into her daytime TV dramatics, voice trembling, eyes wide. "I've done my best for Lola, but this whole thing makes me feel like I've failed her in some way. I want to save her, but I can't save her from herself."

She certainly can't.

"On the contrary," says Koch. "You *have* saved her. You have brought her to me."

Mom bows her head as if awaiting the Crown of Motherhood.

Dr. Koch looks ready to bestow it.

I close my eyes and think of Wade. Wade lost and tripping over his feet his first day on set, and then a few days later after I'd shown him the ropes, singing, dancing, and acting up a storm, slaying his first zombie, so talented, so cute it nearly killed me, and after the day wrapped, coming at me with eyes brimming and wrapping me in a massive hug. These memories are familiar and worn, like a favorite T-shirt. But soon I'll have new ones, and a deeper bond. Soon he'll be right in front of me.

"Miss Carlyle?"

I snap to attention. "What was that?"

"I was explaining our philosophy and about the Level System."

"Yes. Sorry." Sydney mentioned the levels, actually. But all she said was, "Make sure you get a Level Three card."

"Unlike many teen rehabilitation centers that are run like jails, you will have a sense of freedom here. We treat our patients with respect and use peer policing, which helps foster responsibility and social accountability. Yes, there are rules and a structure to each day, but within that structure you will have some choice, opportunities to increase your privileges, and overall, an experience of empowerment."

"Empowerment." I nod enthusiastically. "Sounds good."

"Here is your level card." Dr. Koch proffers a small plastic card that looks like a hotel key. "Since it's your first week, you start at Level One, which means you may move freely within the building, but you need a Level Three patient or a staff member in order to go outside."

I frown but take the key.

"Normally your access to the studios would also be restricted until next week when you reach Level Two, but I've modified your card. Coming from such a creative family, you surely need to express yourself artistically, and so you'll have access immediately. The studios are equipped for music, performance, writing, visual arts, and so on."

"Um…thanks. So this is a Level One card? Or a Level Two?"

"It is a Level One…as far as anyone needs to know."

"But it acts like a Level Two."

"Yes. Please come to me for anything you need and I will do what I can. All I ask is you be discreet. We don't want the other patients or the staff thinking you're getting special treatment."

"Even though I am?"

"Of course not," he says, and then winks.

I'm all for special treatment and everything, but suddenly I want to take a shower.

Speaking of showers, now that all this arrival business is taken care of, it's time to find Sydney and get to the spa, because if possible, I'd like to be relaxed when I finally see Wade again.

Chapter Four

To my surprise, the arrival business is *not*, in fact, fully taken care of, and soon I am the opposite of relaxed and am instead thinking about strangling Sydney.

After a dramatic good-bye from my mother and a warm one from Elise, Dr. Koch takes me to a suite of rooms that looks like a doctor's office, and introduces me to a Grinch-faced woman…who turns out to be a doctor of the medical variety.

"Nice to meet you," I say with what I hope is a friendly wave.

"And this," Dr. Koch says, turning toward a guy who's just come into the room behind us, "is Adam."

"H-hi…" I squint at Adam, trying to figure out if he's a fellow "guest" or what. He's young—early twenties at the most—too young to be a doctor, that's for sure. Unless he's some kind of prodigy. But he doesn't look like a prodigy. He looks like a Jonas brother—medium height; thick, dark brown hair; brown eyes; broad shoulders; wears the hell out of a pair of jeans without seeming to know it. without seeming to know it. But he's not cute; he's intense, stern-looking for his age, and could probably eat a Jonas brother for breakfast.

"Adam is one of our summer placements," Dr. Koch says. "A college student on track to become a social worker."

"Cool," I say, giving what I think of as a winning smile, but receiving nothing but a deadpan gaze in return.

"As part of his duties, he has been assigned to you."

Uh-oh. "Assigned to me?" The somber demeanor is getting to me already, and I decide to poke him a little and see what happens. "Oh, you mean like a valet?"

Ha– now he looks like he's going to choke.

"Not exactly," Dr. Koch says, looking mildly amused. "He is your adviser, your mentor."

"Too bad," I say to him. "Because I have a lot of stuff to carry."

"Speaking of which," Dr. Koch says, glancing at my suitcases, sitting just inside the door, "I'll let you get to it."

He glides out, leaving me with the doctor, who is busy making notes on her laptop, and Adam, who looks like he's swallowed a cactus.

"I was only kidding," I tell him.

"You think you're funny," he says.

"I try."

"Well, don't." Then he turns to the doctor. "You ready

for her?"

"Mmm-hmm…" she says absently. "Just…get on the table, please."

"What?"

Adam points to the examining table, then looks me up and down, presumably taking in my outfit. I am wearing a lacy pale green slip dress that matches my eyes, and ankle boots. It's a cute outfit, and looking in the mirror back at home, I thought it gave a sort of…curvy elfin waif vibe. But with him looking at me I suddenly feel self-conscious and a bit ridiculous, like I should be in something more serious, more substantial, less…flimsy, for entering rehab. And then, as I contemplate climbing up on the table, I realize the dress is really short, and the lace parts are a little see-through, and maybe I should have added leggings.

I turn and walk over to the table.

"You need help getting up?" Adam says when I stop in front of it.

"Nope," I say, then look around for a step stool of some kind, because if I have to jump or climb, I'm going to be giving him a free show.

"No?"

"No, I just need…"

"People don't usually dress up to come to rehab," he says, confirming my suspicions.

"I wasn't…I didn't consider this to be dressed up," I reply, feeling heat rise in my cheeks.

"Here," he says, and then before I can process what's happening, he's crossed the distance between us, picked me up, and deposited me, none too gently, on the table.

"Wha— I was going to…" I rub my arms where his hands were and face him. "That wasn't necessary."

He grins. Which makes no sense because I don't see anything funny going on.

"Why do I need to be up here anyway?"

"Physical," he says.

The doctor clears her throat, comes over, tells me to lie down.

"I'll be over there if you need anything," Adam says, then points to a chair a few feet away, pulls a curtain around the examining area, and then I hear him plunking down onto the chair.

What follows starts as a fairly typical physical exam— blood pressure; bright lights in my eyes, ears, throat; all my glands palpated; stomach pressed on; reflexes checked; lungs and heart listened to. I don't know if there's a way for me to fake any of this to seem more like an alcoholic, so I just do my best to be cooperative.

But then it gets personal. She runs her hands up the insides of my arms, looks closely at my wrists, and then inspects my inner thighs.

"Isn't this a little…intrusive?"

"Drug addicts find many ways to hide injection sites," she says in a creepy monotone.

"Oh."

"Have you ever given yourself an injection?'

"Gross. No."

"Are you sexually active?"

"What?"

"It's a simple question."

"I don't have to answer that," I say to her. "Adam? Do I have to answer that?"

"Yes," he says from behind the curtain.

"Have you ever been sexually active?" she asks again.

"I'm seventeen," I say.

"So, yes?"

"So, nothing. It's none of your business."

"So your answer is no?"

"If you need an answer, that's correct. No."

"Have you ever been pregnant?"

"Oh, so I could somehow have been pregnant without having been sexually active? No."

"Have you ever been treated for a sexually transmitted disease?"

"Uh, refer to my previous two answers, please."

"Respond to the question, please."

"No. No sex, no pregnancy, no STDs. God."

Next, maybe because she doesn't believe me, I have to give a urine sample. Then I give blood for blood work.

"Are you using any drugs?"

"No."

"Have you been using any drugs recently?" she says in her same grating monotone.

"No. I mean, well, I probably inhaled some secondhand pot at a party last week. In fact I'm sure I did, but I'm here for my alcohol problem." I can tell, as she types out my answer, that she thinks I'm lying. I would think I'm lying, too. It totally sounds like I am. But that's probably okay, considering.

"How often do you smoke marijuana?"

"Oh, come on. Is this another trick question? Is this your brilliant way of smoking out the secret pot smokers, so to speak? Well, guess what? Their brains are working slower than mine."

"Answer the question."

"I don't smoke marijuana."

"How often do you take prescription drugs?"

"Um...every couple of years? You know, when the doctor prescribes them?"

"What kind of drugs does your doctor prescribe?"

"Antibiotics, usually. What kind does yours prescribe?"

At this, I could swear I hear Adam trying not to laugh behind the curtain.

"How often do you drink alcohol?"

Here we go.

"A lot. Uh..." Sydney coached me on this—it doesn't have to be that I drink every day; it can be binge drinking, which is considered an equally serious addiction. "There might be a few days when I don't drink at all, but then when I get going, it's a binge. It's a lot and I can't stop. I totally lose control and do...stupid things."

"What kind of alcohol do you consume?"

"Any kind."

"How much do you consume on a given day?"

"A lot. I lose track. But definitely...like, I could drink a couple of bottles of vodka over the course of a day...and then start with more first thing the next morning."

"Why are you here?"

"Because I need to get help or I'm afraid something bad will happen," I say, doing my best to look tremulous and fragile, which is challenging because she's pissed me off with all the badgering, and I have no desire to show her any vulnerability. "I can't control it."

It goes on like this for what feels like ages, with the doctor occasionally looping back to a question she's already asked, to see if my answer will be different.

Finally she lets me go and hands me over to Adam while she goes to take the urine and blood to a lab at the back.

He sits me at a small table.

"Shouldn't she be nicer?" I whisper to him.

"Why do you think she should be nicer?" he whispers back.

"Like, to make people feel welcome? And safe?"

"Sometimes she is nicer," he says.

"Oh! So it's just me?"

"I think it depends on what the situation requires," he says, and then hands me a questionnaire. "Here. You have to fill this out."

"You're kidding me," I say, looking down at it. "This thing is—what—ten pages long? And this first page is all the same questions! Plus more questions!"

"This is more to assess your mental health, Lola."

"My mental health? Well, I can just tell you myself—it's rapidly deteriorating."

fill out the form. It takes forever and includes a bunch of tricky multiple choice questions that are obviously there to ferret out sociopaths, depressives, narcissists, et cetera. This is the hardest part, because I have to keep myself in the zone of being an unhappy, addicted person, without coming across like I need a straitjacket.

Midway through, as my brain threatens to break, I ask Adam if I might have a coffee.

"You'll have to get that from the valet," he says.

"Awesome. Where is said valet?" I ask, although I think I already know the answer.

Adam reaches across the table, puts his index finger to my forehead, and taps. "Right...there," he says.

"Look, I'll get it myself. I just need you to tell me where to go."

"Finish the questionnaire."

I get back to work, and Adam stands up and crosses the room to confer with the doctor, who is presumably showing him the test results and who knows what else. I have no idea, for example, whether the secondhand pot smoke will show up in my urine or blood work. It's something I should have researched. And in general, it makes me itchy knowing they're talking about me but there's nothing I can do about it.

I finish, and Adam hands me another stack of papers, but this is just for signatures—giving myself into their care, committing to the program, stating I've come of my own free will, yada yada. I skim them and sign.

"Okay!" I pop up from the chair. "We're done here, right?"

"Not quite," he says, and goes to get my suitcases, rolling them over to the examining table.

"Oh no."

"This is the one time I'm going to lift these for you," he says, and then hoists each one up to the table and unzips it. Grouch Doctor comes to stand on the other side, bringing two rolling carts with her, and they begin to empty my suitcases, inspecting each item, and placing it on one of the two carts.

"Let me save you the trouble," I say. "I am not smuggling any drugs or alcohol. And I already figured I'd have to surrender my phone—I'll just give it to you."

They ignore me.

"Well, how about you let me help?"

"Sit in the chair and wait, please," the doctor says.

"I think I'll stand."

So I stand, mortified and furious, and watch. They unroll every pair of socks and turn each sock inside out. They study the sole of every shoe, open every tube of lip gloss, page through all six of the novels I brought with me, shake every piece of clothing.

"If you give me some scissors, I should really cut off those tags," I say as the clothing pile mushrooms, obscuring the surface of the cart.

"You bought an entire new wardrobe for this, I see,"

Adam says, rolling his eyes. "Or do you just have a bunch of clothes with tags in your closet all the time?"

"They're not all new," I say weakly. "Hey, don't touch my underwear, people!"

Adam looks down, realizes he's holding a bra, and drops it like a hot potato.

"Doctor, why don't we trade," he says, going to the other suitcase where she's working. "I'll finish this one."

I stalk away, face burning, and slump into the chair.

The doctor gets quickly to the bottom of the suitcase with the underwear, and begins to feel around like she's checking for secret compartments. Meanwhile, Adam is almost finished too.

"Whoa—what do we have here?" Adam says, and the doctor and I both look at him.

He is holding up a bar of dark chocolate and acting like it's crack cocaine.

"It's chocolate," I say. "And it's sealed—nothing nefarious."

"Looks all right to me," the doctor says, and for the first time, I like her a little bit.

"But Doctor, look at this," Adam says, and she looks. "She's got, like, a hundred of them."

"Fifty, actually," I say. "All safely packaged."

The doctor turns and gives me a penetrating look. "Why did you pack fifty chocolate bars?"

I blink. "Because I like chocolate...?"

They both stare at me now.

"It's gourmet. And organic."

They start opening the chocolate bars.

"What is wrong with you people? That's seventy percent dark chocolate—it's a freaking antioxidant."

Adam breaks off a piece, sniffs it, and passes it to the doctor, who takes a small bite.

I clench my fists.

The doctor nods. "It's chocolate."

Adam takes a bite, nods, then puts the bar down.

"Please tell me you're not going to open every one of them," I say. "They'll dry out. I can't eat them fast enough to keep them from drying out…"

Adam and the doctor exchange a glance, then start putting the bars off to the side, on a tray.

"What, are you going to x-ray them or something?" I say, arms crossed and glaring.

"No, we're going to pack them up with the other stuff," Adam says, pointing to my phone and a bottle of toner and some hairspray I can't take in because it contains alcohol. "You can't bring these into the dorms."

"Are you fucking kidding me?"

"There are people here with eating disorders," he says, gazing pointedly at me like I might be one of them. "For some people this could be an addictive substance."

"Of course it's an addictive substance—it's chocolate."

"You can have it back when you leave."

"Can't I keep just a couple? The ones you opened?"

"No."

"Well, that's just great," I say, shaking my head.

If I'd known I could check into rehab for chocolate

addiction, I'd have skipped the tequila.

"Almost done," Adam says a few minutes later when my suitcases have been (messily) repacked and my forbidden items have been locked in a bin and taken away. "There's just one more thing."

"Yay." I am in a full sulk at this point.

"Doctor?" Adam says, gesturing her toward me.

I guess I shouldn't be surprised that she frisks me, then makes me take off my shoes and socks, hands them to Adam for inspection, and proceeds to look between my toes.

"When's the anal probe?" I say darkly.

She looks up from my feet, expression flat.

"Because, you know, I might be smuggling in a few M&M's."

She doesn't even crack a smile.

"Don't press your luck," Adam says, and hands me a shoe.

Chapter Five

Adam leads me back out to the entrance foyer and stops near the fountain.

"Done," he says. "Was that so bad?"

"Um, yes," I say, wheeling my suitcases up and stopping beside him. "Listen, I need you to book me a massage for this afternoon."

He tilts his head and narrows his eyes.

"Please," I say.

"I'm not the concierge, either," he says.

"Well, what good are you? I mean, what do you do besides force me into stuff I don't want and give me shit and confiscate my things?"

He just looks at me.

"Fine. Tell me where to go and who to talk to and I'll book it myself. I'm very stressed out."

"No massages on the first day," he says.

"What? Why?"

"I'm not the expert on this, but apparently your energy may be too fragile at first for body treatments."

"I assure you, my energy is not fragile," I say, walking closer to him as if to prove it. "I have very tough energy."

"None of that on day one," he says, refusing to back away, which leaves me standing awkwardly close to him — close enough to see he's had his nose broken at some point, and not reset quite right. "Period."

"Well then, I'll take a pedicure or manicure—whatever you recommend."

"I said no." Suddenly, his eyes get kind of fierce and wolfish, and in spite of myself, I take a step back.

"Okay." I put my hands up in surrender. "Sorry."

"You need to establish a rapport with your therapist first," he says. "And your roommates."

"I have *roommates*?"

He nods.

"Eww."

"You might want to avoid saying that to them," he says, and heads for the stairs. "Now move it."

You would think, considering everyone here is supposed to be all screwed up and vulnerable to ridiculous things like chocolate and hairspray, that they'd give us some privacy, that they'd avoid sticking all the crazies in rooms together where they risk making one another more crazy.

Case in point: I heave my own bags up two flights of stairs and follow Adam to my room, where there are three double platform beds lined up on one wall.

"I'll let you introduce yourselves. Meet me outside the dorm doors. Ten minutes," Adam orders, and then leaves me there.

Someone is lying faceup and surrounded by an almost visible funk, on the farthest bed.

"Uh, hi…?" I say. Her eyes are open but the girl doesn't move.

"She doesn't talk," a voice says.

I jump, look to my left, and find a tall girl with brown corkscrew curls; a rash of freckles across her nose, forehead, and cheeks; and intense, close-set blue eyes.

"She just moans," says the freckled girl. "And screams sometimes at night."

"Wow, that's so *Paranormal Activity 4*," I say.

"Oh, you're funny."

"Thanks."

"I don't know how she does it—the not talking. She's… There's a term for it… Anyway, she's mute by choice. *Selectively mute*, that's it. Apparently she hasn't spoken a word in years. She's cross-addicted and co-occurring like most of us, but I think her big thing is heroin. And she looks like a cutter to me but she hasn't said so. Obviously, ha ha. What about you? You look like a cocaine girl, or maybe crystal."

She grabs my hands, turns them, and starts to inspect my forearms.

"OmigodIloveyourbracelet!" she shouts. "Tiffany?"

"Cartier."

"Oh my God, let me see, is it from a *boy*?" She drops one of my arms and turns the bracelet over and sees the inscription: DADDY'S GIRL.

"Aw, from your dad?"

"Yeah." I stare fixedly at the letters while she fingers the chain.

"You have a nice dad, then?" she says, rocking forward onto her toes.

"Nice…? Yeah, he's nice."

"Mine's a fucker."

"Oh. Too bad."

"S'okay. That's what drugs are for, right?" she says, and then laughs hysterically.

"Ri-ight."

"Oh poor you, it's only your first day. I'll stop being such a freak." She finally drops my hand. "I'm glad you have a nice dad."

Nice. Well. My fantasy dad—the one I lead people to believe I have, the one I wish I had—is quite nice. In fact he's better than nice, he's doting and extravagant and I have him wrapped around my finger. The real one, not so much. But that's what imagination is for—I am using my imagination to manifest the better dad, and if I believe it long enough, maybe it'll happen.

"Well, he's a busy guy but he's fun. A couple of years ago he flew me to Prague just to have dinner with him."

He *said* he would, anyway, which in a way means he, too, is imagining a better version of himself, which means we are creating this illusion together. Sort of.

"Seriously?"

"Oh yeah. He sent a jet, actually," I say, warming to the story and figuring it's a good place to boost my alcoholism cred. "It was just the pilots and me and a bottle of Cristal. The restaurant was French and we ate so much caviar—you know, with the little pancakes—that we didn't have room for the rest of the food when it came."

My new roomie gazes at me, eyes wide. "What did you do with the food?"

"My dad said we should be like the ancient Greeks…"

"Huh?"

"You know how they…" I make a finger-down-throat gesture. "They'd just get rid of it so they could keep eating."

"Early bulimia!"

"Of an entire culture, I know. Totally. But, gross. We didn't. We had it packed up specially with ice and stuff, and I took it to school for my lunch the next day…in L.A."

"Crazy."

"And of course I finished the Cristal on the way back, so I was pretty hungover and eating this five-star lunch from Prague—"

"That's a pretty expensive lunch."

"I know, right? But my dad…he didn't care, he just wanted to see me."

"Wow. Sweet," she murmurs.

"So sweet," I say, ignoring the curdling feeling in my gut.

"So, drinking," she says, and then looks down at my arms again. "But no tracks. Didn't think so, since you've arrived in no sleeves. I drink and I like my wacky tabbacky, as my mom calls it. It makes me"—she flaps her arms here like she's going to take flight—"it makes me—woo! Like I still love to talk and all but I'm...I'm just cut loose and relaxed. And, well, I guess this is the end of all that. I've got a sex thing, too, but that's not what I'm in for this time. And I don't know, I think I'd like to keep one vice. Although, group therapy for sex addicts? Everyone knows that's the best place to find someone to hook up with. Ironic, right? Woo! Am I in your space?"

She is. She is right up in my face, but I can't get a word in to say so.

"I'll try not to be in your space." She takes a half step back, not nearly enough. "I have porous boundaries and apparently I'm a little intense. This is your bed," she says, and points to the middle one. "The sheets are so soft you'll just want to strip down and roll around in them. Last time, I bought one. "

"What?"

"Yeah. They sell them—just like a Westin or Hilton bed. You can buy the Sunrise bed."

"Seriously? That's hilarious."

I wheel my two suitcases across the ebony-stained bamboo floors and over to the middle bed. It's not bad— done up with crisp white linens, four fluffy, down-filled pillows, and a duvet. Draped across the bottom is a bed-scarf woven in shades of blue.

"Okay, this'll work," I say, continuing to survey the room.

"Private balcony," the girl says, following my gaze.

"Really? What about when our friend here decides to

jump?" I say, walking over to look outside.

"Shh," she says, coming up beside me. "She can hear. But anyway, there are thick bushes underneath, so it'd be really hard to die that way. I think all that would happen is you'd be scratched up, maybe with a broken limb or two. And you might get an eye poked out or something."

I try to picture someone planting the bushes on purpose, for suicide prevention, and shake my head. Wade and Sydney had better be grateful.

"I'm Talia," the girl says. "The mute is Jade—like the stone. That's what I said when I found out she doesn't— ha ha—doesn't talk, get it? Anyway. I think she's been seriously traumatized. Well, most of us have, but worse for her. Something really crazy, like somebody lit her on fire or killed someone in front of her or something."

I shiver.

"I've been asking her, trying to get her to talk, telling her all my deep, dark secrets to encourage her, but so far nothing. Right, Jade?"

Jade does not move, but I get the feeling that she is, in fact, listening to every word.

"Anyway, our previous roommate's parents yanked her from the program two days ago. They came for the family therapy sessions and I guess things got too real for them or maybe they thought she was going to spill a bunch of family secrets—they're famous. I'm betting she's very, very high right now. Or, like, dead. Wouldn't that be creepy? To be sleeping in a dead girl's bed?"

I stare at the bed.

Jade has not moved except to breathe.

Talia has not breathed except to talk.

"I bet it's happened before. People checking out early, dying the next day because they went on a binge. We should do some kind of smudge ceremony or something. And pray." Talia plops down on my bed and bounces a bit.

I raise my eyebrows.

"Pick your deity—doesn't have to be the Bearded One or anything. So what did you say your thing is?"

She actually pauses for an answer.

"Um." I clear my throat. "Like you said—alcohol."

"Just alcohol?"

"Isn't that enough?"

She shrugs. "Most of us are cross-addicted. Apparently we teens have an underdeveloped—ah, one of the cortexes? In the brain? Anyway, we have less impulse control than adults, less fear of risk, so we tend to try a whole bunch of stuff once we get going. But hey, if it's just alcohol, yay for you. Won't make the recovery any easier, though."

"Thanks for the reassurance," I mumble.

"So are you famous?" Talia asks.

"Me? No." This is the standard celebu-spawn answer, though most of us give it expecting people not to believe us.

"Really? You look like you might be. You've got the *thing*. And I heard you met Koch. Plus, your hair! Is that strawberry blond your natural color? Of course it isn't. This is California. You know who you look like, though? You look exactly like the woman—that soap star who was all over the tabloids with her porn star girlfriend. Julie? No...

Jules," Talia continues. "Jules Carlyle. You've both got that feline thing going on."

"It *is* my natural color, actually. Speaking of famous, anyone interesting here right now?"

"Couple of reality stars, some former child actors, a model," she says. "There's always someone, and a lot more since Koch took over the place. 'Course there are people on staff who think Sunrise is going to hell because of him."

"Really," I say, suddenly feeling my Level card as a sharp weight in my pocket and simultaneously worrying that there's been no mention of Wade—what if he checked out early like this roommate of theirs? I will put a hit on Sydney if that's the case. "So no one major…"

"Oh! Actually, one of the boys from that series—*Drift*?—is here. He's pretty major." She raises a hand and snaps her fingers repeatedly, right next to her ear. "Ahhh… what'shisname…Miller…"

I try to remain casual. "*Wade* Miller?"

"Oh! Yeah. Yeah, that's him."

Okay, no hit man for Sydney.

"Is he… Does he seem all right?"

"I heard prescription drugs," Talia says. "Opiates. They say he was in the infirmary detoxing for days. But then again, we don't see them much."

I'm wrestling with the idea of sweet Wade from Ohio getting so sick from drugs that he had to detox for days, and thinking of Sydney's description—pale, skinny, sweaty—and then adding that to the silence from his team, when her last sentence registers.

"Wait. We don't see who?"

"The boys."

"What do you mean we don't see them?"

"Well, we see them but we don't *see* them—you know, because they have us sign that 'no fraternization' contract—"

"What?"

"Don't worry, you signed it. It basically says you'll be booted if you're caught screwing around with someone. The programs are separate and we're discouraged from hanging with each other. I mean, there are some supervised social events and stuff, and it's not like you can't have a conversation, but the staff are breathing down our necks the whole time. Too much potential for trouble otherwise, especially with people like me around, ha ha. I have to say I'd really like some of that kind of trouble. I have not had a chance to get my freak on at all."

"I'm...sorry to hear it..."

"Anyway, I have an art class in five and you'll be off to therapy. I hear you have Madam."

"Madam?"

"Yeah. Not because she's French or anything, but because she's, you know, like a madam. Of the whips-and-chains variety. And she *will* whip your psychological ass."

I frown.

"It's, like, her mission in life to make everybody break down. You know, it's the 'tear you apart then put you back together' method. Of course, you're supposed to be much stronger once put back together but, woo! Not fun! Whatever you do, do not try to lie to her. No one can lie to that woman. You look a little pale; are you all right?"

"I'm fine. I can handle it. You have her?"

"Ha. Not this time. My doctor this time is a sweetie. Total earth mother. Guess they figure if you're a repeat patient, they need to try a new approach."

"What about Jade?"

"Well, I have no idea how she even does therapy—smoke signals?—but no, she doesn't have Madam. They probably think she's too fragile."

This time, I groan out loud.

"Oh, don't worry. It's only an hour of your life. Well, an hour every other day. And it's for your own good." Talia picks up her bag and moves to the door. "Gotta go," she chirps.

Scary therapist, strange roommates, no-fraternization contract, different program from the guys…when I find Sydney we're going to have a *serious* talk.

"Wait," I say, and Talia pauses.

"Yeah?"

"About the…the boys. When *do* you see them?"

"You sure you're not a sex addict, too?"

"Uh, not so far."

"There's still time. Ha ha! Anyway, the boys are at the evening meetings, and you'll see them on weekends at the big Family Group extravaganzas. Plus they have their meals in the dining hall right after us, so we see them in passing, but they keep us so busy it would take a major effort even if you did want to fraternize."

"I'm going to kill Sydney."

"Sydney?"

Oops, I didn't mean to say that out loud.

"Just a friend from school," I say.

"Oh," Talia says, somehow seeming to bounce even while standing still in the doorway. "For a second I thought you meant *Sydney* Sydney."

"*Sydney* Sydney?"

"Yeah. You know, our former roommate?"

"Your former…"

"Sydney Leoni."

Shiiiiiittttttt.

"She was pissed about the no-boys thing, too."

Chapter Six

So, I get the purse, then kill her.

If she's still alive, that is.

Because she did fall completely on her face at some opening. I wasn't talking to her at the time, but I heard they found cocaine on her, so she might actually have a problem, as opposed to it being a onetime thing followed by an overreaction of her parents that she went along with in order for the chance to ditch the last couple weeks of school, which is what she told everyone.

Either way, she's gone and I'm solo.

Maybe I should retract my supposed alcoholism and get out of here. Nobody said anything about hard-core therapy or male/female segregation, or roommates, and although it seems obvious now, I didn't realize I'd have to lie constantly once I got here.

Plus Mr. Adam Mentor Dude is super uptight, and what is the point of going through all the pain to get bouncy butt cheeks if there's no one to appreciate them? (It's kind of like that thing about the tree falling in the forest. If a quarter bounces off my butt cheeks but there's no one to see it, did it really bounce? If Wade is here but I can't rescue him, is he really here?)

Worst of all, to get busted as a fake alcoholic would be horrifying. My mom would lose her mind, my dad would be even more certain never to speak to me again, Wade would think I'm a total idiot, and it would probably be all over the internet, making me a laughingstock and pariah all at once.

On the pro-staying side, I have put a lot of time and energy into this project.

And it *would* be nice to be pampered a little, and gain muscle tone.

And if I leave, I'll just have to go back to my boring life where there is no chance at all to help Wade, much less make him fall in love with me.

And it looks like my mom would make a big freaking deal about it no matter what, and then probably send me back, either here or somewhere worse, without the gourmet food and the possibility, at least, of saving Wade.

And leaving might be kind of like chickening out.

So in that sense, staying is a matter of bravery.

And selflessness.

And honor.

Exactly.

And really, how hard can it be? I've dealt with therapists

before. Mom made me go during the divorce, and if anything it was more boring than scary.

Talia was exaggerating. Everything will be fine. I just have to get through the first couple of days, and then the rescuing, relaxing, and getting-fit part starts.

Besides, no one said it's *impossible* to see the guys.

Everyone else is just too busy dealing with their co-occurrences and cross-addictions to try. Whereas I am not hampered by such trivialities and can focus my full arsenal of undiminished talents on the project.

I am a celebu-spawn, after all. And though we celebu-spawn are universally disparaged and generally expected to come up short in looks, talent, and moral fortitude and very often do crash and burn, we survive in a world that is completely wack, so we are also smart, resourceful, creative, and endlessly determined to get what we want.

Do not mess with a celebu-spawn, in other words.

Do not mess with *me*, because I will find a way to get what I came for: Wade Miller.

I just need to orient myself, get through a bit of red tape, and then figure out a way to explore. Obviously we do get some free time if Jade is allowed to lie around on her bed like a lump of congealed angst.

Yes. Onward.

I stand up, lift my suitcase onto the end of my bed, and open it.

"So what should I wear for therapy?" I say, glancing at Jade. "Topshop? Prada? Full body armor?"

Her gaze flickers to me and then back to the ceiling.

"You really mute?" I say. "Or just don't feel like talking?"

I detect a smirk.

Ha. She's totally normal. I knew it. Talia is the world's biggest exaggerator.

"Seriously," I say, taking a step toward her bed, "you can talk to me if you want."

I'm about to take another step when she sits bolt upright and hisses at me—*hisses*—loud and sudden as if she's a snake and I just stepped on her tail.

"Whoa!" I hold up my hands and back up. "Jeez. Take it easy."

She stays there, panting and glaring at me, and I get my first real look at her. She has big dark green bruised-looking eyes and stringy, straight, shoulder-length dyed-black hair with brown roots growing in, and her vibe is all wannabe Demi Lovato crossed with Kristen Stewart, but in sweats, and the overall effect being more Avril Lavigne—ie, trying way too hard. And even though she's stick-skinny, she looks like she could kill me.

"Okay, no worries." I step away. "I can choose my own outfit."

Back at my bed, I contemplate leggings and a different dress—tight and red with cutouts—but I'm rattled. I don't feel like getting undressed and changing bras, et cetera, with Snake Girl in the room, and I don't have time to look around for a bathroom, either.

I re-zip the suitcase and settle for changing into sandals and putting on a fresh coat of Stila lip stain.

At the door, I risk a look back, half expecting Jade to

be staring at me with her teeth bared. Instead, she's on her back again, but now her chest and shoulders are shaking and there are real tears rolling down across her temple and into her hair.

Shit.

I blink and lick my lips, then open my mouth to say something but cannot think of anything helpful. Finally I just tiptoe away.

And if I thought that was weird, on my way back to meet Adam I glance into one of the other rooms and see a blond-haired girl curled up and moaning on the floor.

Wow. The rooms are nice and the view is pretty…but these people do not look like they're at a spa. They do not look like a steam, a pedicure, and a light lunch will fix them.

Adam is sitting with his compact body flopped, legs splayed on a couch just outside the girls' dormitory. There's a TV on the opposite wall and all he needs now is a bag of chips to make the scene complete.

"Awesome," I say, sitting down next to him, kicking my shoes off and pulling my feet up under me. "What are we watching?"

The couch is small, so our legs touch for a couple of seconds, but then he leaps up like it burned him.

"We're not watching anything," he says, and clicks off the TV.

"You get to relax; why can't I?" I say, stretching out and

wriggling my toes.

"Much as I'd love to sit around watching movies with you," he says, making it clear he would not love it, "I have a job to do."

"You would be much cuter if you smiled once in a while. Let me guess—you're afraid to."

"What?"

"You know, because you're so young and you think we won't take you seriously, so you've decided to act super authoritative all the time. Like, to keep your professional distance."

"I have no problems with my professional distance."

"If you say so."

He opens his mouth, shuts it, glares at me. "And cuteness is not my job, either."

"The list of things that aren't your job is getting really long, Mr. Mentor."

"Let's just go," he says, shaking his head.

"Fine," I say, and stand. "Oh! But, um…you should probably know, my roommate? Jade? She's all crying and weird. And there's another girl lying on the floor of her room looking like she's about to die."

He grunts. "Ar'right."

"Should someone…I mean…"

"Eyes on the prize, Miss Carlyle."

"Oh yeah? What's the prize?"

Finally, an unwilling grin quirks at the corners of his mouth, and it changes his face. It's not cute, it's something else. Just for a moment there is a flash of humor, of intelligence, of other layers existing below the inflexible persona he's projecting.

"Look to your own recovery," Adam says, and locks eyes with me.

"Sure, but…"

"We're aware of Camille's situation. And of Jade."

"But don't you even—you act like you don't even care."

"You have no idea what I care about," he says in a suddenly cold voice.

"Sorry. Jeez. Who pissed in your corn flakes?"

For a second, he looks like he wants to throttle me.

And then he lets out a bark of laughter, showing yet another side of himself, and shakes his head.

"Well, aren't you something," he says.

"Uh…thanks."

"It's not really a compliment."

"I kind of got that. What about Jade and the other girl? Camille?"

"Yes, yes. I'll send someone to check on them both after I've dropped you at therapy. Happy?"

"Ecstatic."

So, fine. They're on it. I don't have time to be getting all involved and overwrought about people I've just met, people who certainly don't give a crap about *me*.

I have my own problems. Many of them.

Like remembering the stages of recovery so I can fake the right sequence of emotions for my apparent terror of a therapist. Figuring out how to get myself a Level Three card, finding the pool, discovering where the guys' program happens and where they hang out when they're not doing… whatever they're all doing.

"Oh, here's an orientation package," Adam says, and passes me a folder. "In there is a copy of the rules, plus your schedule. Memorize it. You're going to be busy."

I glance at the schedule and see that there is, indeed, a long list of activities including drama therapy, creative dance, music, painting, yoga, surfing, group, twelve-step meeting, therapy, reflection, AA, and something called "Vision."

"Also, you'll find a map in there."

A map. Finally something useful.

"The building is obviously big enough and the property is almost five acres, not that you'll be unaccompanied until you're a Level Three, but I suggest you keep it with you."

I flip through and find the map. What I need is one of those stars that says "You are here" and then a Google Map that shows me the way to the male dorms. Wade's location via GPS would also be helpful. But no luck—it's just an ordinary map.

"Now, follow me," Adam says, and lopes away without even looking to see if I'm coming. I have to jog to catch up, and my sandals make a conspicuous clip-clop on the terra-cotta tile.

"So, Adam…" I say, once I've fallen into step with him.

"Yeah?"

"The male and female programs are separate?"

"Yup."

"I'm relieved to hear it," I say.

"Really," he says, without so much as a sideways glance.

"Yes, really. I think my healing process, my, uh, recovery, will go faster if I'm surrounded by women. I mean, not counting you. No offense. Come to think of it, why *do* they have a guy working with us?"

He grunts for an answer, then takes me by the elbow to steer me left and produces an access card to get us through a doorway. We're now in a hallway with what are obviously office doors on one side and massive windows overlooking the grounds and ocean on the other.

"Wow," I say, and stop to look, though since I live on the ocean I'm less moved than I'm pretending to be and really trying to stall while I get information. Also, I need to use up some of the minutes of my therapy appointment—the shorter it is, the better.

"Yeah, it's nice," Adam concedes.

"So what's your deal?"

"My deal?"

"Yeah, like, what are you doing here? Where are you from? Why do you want to spend all your time with alcoholics and drug addicts and so on?"

"Why do you want to know?"

"Well, you know a lot about me. Including every single thing I packed to come here and all the answers on that questionnaire probably—"

"I haven't read your answers, actually."

"The point is, it doesn't seem fair. Or balanced, or whatever. And I'm supposed to trust you, right?"

"All right. I grew up here—Venice."

"California boy."

"Yep."

"Venice is nice."

"Depends where in Venice you live," he says with a grimace.

"Parents?"

"Mom's a social worker—"

"Aha!"

"Yeah, runs in the family, kind of."

"And your dad?"

"You're nosy, you know that?"

I wait.

He sighs. "My dad was in the business—like yours—"

"How do you know who my dad is?"

"Your last name, to start, and you're a dead ringer for your mother. Give me some credit."

"Fine. So your dad?"

"He couldn't stick it out."

"It's a hard business. What'd he do after?"

"Can we move on to something else?"

"Sure. Why are you allowed to work with female patients? Clients?"

"Patients. Why do you ask?"

"Oh, I guess because if the male and female programs are separate, I figured they might do the same with the staff."

"We're professionals."

"I thought you were a college student—how can you be a professional?"

"I met the criteria to work here, I was hired, I signed contracts, I get a paycheck every two weeks, therefore I am a professional."

"Is there a special training to be a mentor?"

"I've done courses in mental health, addiction therapy, recovery, prevention…so yes."

"Hmm." I lean against the window and tilt my head so the light shines through my hair. I've learned a thing or two about lighting from Mom over the years. And yet, Adam does not appear to be moved. Not one bit. "You must also be good at fending them off."

He frowns. "Fending who off?"

"You know," I say, "the sex maniacs. *Addicts*, I mean."

He gives me a disappointed look.

"No, no, listen," I say. "I've already heard about this from Talia. Since we're all locked up like Rapunzel with no access to the opposite sex and there you are, the only somewhat attractive, red-blooded male around…"

At this, Adam cocks his head and lifts his eyebrows.

"Nobody's locked up," he says.

"No?"

"No. We try to foster an atmosphere of respect and trust. It's a 'respectful separation.' The guys are just in another wing."

"Ah."

"But don't pull that 'attractive, red-blooded male' shit on me, Lola."

"I said *somewhat* attractive."

"I said, don't pull—"

"I'm not pulling any—"

"Stop."

He gets up in my space and he's suddenly less Jonas brother, more Hemsworth brother in kick-ass superhero mode, which is to say large and intimidating.

I shut my mouth.

"Thank you," he says.

I nod.

"People come here because they want to get better."

"Of course."

"And as for me," he says, "I think I have a pretty good handle on the teenage psyche."

"Yes, well, it can't have been that long since you were one yourself."

"You don't give up, do you?"

"Not often. How old are you?"

"I can handle myself."

"What a relief," I say and, even though my celebu-spawn flirting doesn't exactly work on him, and obviously he isn't going to tell me his age, it did help me get the information I need, sort of.

He checks his watch. "Let's move along."

"Sure."

There are a couple more turns and then we're at the door, a big oak door behind which lies Madam. Outside is a chair, presumably for those so keen they want to get here early. Unlike me.

I would not call myself keen.

In fact, I think I would really be better off without therapy.

Adam puts up a hand to knock.

"Adam?"

He pauses.

"I…I think it might be too early."

"No," he says, "we're right on time."

"No, no. I mean, for me. Too early for me."

"To have therapy?"

"Yeah. I mean, it's a big day. I just met my roommates and I'm trying to get integrated. It all feels like a little bit… too much, too stressful. And…and stress is the biggest trigger, right? I read that somewhere. And God forbid I should be triggered on such an important day."

"You'll be fine."

"I don't think so."

"Regardless, there's no negotiation. You have to go."

I look at the big oak door again and my insides twist. It's not that I'm *afraid*, exactly. But if Madam really is some kind of psychic, truth-seeing ass-kicker I cannot handle with my celebu-spawn powers, I could be unmasked, humiliated, and booted from this place before I even *see* Wade, much less save him so we can run off into the sunset together.

"Are you coming, too? For the session?"

Adam shakes his head. "I don't take part in one-on-one therapy sessions. I'm like…more like a guidance counselor. I'm the guy you come to if you have an issue — "

I snort.

"—if you *have an issue* or you want to change your programming."

"Okay, perfect: I want to change my programming."

He raises a thick dark eyebrow and hooks his hands in

his belt loops.

I pull out my schedule.

"Right. See here, it says 'Vision.' That sounds like something I need right away. I would like to switch that to now and therapy to…tomorrow."

"No." He puts his hand up again, ready to knock.

"But Adam!"

"What now?"

"What about the energy thing? If I can't handle a massage or spa treatments, my energy really might be too fragile for this today."

He drops his hand from the door, steps closer, and looks into my eyes.

"Everyone's scared when they get here, Lola," he says, attitude gone for the moment.

"Not the way I am."

"Exactly the way you are," he says. "Without alcohol, drugs, whatever the addiction, you feel stripped down, vulnerable. How many days have you been sober?"

"My last drink was three days ago," I say, happy this, at least, is true. "As you know."

"Right. So the worst of the physical is probably over by now, but there's the psychological, the emotional withdrawal. You're without your crutch for the first time. Counseling will help with that."

Unable to sustain his gaze, I look down at my feet. And then I wonder how many addicts take time to get a pedicure before they come in. Not many, I'm guessing. Most of them probably go on one last binge instead.

Crap. I really might not be as well prepped as I thought.

"Everyone here has been through it, Lola. Everyone. So you don't have to pretend to be brave and you don't have to bullshit."

"That's what you think."

"It's what I know."

His sincerity, combined with his intensity, slays me. It's one thing when he's uptight, or acting tough, but this side of him is disturbingly, disconcertingly compelling. Looking into his eyes at close range, they're focused and full of conviction, and it's almost like he has a superpower—this thing he can turn on that will cause me to be willing to do anything he wants. Whatever he wants. Mixed with that is another factor—that Adam being nice is much worse than Adam being a jerk, because suddenly I feel like a terrible person.

"Fine," I say, and my shoulders slump. "I get it. I'll do it."

"Good."

"I don't have to like it."

"You probably won't."

"Nice," I say. "Okay, I just need a minute."

"Sure," he says.

I pull myself forcibly out of his physical zone, then sit down in the chair and wait for him to leave, but he just stands there.

"You were going to talk to someone about Jade…?"

"It can wait."

"No, no. You go. I'll be fine."

"I have to deliver you to her, Lola," he says, and then

before I can stop him, he knocks.

"But you said I could—"

"Calm down. I'm just going to tell her you're here," he says, and then opens the door a crack, sticks his head in, and finally goes all the way inside.

I hear the low tones of a hushed conversation and then Adam's voice: "Yes, I'll tell her."

He reappears, leaving the door mostly open behind him.

"I said you need a moment," he says, "and she's just finishing some paperwork, so go in whenever you're ready."

"Thanks," I say. "I'm good from here."

"You want me to wait and introduce you?"

"You know, this feels like something I need to do myself," I say, channeling some melodrama and standing up.

Adam smiles, nods his approval, then starts off down the hallway.

I'm turning to knock on the doorframe as he reaches the corner and looks back.

I wave.

He waves, and then disappears.

I wait a full five seconds…then I turn in the other direction…and run like hell.

CHAPTER SEVEN

So, I look like a coward.

But if I can't actually do what I came to do, maybe I *should* bail and leave the space for the real addicts.

Because, just possibly, I might be in over my head.

Also, if I decide to stay but I'm going to act like a total idiot and possibly get caught somewhere I'm not supposed to be, assuming I can *get* to the place I'm not supposed to be, I'll be cut more slack on my first day than I will later on.

Also, yeah, I am a coward.

I don't want my inner life taken apart and examined. I don't want to talk about my feelings, my childhood, my repressed sexual desires, or any of that stuff.

I come to a locked door, slide my card into the slot, and cross my fingers. The light goes from red to green and the door clicks open. *Thank you, Dr. Koch.* I step through, look around, and realize I've found my way to the studio section where I had a brief tour earlier on. I duck around a couple of corners and run down a set of stairs, hoping to put some distance between myself and the possibly pursuing sadistic shrink. I get to a door that goes outside. Through the glass I see palm trees, flowers, a blue sky. I send out a prayer and put my card in the slot.

Red light.

Wow. I really am locked inside like some kind of criminal.

Somewhere to hide, then.

I scan the nearby studio doors and see one whose window is dark. Perfect. I turn the knob, go in, close it behind me, and prepare to take a few deep breaths and maybe collapse on the floor.

Except I hear music. Piano and a stunning, heartbreaking voice. And through the dim light coming through the closed blinds, I see a baby grand piano and the singer sitting, playing it.

The notes are melodic, the song like a dirge, albeit a bluesy, sexy kind of dirge.

I step farther into the room, but the singing cuts off mid-note and the singer pushes back abruptly and slams the lid down over the keys.

"Well hello there," I say once I've recovered from the shock. "Nice to see you, *roomie*."

She stands rigid, looking at me.

"So…you're singing? Does that mean you're cured? That was fast."

She shakes her head.

"Not cured. Faking?"

She shakes her head, more vigorously this time.

"So…the selectivity is selective, is that it? Personally I'd call that faking, but hey, no judgment here. Song's a little depressing, but you've got a wicked voice."

She crosses her arms, glares.

"Don't worry, I won't tell anyone. At least, I don't plan to."

She points imperiously to the door.

"Yeah, I'm going. You don't have to pull your snake girl routine or anything."

I'm turning to go, then remember the map in my hand and the reason I came in here in the first place, and turn back.

"Wait a second! Jade? Any chance you're a Level Three? Because I'm desperate for some fresh air."

She stares at me with her freaky, piercing gaze, calculating.

I stare back.

Of course I wouldn't tell her secret. But she has something I need right now and there's nothing wrong with a little friendly, mutually beneficial deal-making…provided she doesn't stab me first.

Fifteen minutes later, I'm skulking through a series of courtyards, like Harry Potter looking for the Slytherin Common Room, but without the invisibility cloak.

I have not seen a single male, teenage or otherwise, plus it's hot as hell, I'm stressed out, and I'm starting to sweat. If I were a real alcoholic, this would definitely send me over the edge.

I'm taking a rest on a stone bench and getting ready to look at the map again when I spot my heart's desire. Well, my heart's current desire—not Wade, but a teenage male.

Hallelujah.

He's short, with white-blond hair, and he's wearing a wetsuit—a surfer. As he comes along the path, I hunch down, pull a large leaf in front of me, and concentrate on becoming one with the foliage.

He comes so close I can smell the ocean on him, but he passes without noticing me. I wait a few moments, then get up and follow him on tiptoe.

Five minutes later, I'm trying to stand casually behind a clump of hibiscus plants—I say casually because while I want to be inconspicuous, I will obviously give myself away if someone sees me actively crouching and peeping, and God forbid I should get mistaken for a paparazzo or something and get publicly humiliated and/or turfed from the premises before I have a chance to explain myself, much less get sober and fit and fall in love.

Up ahead, through an iron gate on the opposite end of the property from the building I'm staying in, and connected by the series of courtyards I got lost in, is a whole other building, also in Spanish Colonial style.

Adam said the guys were in another *wing*.

This is not a wing, it's the whole freaking bird.

The building is similar to the main one, including the private, suicide-proof balconies that must be attached to the dorm rooms, but slightly smaller—I'd have to guess without the dining hall and infirmary.

I've got nothing but my Level One card, but I need to find Wade, or find his room or his balcony at least, so I can come back at a more auspicious time—by moonlight, for example.

I check my watch. The hour allotted for my therapy with Madam is almost over and things are quiet. Ten minutes from now, I'm guessing, people will be out and about, moving from one session to the next.

In the meantime, my surfer boy has his card out and is getting ready to go inside.

What the hell.

I take a deep breath in, straighten my shoulders, step out from behind the hibiscus and up to the gate, just as surfer boy gets the green light and opens the door. I catch the door on the backswing and follow him into the foyer, which is almost identical to the one in the other building, right down to the double stairway and tiled fountain.

Surfer boy turns back, gives me a questioning look.

"Thanks," I say with a confident smile and a wave of my card.

"Uh, okay, no problem," he says, then shrugs and takes off up the right staircase, leaving me alone, at least for the moment.

Too late to get a maid's costume, I suppose.

I step lightly onto the left staircase and make my way

up. Below me, two guys come into the foyer, but their heads are together and they're in deep conversation, so they don't notice me.

At the top of the stairs, I check my map again, make a guess, and go left.

I'm halfway down the next corridor when someone, another teenage boy, this one super nerdy, comes toward me. He glances at me, frowns.

"What're you looking at?" I snap.

He ducks his head, walks faster, and I feel a pang of remorse for picking on someone who looks so downtrodden already. But I didn't exactly have a choice.

Besides, it worked.

I get to the doorway of the dorms but see the already familiar key-card thingy.

I try my card, but of course it doesn't work, so I turn and make my way back. Maybe I can find the lounge. I'm rounding a corner back near the stairway when I hear voices behind me—multiple voices.

Crap.

I cast about for somewhere to hide and realize there's a door just ahead. Unfortunately, it's the men's room door.

No choice.

I push on it, and it gives.

I push harder and then hurl myself inside, shove it closed behind me, and lean backward on it, safe for the moment.

And, as luck would have it…there stands sexy Wade Miller.

The only problem is, sexy Wade is…peeing.

He's standing at a urinal, peeing.

We haven't even kissed yet and I'm watching him pee.

Oh my God, kill me.

This is not the first encounter I want to have. I cannot have it. I'll have to throw myself back out the door and pretend it never happened. I start to move but, crap, it's too late—our eyes have met in the mirror.

"Uh, hi…" he says, less fazed than you'd expect, considering.

"I am *so* sorry! I'll just…" I turn to go.

"No, no, wait," he says, and I do because there are still voices in the hallway. I stand with my back to the room and close my eyes.

All these years I've dreamed of us meeting again, I imagined myself cool, self-possessed, and glamorous—nothing like the awkward kid I used to be. And we'd be on a red carpet, or in a field, or on the cobblestoned streets of Europe.

A bathroom in a teen rehab center falls rather short from a romantic perspective.

Add the fact that he's peeing and it becomes unspeakable.

I hear a flush, some rustling, water running at the sink, and then the sound of a paper towel dispenser.

"I'm really, really sorry," I say again, talking straight into the door.

"Hey, I'm the one who's sorry," he says.

"You… Why?"

"First girl I've been alone with in days and she catches me with my pants down."

"Oh. Ha ha." This would be a good time for the long-awaited big earthquake to come and swallow us both up.

"You can turn around, I'm decent."

"I'm sure you are," I say, still not turning because maybe I can keep my back to him the entire time and then he won't recognize me yet (he might not anyway—my being transformed into a totally different person is kind of the point   he's not supposed to associate me with the *old* me until he's at least met, and ideally started to fall for, the *new* me, at which point I can also begin the rescue mission) and then next time we meet we can start over.

"Come on, now you're making me feel weird," he says.

"*Now* I'm making you feel weird? As opposed to when I walked in on you in the bathroom?"

"Well, then, too."

I turn, putting my back to the door again, ostensibly to keep my distance from him, but also hoping to prevent anyone from coming in.

He's standing in the middle of the room looking... ridiculously good. I may not be able to breathe enough to manage a conversation with him. Rehab and recent detox notwithstanding, the slightly odiferous orange bathroom, the lighting of which does not do his coloring justice notwithstanding, this guy who was charming and deadly cute a couple of years ago is now dazzling. He's grown taller, his shoulders have filled out, his face is more chiseled—those are the biological facts, the on-paper differences. Meanwhile the sandy hair and cappuccino-colored eyes are the same. But...what is that saying about the whole being greater than the sum total of its parts? The sum total of Wade and his parts is devastating, is heart-stopping.

Bam.

I'm not going to rescue him. I'm not even going to talk to him. I'm just going to melt into a worshipping puddle at his feet, or throw myself, naked, into his arms.

Unless I can get a hold of myself, stat.

He shoves his hands into the pockets of his jeans, meets my eyes, then gives me a definite and not-subtle once-over.

I try not to hyperventilate, or giggle, or look away, and somehow manage to stand my ground.

He smiles his now-famous smile—some teen magazine actually awarded him "best smile" last year—and I watch his eyes for signs of recognition.

"So," I say, schooling my insides to calm the eff down, "how's your day going?"

"Looking up," he says.

No way he'd flirt like this if he knew it was me. And I doubt he'd be so cocky talking to Ben Carlyle's daughter, either. Mind you, he *is* cocky compared to the old Wade— he's grown a swagger. But you need some arrogance, or at least the appearance of it, to thrive in Hollywood, so it's not a bad thing.

Underneath, I have no doubt sweet Wade Miller from Ohio is still there, and I may be one of the only people in the state of California who knows him. All I have to do is cut through to that guy, make him fall in love with me, then escape from the bathroom without getting caught, and we'll be set.

Yes, he's gorgeous. But he also knows he's gorgeous, and that fact somehow helps me chill.

"So, I'm Wade," he says.

I smile. "Nice to meet you, Wayne."

"No, Wade. Wade *Miller*."

It's annoying yet adorable how he expects this information to make me swoon. Sure, the sight of him might have given me some heart palpitations and robbed me of breath for a few moments, but celebu-spawn do not swoon over TV stars, or any stars for that matter. Much better to put them in their place. Putting him in his place is also part of the Save Wade program, the program to get him off the Hollywood/Wade Kool-Aid, because that's got to be at the root of whatever other addictions he has.

"Huh. You one of the counselors, Wayne?"

"No, I'm not a counselor," he says, charm giving way to disbelief.

"Phew!"

"And it's Wade. W.A.D.E. Wade Miller. From *Drift*."

Everyone knows *Drift*. It's huge, the network has spent a fortune promoting it, and Wade has been on a zillion billboards.

"Hey, relax," I say. "Your nostrils are starting to flare and stuff."

He frowns, touches his nose.

"So, *Drift*…is that down the coast?" I ask.

"Down the coast? No!" Wade almost shouts. "*Drift* is… It's a show. A TV show, and I'm the— I'm on it."

He's both irritating and sexy, all flustered and pissed off

at the same time, and I love how he barely stopped himself from shouting, *I'm the lead!*

I take a few steps toward him, close enough to catch his scent—soapy and boyish and exactly the same but somehow *more*—and study his face like I'm trying to place it.

"*Drift*...hmm, I might have flipped by it late at night. But I don't watch reality TV."

He blinks, opens his mouth, then closes it.

"Anyway, W.A.D.E., I hope you win the...whatever it is you're all trying to win on that show."

"I—"

I start to leave.

"Wait! Where are you going?"

"Well, if you haven't noticed, I've kinda lost my way, and I'm pretty sure it won't go over well for me to be found in here, especially with you."

"Why especially with me?"

"On account of the male/female segregation, ahem, *respectful separation*, and the fact that there are supposedly a bunch of sex addicts running loose in this place. I might get mistaken for one of them and end up with a whole lot of extra therapy I don't need."

He frowns, shakes his head, looks bemused.

"Or *you* might. And I'm guessing you've got enough problems already, what with your reality show going on without you and stuff."

Now he laughs, a real, rumbling, nice kind of laugh, the arrogance finally gone.

"Yeah," he says, "I've got one or two problems on the

go. It's not a reality show, though."

"I know."

"You know?"

"Yeah, I can tell. You're one of those *real actor* types, right? Chops galore, very serious guy."

"Ha. I guess."

"Changing the world and stuff…"

He puffs up a little. "Sometimes. Not all the time, though."

"Oh well."

I should be leaving, but my feet seem overly heavy and we're kind of…staring at each other and he is so damn beautiful it's hard to stop.

"Wait, do I…? You look familiar, except… No way, I would have remembered," he says in a tone that makes me hot all over. "But it's more like you…you *seem* familiar."

"You think?"

"Yeah, I'm just trying to—" He breaks off as the door starts to open behind me.

"Shit!" I say, looking for somewhere to hide.

But Wade's reflexes are fast, and in seconds, before the person on the other side actually gets in, his arms come on either side of me to push the door shut again.

Lucky me, I'm between him and it.

"Hey, what the fuck!" says a voice from outside.

"Listen, man, I need a minute."

"Wade?"

"Yeah."

"Dude, let me in."

"Come back in five. You don't want to be in here, trust me," Wade says, and mouths *my roommate* to me.

"Okay, whatev," the guy says. "Thanks for nothing."

And then things get quiet again. Quiet with me essentially pinned to the door by Wade. Not counting the peeing thing, this bathroom venue is turning out much better than I expected.

Now if I could only breathe.

He looks down at me.

"Thanks," I say, trying to stay cool despite the record levels of hormones screaming through my veins.

"So," he says, still right up in front of me, "you said you were lost?"

I nod.

"You're *really* lost," he says.

"Oh?"

"It takes a special talent to get this lost. I mean, you ended up in a men's bathroom on the other side of the compound."

"It's my first day," I say, as if this explains it.

"What are you going to do on your second?"

I grin. "Don't know. You have any suggestions? Because I plan to get lost every time I have therapy."

His eyes widen and sadly, he takes a step back to look at me.

"You ditched therapy? On your first day?"

"Kind of. Yeah."

"Uh, that's not exactly the height of compliance."

"Hey, I'll comply. I'll do yoga and group and swimming

and 'Vision.' I'm not going to drink or do any drugs. I just don't want therapy. I don't need it."

"At the rate you're going, you're going to have it twice a day."

"Not possible. I'm going to be way too busy doing downward dog and rock climbing. Assuming I can get back to the girls' dorms."

"You need some help?"

I draw myself up. "Do I look like I need help?"

"Uh…"

"Don't answer that," I say, and reach for the door handle.

"Let me check the hall for you at least," he says.

"No, I'm good," I say. "But you're very cute to offer, W.A.D.E. Very cute in general. They should give you a bigger part on that show of yours."

"Actually, I'm the le—"

And that's when I kiss him.

I swoop up, give him a fast but firm kiss on the lips, then pull away and open the door while he stands there, blinking.

"Hmm," I say, doing my best not to hyperventilate or, God forbid, *swoon*, "not bad."

"Not bad?"

"Yeah," I say with a casual shrug. "It'll do."

CHAPTER EIGHT

I'm sure the only reason I make it back through the grounds and into the main building without getting caught is I'm floating.

I kissed Wade.

The last time I saw him I had a plan to kiss him. It was at the wrap party and I was thanking him for letting me hide out in his trailer when my dad was in a mood, and he was saying he owed me big time for showing him the ropes and so on. My plan was to tell him I liked some guy and wanted to kiss him and Wade could pay back his big debt by helping me practice in advance. And then we'd have to practice a lot and in the process fall madly in love and he'd beg me to ditch the other guy and we'd live happily ever after. He probably would have done it, too. He was that nice of a guy, and I tend to be pretty convincing. Except I was too chicken to ask and so there was no kissing, for practice or otherwise.

Until now.

Swoon.

I am totally staying in rehab.

I wait all day for the hammer to come down. I mean, yes, I didn't get caught with Wade, or even outside on the grounds where I'm not supposed to be yet, but there's no way Madam didn't tell someone I never showed for my session. Adam, most logically.

I tell myself that I'm already in rehab with limited privileges and access, so really, what can they do to me if I am in trouble, other than lecture me or kick me out? And they're not going to kick me out, at least not yet. Still, alongside my giddy, Wade-induced bliss is a knot of tension I can't quite shake, and I am dreading my next encounter with Adam.

When I see him outside the dining hall before dinner, I have to force myself to look him in the eyes, and then looking him in the eyes gives me a full-body flush that's obviously related to my guilty conscience, which makes my act of wide-eyed innocence hard to pull off.

"What's up?" he says.

"Not much," I say.

And then…a too-long pause as he just stares at me.

"You changed," he says, finally.

"W-what?"

He glances down at me, taking in my jean shorts and

cropped tee.

"Oh," I say, and then start breathing better, feeling like I'm out of the woods. "Yeah. You know, just in case I have to climb up onto any more doctors' tables."

He doesn't laugh. Instead, he says, "I think the doctors from now on will have couches or chairs, not tables."

I give a weak laugh and curse at myself inwardly for bringing up doctors of any kind.

"So, speaking of doctors...?"

"Let's not, actually—"

"How was therapy?"

"Therapy?" I say, as if it's a distant memory. "Oh. Well it was...as expected, pretty much."

"Oh yeah? What was it you expected?"

He knows. Shit, shit, he knows.

In case there's any doubt, though, better to go on the offensive.

"Do I have to talk to you about it? I mean as your mentee? I thought that kind of thing was confidential."

"Yeah, it's confidential," he says, eyes narrowing. "But you can talk to me if you want to."

"Awesome."

"So?"

"I don't want to."

"All right, Lola, but—"

"New subject," I say brightly. "How are you? What did you do this afternoon? Do you have other patients to mentor, or is it just me?"

"I'm fine. I did paperwork and prep work. I have other

duties besides mentoring, as you'll see. And I've got a couple of other patients I mentor but they're settled into the program—progressing and complying nicely."

Complying nicely. He knows. He knows but he's not saying. Why?

"I'm not your full-time job, then?"

The corners of his mouth quirk up, just a bit.

"No," he says, a glower replacing the almost-smile. "But you should be someone's."

After that, he walks me into dinner without saying anything about Madam, and leaves me with Talia while he goes off to sit with some of the staff.

I glance repeatedly at him throughout the meal—to the point that Talia asks me if I'm looking for someone—but I'm trying to figure out if he knows, and if he does, why he didn't say anything. Maybe he knows and he's just being patient—giving me a pass because it's the first day. Or he knows and he's playing some kind of mind game with me, trying to wear me down, make me feel shitty, drive me to confess. Or he knows but doesn't have the authority to do anything about it because he's just a summer student, and I will be getting in trouble later, from Dr. Koch. Or he doesn't know, because he was busy and/or Madam decided not to tell him because *she* is playing games with me—gathering information and waiting to see what I'll do, the better to strip my psyche with.

None of these are good scenarios.

And yet, it occurs to me that if I'm going to succeed at this masquerade and subsequent rescue mission and love connection, et cetera, I can't afford to get all fucked up and stressed out like this every time I break a rule. I'm going to break a bunch of rules. I broke a bunch already just by coming here. This problem is not a problem until it *is* actually a problem. When it comes to me as an actual problem, I'll deal with it. In the meantime, I have to forget about it. Stay focused.

Exactly.

My schedule says, and Talia confirms, that every evening there's a big meeting—everyone at Sunrise can attend. Sometimes it's a guest speaker, sometimes it's an AA meeting.

"Even for the people who aren't alcoholics?" I ask Talia, who is sitting across the table from me, noshing on a piece of spelt-crust pizza.

She nods vigorously. "It's a catchall. It's called AA but it addresses and includes all the types of addictions. Because really, the disease is the same no matter what the substance or substances."

"But it's not, like, the TV thing where you have to stand up in front of everyone and say, 'My name is so-and-so and I'm an alcoholic,' and tell them your sob story, is it?"

Talia starts laughing.

"What?"

"It's totally that," she says.

"No."

"Oh, yes. Unlike how with police procedurals and legal dramas where it's totally different from real life? AA is, well of course every meeting is different, but that part? That's it exactly."

"Oh my God."

"Don't worry, you'll be great."

"No, no. I won't be."

"Well…you don't actually have to go," she says. "You do, but not every night. People don't always go on their first day. I mean, half of us are still detoxing and totally unable to go the first couple of days. There's a certain number of nights per week that you have to attend, but I can't remember what it is because I always go. I like to see people, keep busy."

"Huh."

I decide to skip AA.

No need to overexpose myself to Wade on the first day.

And, well, yuck. I'll sit through whatever class or group, but I'm not standing up in front of a bunch of people and making a big mortifying speech about my supposed alcoholism. I'm not into telling my business to strangers— even my fake business. Plus, the longer I'm here the more I realize that I cannot possibly be well rehearsed enough to do it.

In addition, I need to call Sydney and find out what the hell is going on and why she left me to fend for myself here, so on my way back from dinner I stop in the lounge—a cozy room in an odd Starbucks–African safari fusion style— where one corner has a wing chair and side table with a landline with a cord (seriously) on it.

It's funny, but I feel sort of naked, twitchy and disconnected without my phone. I keep going to check it every few minutes and then it's just not there.

Anyway, time to make some calls on the dinosaur. Thank God Sydney's number is one of the few I have memorized, due to her being allowed to get a cell phone a full six months before me, and my having to call her on a landline that entire time.

But when I reach for the phone, a staff member (one of the nonmedical, non-counseling staff who're apparently called "techs") materializes to inform me I don't have privileges yet.

"To make a phone call? Are you serious?"

"It's on the first page of the rule book."

"I haven't gotten that far yet."

"Well, I suggest you get started."

As I'm stalking to the door I spot Jade, sitting in a corner smirking at me. I stop and turn my glare on her.

"What?" I snap. "Doesn't look like you can make any calls either, Miss Mute."

She smiles and gives me the finger.

Just before dawn, the center seems to go up in flames. I am yanked out of a deep sleep by a screaming bell that is obviously the fire alarm and leap out of bed, stumble to the door, and lurch into the hallway before noticing I'm all alone.

Shit.

I dash back into our room.

"Talia! Jade! Get up!"

I flip on the lights. Talia, already sitting up, squints, and Jade, also awake, flinches away from the light like a vampire. That would explain a few things, actually. Regardless, at the moment it's my job to save her life.

"Girls! Get up, we have to go!"

"Well sure, eventually," Talia says.

"Not eventually. Now!"

"Where's the fire?" Talia says.

"I don't know! I don't smell any smoke but —" I pause, realizing abruptly that the alarm has stopped ringing. "Okay, it's stopped, but we should still evacuate just in case."

"Hunh?"

I walk over to her and wave my arms in front of her face. "Fire! Hello? There was a fire alarm! I'm having a freaking heart attack here and nobody has moved." I turn to include Jade in my rant. "Is everyone in this place so depressed they're not afraid of burning to death? Are you deaf as well as mute? Joan of freaking Arc?"

"Um, Lola?" Talia says.

"Yes, okay, that was insensitive. Sorry, Jade. My point is—"

"No, Lola, it was just the wake-up bell."

"May I point out it's the middle of the night?"

"Six a.m."

"Exactly."

"Six a.m. is when we get up."

"We get up at six."

"That's what I said," Talia replies. "For Contemplation."

"Contemplation? Related to, or as opposed to,

Reflection, which I believe we do every night?"

"In the morning we Contemplate, in the evening we Reflect. I know, I know. But it's on the schedule: Contemplation, six fifteen. We're supposed to make our beds first and I suggest you do it fast. Hey, I love how you keep repeating everything I say, by the way." The sincere grin that accompanies this last statement only irritates me more. How can she be so sunny and helpful and devoid of sarcasm, even this early in the morning?

Fifteen minutes later, I've pulled on a pair of distressed jeans and a cropped sky-blue sweater, thrown my hair into a ponytail, and grabbed one of my pairs of Ray-Ban Fat-Asses, though I could have sworn I packed two pairs and I only see one in my dresser. We arrive in the lounge, which reminds me of last night and being denied use of the phone and the fact that I'm not supposed to leave the damn building, much less get a massage.

To top it off, Adam is sitting on one of the khaki linen-covered couches with a steaming coffee and a binder, looking perfectly awake and well-groomed, and still not mad at me, not even noticing me at all, in fact. He is almost chipper, sitting there laughing and talking with one of the prettier female patients from my hallway.

She's probably one of his mentees. A better behaved, more compliant mentee who doesn't actually even need his help or attention and now just likes to sit around having cozy talks with him and telling him how great he is. Or maybe he's telling her how great she is. Whatever. It's irritating. Everything this morning is irritating.

Talia and Jade make a beeline for the coffeepot.

I march up to Adam, who finally notices me, and then has the nerve to smile.

"My parents would never have sent me here if they knew about the human rights violations," I say.

"What?"

"My dad especially. Communication is very important to him and he's going to be seriously pissed when he finds out I can't call or even text or email him."

"Contrary to popular belief, Lola, use of the telephone and internet is not a human right." He swivels back to talk to the pretty female patient again.

"I beg to differ. Freedom of speech. And another thing," I say, running over him as he turns to me and starts to speak, "there are studies—*scientific* studies about teenagers and sleep. It's proven we function much better when we are not woken at the crack of freaking dawn."

"Is that the *scientific* wording? Crack of freaking dawn?"

The girl laughs. I hate her. I hate him.

He leans back on the couch and studies me, again with that gaze that seems to hold superpowers. There is something about Adam, about the way he looks at me, at anyone he's talking to actually, that's very intense, very present. He locks on, pays attention, sees. He doesn't seem to care if it's weird or if it creates an awkward silence. It's disconcerting, annoying, and yet when it stops it always leaves me feeling a little bit...less. Relieved, but less there, less colorful, less interesting. At the moment, though, we're still in the disconcerting, uncomfortable zone.

"What?" I demand.

"Nothing," he says, pleased with himself, obviously.

"Stop smiling at me, Adam," I say through my teeth. "And don't mock me, either. And one more thing: being so rudely awoken by a bell that sounds like a damn fire alarm is very bad for the overall mental outlook of any teenager, much less a bunch of addicts who are obviously easily upset!"

The other girls, eighteen in total, plus a few older people who must be the other mentors, are filtering in and sitting with their mentees, but the room has gone quiet.

"Ah. You're *upset*?"

"Yes, I'm— No, I'm…I'm just making a point."

"Okay," he says, then dismisses me with a shrug, leaving me less, and with everyone looking.

"*Okay?* What do you mean, okay?"

He opens a binder that's sitting beside him on the couch and starts to read, but I am not going away because now I've got a real fire—a fire burning up my belly, chest, and throat.

"You know what?" I say, pointing an accusing finger at him and willing him to *look* at me. "This is not a spa."

Adam looks back up again, finally. "Sorry?"

"This is not a spa! It's not like a spa *at all*. It's nothing *like* a spa."

I'm shouting. Everyone is staring at me. I'm making an ass of myself, I know, but I can't stop.

"Nope," he says calmly, "it's rehab."

"Well, *obviously*! But regardless whether it was supposed to be a spa, or *like* a spa, and that it's actually fucking *rehab*, this...this is not a reasonable time of day to ask a person to get up. Unless there is a *fire*."

"It seems she's not a morning person," says Talia, who has come up beside me with a mug in each hand. "Coffee, roomie?"

I'm shaking. I'm losing it. I'm staring at Adam, glaring at him and shaking with a sudden, choking fury that has to *go* somewhere, a fury that, if I were in my right mind, might seem unreasonable and out of proportion and even a little bit crazed.

But I am very much *not* in my right mind, and so I reach a hand out and take the coffee without looking away from Adam, who makes things worse by ignoring me and turning back to his damn binder.

"I am not having a good time," I say through clenched teeth. "And I don't like this kind of coffee!"

And then I reach out and slowly, purposefully...

...pour coffee all over Adam's binder.

CHAPTER NINE

So there's a cold, ugly white room with no windows for people who pour coffee on their mentors' binders. It's called "solitary" and it's quite a bit more jail-like than spa-like.

I spend the morning there.

Breakfast is pushed through a slot in the door, but there's nothing on the tray I want to eat and anyway, I'm not hungry. No one talks to me. I am left, presumably, to think about what a bad thing I've done.

I know it was a bad thing. And sitting all alone in the silence, my brain goes on a loop, repeating it over and over, and it's all I can do not to curl up into a ball in the corner and moan. I am an idiot. I made an idiot *of myself*. And for a person who considers herself to be relatively "together," I really lost it.

But the thing I feel the worst about is Adam, who may be uptight and irritating but who obviously has a difficult job and didn't deserve to start his day like that. Not to mention it's not his fault he gets under my skin the way he does—he's just doing his job. Meanwhile I'm being an asshole.

A few hours later, I'm starting to think I'm locked in the white room permanently and pondering how I'll fend off boredom and eventual lunacy when the locks finally turn and someone comes in. My insides lurch. It's Adam. While I'm super relieved someone has come, and even almost happy to see him, I can't quite look him in the face. Instead I sit, slumped at the edge of the single bed that is the only piece of furniture in the room.

He leans against the wall inside the door, arms folded across his chest, and I can tell he's looking at me by the way I want to squirm away.

"Lola."

Of course there's nowhere to go.

"Yes."

"You're lucky Dr. Koch likes you, because we have zero tolerance for violent behavior."

"I wasn't being—"

"*Zero.* That's company policy."

"Okay."

"And I personally have a no-tantrums policy."

"Look," I say, head snapping up finally to brave his gaze, "if you would stop giving me shit for five seconds, I would apologize!"

"Wow," he says. "This should be good."

"Except you're annoying me again *already*, and that makes it hard to keep feeling remorseful. Which I *am*, actually."

He shakes his head and turns, as if to leave.

"Wait!" I stand. "Please don't leave."

He turns back. Still having trouble looking into his eyes, I glance down and notice he has changed his clothes into a darker pair of jeans and a rather tight T-shirt. I wonder if he keeps extra ones here, or if he went home to Venice. I wonder when he finds time to work out, because obviously he does. Maybe he does it in one of the gyms here...

Amazing what my brain will jump to when I'm avoiding something difficult.

Focus, Lola.

I yank my gaze up—God, what if he thinks I'm ogling him on top of everything else?—then I fill my lungs with air and let it all out in one long sentence. "I really am sorry; it was totally out of line to pour coffee on your stuff and I truly, honestly feel terrible about it and I really, really promise I won't do it again."

"Okay."

"And I want to add that it was very uncharacteristic behavior for me and I'm sure my parents will pay for the dry cleaning bills for the couch and your clothes, and for replacing your binder or the paper, or whatever. Seriously. In fact go ahead and get yourself a designer leather binder and, like, paper made from Indonesian silkworms or Mexican bark or whatever. I know you're actually a hardworking guy."

"Uh…thanks."

"That's it? 'Thanks'?"

"But I'll pass on the silkworms. What were you expecting?"

"Well…it was a big step, I thought."

"To apologize?"

"Yes! And I was very sincere, Adam."

He walks closer, never taking his eyes off me. "Good."

"And I'm embarrassed. I have no idea what came over me."

"Because you're usually one hundred percent charming," he says with a smirk, now only a step away from me and staring right into my eyes like he's trying to gauge my sincerity.

"Exactly," I say, but then, again, I find myself looking away. "And I don't want you to think I'm…I don't want you to hate me."

I must be looking pathetic all of a sudden because Adam puts his hands on my shoulders. His skin is warm but instead of soothing me, it makes me jumpy. Then he squeezes and says, "Relax, Lola. It's all right."

I reach up, thinking I need to pull his hands off my shoulders and step away, but instead I find myself—WTF?— falling into him for a hug like some kind of desperate little girl, or not-so-little girl. And he lets it happen. He actually wraps his arms around me and pulls me closer, and it feels— crap, I can't put words to it; I don't know. We're not that physical a family and in general I don't hug a lot of people, so it's kind of a shock. He smells really nice—clean and somehow sharp and he's so warm and solid, and it…aches. Shit. To my horror I suddenly feel like I might cry.

"You'd have to dish out a lot worse than that for me to hate you," he says.

"Okay," I say, blinking hard, swallowing, keeping my face turned away, head on his chest as I try to pull myself back together.

"But please," he says, "don't take that as a challenge."

Chapter Ten

After swearing up and down to behave myself and rhapsodizing about how excited I am to rejoin the program (and I am, especially in contrast to being locked up), I am released from solitary. Adam escorts me to the dining hall, where I'm just in time to grab some lunch before the afternoon program starts.

First up on my schedule is meditation. Like I need that after five hours alone in a jail cell. But fortunately with the morning's drama out of the way, I can get back to thinking about Wade, which gives me something to meditate on.

I meditate on the sound of his voice, his extreme handsomeness, on the surprise in his eyes as I swooped in to kiss him, on the way he caught his breath, on the strong-but-fleeting warmth of his lips on mine…

And then, like the way it happens in dreams and things

don't make any sense, Wade's face morphs into Adam's and he's not kissing me but staring, disappointed, like he saw me kissing Wade and knows I'm here for less-than-legitimate reasons…

"When a thought comes, observe it, then dismiss it."

Yes.

It's not *my* fault I'm not a real alcoholic.

Well, depending on how you look at it…

And anyway, since yesterday when I saw (and kissed) Wade, I now know for sure I have a purpose in being here.

I am here for him.

It's not like I'm hurting anyone—I'm trying to help.

Exactly.

Drama is next and, despite my new and improved attitude, a bit of a nightmare.

Clarice, the drama teacher, has a bad weave and manages to mention how she was in *Rent* on Broadway about every five minutes.

"Failed actor?" I whisper to Talia.

"You're such a bitch," Talia whispers, and then cackles with delight, earning us a long, level gaze from Clarice.

"Today we're having our class outside," Clarice says, and proceeds to lead us from the delicious air-conditioning of the studio out the back door into another sweltering day. We go through a wide archway to one of the numerous courtyards I saw on my tour yesterday. It's rectangular and very pretty, with high ivy-covered stucco walls and an arch on each wall, a large patch of springy grass at the center, and multicolored tiled fountains tinkling on either end.

"All right," Clarice says, once we've all settled on the grass. "I want you to close your eyes and go to your quiet place."

"Not again," I mutter. The meditation teacher was also very keen on this supposed "quiet place."

Talia, beside me, giggles like she's reading my mind, then whispers, "It's all about the quiet place. You'll be going there a lot. One time—"

"Talia," Clarice says, a warning in her voice.

"Sorry."

Talia must have a lot of trouble finding her quiet place.

"Okay, eyes closed," Clarice continues. "Now I want you to think about your addict."

"My what?"

"For those of you who are new, ahem, that's the persona, the part of you inside that takes over when you get high," she says. "A lot of us try to simply lock this part of ourselves away, but it doesn't work. The addict always gets loose. What we need to do is learn to handle it when it happens rather than deny it exists. We need to hear what the addict has to say and come to terms with it. This is the path to both healing and coping."

Aha.

"All right. Go deep and connect with the addict."

Talia giggles again, then for a few moments all is quiet.

"Now, we are out in nature because I want you to think

of an animal. Think of the animal that is most like your addict."

My mind draws a big fat blank on this one.

"There is no right or wrong here," Clarice says. "If you look deep enough, you will find it."

I press my lips together and concentrate.

Alcoholic, alcoholic…what kind of animal would I be if I were an alcoholic and harboring an inner addict? Something thirsty, I guess. Thirsty and hungry and kind of desperate. Rat, vulture, squirrel, fox, bear, crow…perhaps this is where Jade got her snake thing. Snake. No. Guinea pig. Wolf. Dog. Lion.

A lion's not a bad choice.

"Now I want you to keep your eyes closed and find the voice of your animal addict…"

Oh ho, wait a second. I think I know where this is going…

"And now…speak with that voice."

Yep, here we go with the capital-D Drama Exercises. All I need now is a unitard and a dog-eared copy of *An Actor Prepares*—I've seen the old pictures of my mom in theater school and heard the stories—and I'll be set.

Scrap the lion. The goal is to fly under the radar.

Maybe the crow?

All around me, people are embracing the exercise, and the air is filled with roars and squeaks and barks.

"Caw, caw," I say halfheartedly.

"Beautiful," Clarice says to us all. "Now with the voice connected, let your animal addict inhabit your body, all of your body, from your core to your fingertips. And, keeping that deep connection to voice and body, you may open your eyes and begin to move."

Oh, give me Lady Macbeth. Give me freaking *mime*.

Do not make me flap around like an alcoholic crow.

And yet, I promised Adam I would behave.

"This is for you, Adam," I mutter as I crouch low and say, "Caw, caw."

After a couple more "caws," I open one eye and survey the group.

Talia has found a very sexy cat in her quiet place and Jade is face-first in the grass, animal indeterminable. A tiny girl with blond ringlets scuttles about wiggling her butt and oinking. Seriously. Actually, she looks familiar...I think she used to be on one of those kids' shows, maybe *Barney & Friends*—everyone's been on that.

Caw, caw. Flap, flap.

I notice Clarice giving me the hairy eyeball and starting to come my way, so I rise to my feet, sigh from the bottom of my soul, and then flap my arms with more enthusiasm. "Caw, caw."

"Don't just move, inhabit the space!"

I jog a little. Flap some more. Channel my inner alcoholic crow.

"Caw."

It's excruciating.

"Don't be afraid!" Clarice calls, her voice rising along with her enthusiasm. "Become your animal, inhabit the space, face your fear! I want to see you louder, bigger, faster!"

I think the phrase is "Louder, faster, funnier," but I doubt she'd appreciate my saying so. Around me people are going wild. Some look like they're actually having fun, and most of them don't even look embarrassed. Two are crying, which makes more sense to me. Except I realize it's more catharsis than mortification, and Clarice actually seems quite thrilled with them both.

Must be one of those addict things I just don't get.

I feel Clarice's eyes on me again and add some frenetic movement to my crow dance. She moves on but keeps glancing over her shoulder, so I keep it up.

Talia meows over, head swiveling (in character), looking for Clarice before whispering, "Lola. Look."

"Look at what?" I whisper back.

"Boys!"

Oh no.

"Me-ow..."

"Where?"

She jerks her chin toward one of the archways and meows again.

I am already frozen, mid-flap, but now I turn my head, slowly and carefully, to look.

And then I wish I hadn't.

Because three shirtless guys are standing, peering through the archway, and of course, one of them is Wade.

And *of course*, I've been cawing and flapping my wings like a total, complete *loser* and he is looking right at me, an unmistakable shit-eating grin on his face.

All the romantic moments I've imagined, all those times I've daydreamed about seeing him shirtless, I never imagined this.

Chapter Eleven

Sadly, I can't skip group. I was really only interested in attending if Wade was going to be there and I could support him through some angst and emotional drama, or at least flirt with him. Since that's not going to happen, I'm not enthused.

And besides, despite my talents for verbal embroidery, I do worry about being unmasked.

But hopefully I can get through it by remaining inconspicuous. Otherwise I'm probably going to have to make up a bunch of lies about myself and my family, which is hard work, not to mention risky. Things are supposed to be confidential here, but please; I'm not that naive.

Sadly, the second I walk in, flanked by Talia and Jade, I can tell inconspicuous is out.

First, there are only six of us in the group.

Second, the woman who must be the therapist—an African-American woman with strikingly deep dark eyes and a mane of beaded dreadlocks—gives me a long, hard look, then a curt nod, and motions me to sit at the large round table. I can tell already that this is a woman who takes no shit, and who is expecting trouble from me. I guess I left inconspicuous behind when I freaked out in the lounge this morning.

"I'm Mary," the therapist says. "I'm a recovering addict with eight years."

"Hi, Mary," I say. "Wow, eight years. That's great."

"Perhaps you could introduce yourself," she suggests. "And tell us why you're here."

"Um, okay. I'm Lola. Lola Carlyle."

Talia's eyes widen.

"Carlyle, oh my God, Jules! I knew you looked like her! And Jules and Ben! Didn't they have, like, the worst breakup ever?" she says, almost jumping out of her seat. "I knew you were famous!"

"I'm not really—"

"Whoa, whoa," Mary says, then turns to me with a glare. "We don't normally use last names. None of that matters here."

"Sure it does," one of the girls pipes up.

"Why would you say that, Emmy?"

"Uh, because if she didn't have famous parents she'd still be in solitary after the shit she pulled this morning," Emmy says.

"That's bullshit!" Talia says.

"Yeah? Then how come I was stuck there for two whole days last week?"

"Maybe because you were acting like a psycho!"

All of a sudden, the two of them are standing up, shouting and swearing at each other across the table. I look around, amazed at how the rest of the group, including Mary, is taking this in stride.

Finally, just as I'm starting to worry there's going to be an actual fight, Mary raises a hand and says in a loud, low voice, "That's enough, girls. Sit down."

And after a moment, they do.

"Emmy," Mary says, "Lola and Adam have dealt with what happened, and we are moving on. Lola may have some anger issues to work through and if so, we'll get to it. Talia, Lola can defend herself if need be. Everybody here is responsible for *themselves*, and for treating everyone else with respect. Let's move on. Please continue, Lola. Why are you in rehab?"

Because I'm a fool.

"Uh, binge drinking."

My one main drinking episode *was* a binge.

"Why do you drink?"

"Wow," I say. "That's really getting to it."

"Why?"

"Well…lots of reasons. Lifestyle, partly. I mean, everybody in Hollywood drinks and no one cares if you're underage. So, I let it get a little out of hand. You know how it goes."

"I don't, actually. I don't know how it goes for *you*."

"Oh."

"We're not so interested in the surface reasons here, Lola. Like, what pain are you medicating for, what's missing in your life? We want to know the *deeper why*." This doesn't even sound cheesy, coming from Mary.

"The deeper why. Gotcha."

"So?"

"I suppose it's related to the quiet place and my inner addict?"

"Sarcasm isn't going to help you."

My heart thumps as I feel everyone staring at me. Staring at me like predators, like vultures, waiting for me to show the right weakness (disguised as the deeper why) so they can tear me apart.

As if.

And yet I have to give some kind of answer, and the best lies are ones that are closest to the truth.

"When you put it that way," I say, speaking slowly like I'm searching deep inside, "I guess my life might be lacking normalcy. And…stability? Like, it sounds so glamorous, the parties and awards ceremonies—my dad loves to take me to those. And I can buy whatever I want, do whatever I want. But it's disruptive, right? It's lacking in structure. And I guess on some level, you know, talking about the deep why thing, I'm restless and looking for something to fill the void."

"The void, huh? Are you lonely?"

"Lonely? No," I say quickly.

"But that question bothers you."

I shake my head and give a baffled look.

"Hmm. How much do you drink?"

"Oh my God," I say with a shrug and a big, self-depre-cating roll of my eyes, "I lose track. But I *love* tequila."

Talia and one of the other girls give sympathetic chuckles. Mary studies me; I stare back.

She asks a few more questions. Everyone seems to be watching and listening to my every word as I fill in more of the story about my supposed addiction. I'm glad I spent time working on my "history" before I arrived because Mary has some very specific, pointed questions—everything from what was my first drink and the reason I took it (I say some-one handed me a glass of champagne at a party when I was thirteen) to whether I've ever blacked out to what made me realize I had a serious problem.

I admit to having blacked out—I actually did—and make up a story about partying too hard and passing out in a bathroom stall at an industry party as my rock-bottom moment.

"Sort of like Charlie Sheen, but with my clothes on and without the porn star or the coke on my face," I say. "But it wasn't good when my dad's assistant found me and had to sneak me out back into the limo. That's when I realized, you know, that I needed help. My parents are so awesome; the last thing I want to do is embarrass them."

Around the room, heads are nodding and I feel simulta-neously exhilarated and ill.

"Congratulations on taking the first step," Mary says, and everyone claps.

And I exhale. They believe me. I can do this.

CHAPTER TWELVE

Tuesday night, I go to the evening meeting and covertly study beautiful Wade, who started out as earth-shatteringly hot and is getting more tanned and fit by the day, while pretending to listen to the guest speaker—some famous hockey player who trashed his career and almost died from taking a variety of drugs and drinking like a maniac.

Wade catches me looking at him and winks, and I duck my head to hide my smile.

Emmy and Jade sit nearby shooting killer glances at Talia and me, and Talia practically sits on top of me. I'm not sure if she thinks she's protecting me, which I don't need, or wants to adopt me as a pet or what, but I don't want to hurt her feelings, so I just try to deal with it.

There's no chance to talk to Wade, since he's on the

other side of the room, and Adam herds us girls out of the meeting and back to the dorm as soon as it's over.

Wednesday morning, Adam stands up in the lounge and reads from his coffee-stained binder: "'Every day is a new day with a new beginning and a new end. I greet each minute with renewed enjoyment.'"

Around me, people are scribbling in their journals and I know I should be too, but…really?

"Lola?" Adam says. "Why the eyebrow?"

"Eyebrow?"

"Yeah, eyebrow," he says and points. "That one there."

"What, you're not greeting my eyebrow with *renewed enjoyment*?"

Talia snorts and a couple of other girls chuckle.

Adam looks at me, not amused, and suddenly the shame over my behavior yesterday comes back full force. And it occurs to me this is why he's still using the stained binder — in order to constantly remind me. Suddenly I feel like I should apologize again, and get another one of his very nice hugs. Although the severity of his gaze makes me feel like I imagined the niceness of the hug, or imagined that it even happened in the first place.

"Oh, God, I'm sorry, Adam," I say. "I'm really not a morning person. But, new day. I'm all over it."

"Good."

After Contemplating, we rock climb at the beach.

In group we each make a collage with the theme "Crossing Over," with images from our addicted pasts, the idea being to use the image of a bridge or a road and show our bad behaviors and unhealthy thought patterns on one side and our new, good, and healthy behaviors and patterns on the other side. Apparently most days (when there isn't someone brand-new to interrogate) we have some kind of themed artistic project in group and it's supposed to lead to all kinds of discussion and growth, et cetera. Kind of "Arts & Crafts with Angst."

I'm just starting to relax into it when Jenny (the blonde who *was* in *Barney*) gets raked over the coals by Mary—some big thing about "not surrendering." There are heated words and then Jenny has a huge meltdown where she admits a bunch of horrifying, painful things about her life as a child actor and Mary chars her butt for feeling sorry for herself. (Harsh in my opinion—I would feel sorry for myself, too, if I were her.) And all of it makes me realize I got off easy yesterday.

Worse, I have therapy again this afternoon, which is going to be more of the same, but without anyone else for the therapist to get distracted by.

This is all getting kind of annoying—I should be saving my mental energy for figuring out how to get some more time alone with Wade, rather than dodging psychological traps.

Yep, somehow I've got to get out of therapy.

I am so distracted in kickboxing I get myself kicked in the ear by Jade.

"Oww! Watch it!"

Jade grins and holds both arms out as if to say, *What?*

"Watch it, emo girl. You could have knocked out my diamonds," I say, and press my hand to my throbbing earlobe and the one-and-a-half carat there. "They are expensive, and my dad would kill me if I lost one of them. And he'll kill *you* if I end up in the hospital."

Jade scowls, gives me the finger, and comes back in for more sparring. Somewhere near the front of the studio, the instructor is going on about finding safe places to vent our aggression.

Surely he doesn't mean each other...

Dr. Koch pops his head in toward the end of class and gives me a thumbs-up, which I return with sincerity because seeing him has just given me an idea...

When the hour is over, with thirty minutes to go until therapy, I head downstairs for an impromptu meeting with Dr. Koch.

It goes well.

Back in the dorm, I shower and change, then lightly crumple my schedule and toss it off the balcony into the bushes below, pack a few things in my purse, and exit the building...with my new Level Three access card.

All it cost me was a couple of VIP passes to my dad's next premiere. It's not until January and I'm sure I'll think of a way to get them by then.

Out in the maze of courtyards, I manage to avoid another drama therapy class, Talia in deep conversation with her therapist (the earth mother apparently likes to therapize outdoors), and some guy playing a bongo drum, on my way to my destination.

It would be too much to hope that I'd run into Wade again, and wandering all over the grounds is sure to get me caught. But I'm not going to spend the hour cowering in a corner either.

Nope, I'm going for a swim.

Sure, I'm not supposed to be at the pool even though I technically have access now. But that's exactly why no one will think to look for me there. And if someone does happen to find me, it won't look like I'm hiding, just confused.

Because, of course, today I "can't find" my schedule.

On Friday I will *misread* my schedule.

And on Monday perhaps I will sit by the ocean and go into such a deep meditation that I lose all track of time and *forget* about my schedule. Or something.

There's a small problem when I get to the pool—I can see it, but the iron gate is locked and the rest of it is surrounded by a high vine-covered fieldstone wall. Of course, I am a decent climber due to spending many bored hours as a child in a neighborhood where every house is surrounded by these types of walls.

I am not to be stopped by a mere wall.

I move back to assess the thing, then step out of my shoes, put them in my purse, zip the purse, and throw it over the wall. Thus committed, I take a last look in both directions, reach both hands up into the vines, scramble for a foothold, and start climbing.

The thing is probably ten feet high and it's not an easy climb. In fact it almost kicks my celebu-spawn ass to the curb more than once. I slip and scramble, skin one knee, and cut my forearm on a stick. But somewhere along the way, the sheer exhilaration of the effort kicks in and that, combined with the buzz of doing something so sneaky and fun, gives me the hit of extra strength I need to persevere.

Before long I am up and over, then dropping down behind a hedge of yellow and purple hibiscus and collecting my purse. Stepping out onto the flagstone patio, I see the deserted pool with its small grotto and tiny waterfall, all surrounded by the giant wall and a lush, wild-looking flower garden

It's paradise. And it's mine, at least for now.

I let out a long, satisfied sigh, then strip down to my polka-dot boy shorts and bikini top, and dive in. I glide through the water, relishing the luxury of solitude, the relief of spending a few beautiful minutes where I don't have to think or talk or lie about addiction, or talk about thinking about addiction—a few minutes where I don't have to think or talk (or lie) to anyone at all.

When my limbs start to feel heavy, I climb out, pull one of the lounge chairs into the remaining sunlight, and lie down on my back.

Sometime later I start to drift off, which is probably why I don't hear the gate opening.

But then a shadow falls over me.

I open my eyes.

The shadow is Adam's.

"Have a nice swim?" he asks, the hands on his hips belying his friendly tone.

Clearly, I'm busted; it's just a matter of what for.

"How lovely to see you," I say, and reach my arms above my head to stretch as though I'm completely relaxed and clear of conscience. "I did indeed. In fact, I'm going to do this every day."

"Really."

"Absolutely. In fact, it really *renewed my enjoyment*. Did you know that exercise is one of the best and most important coping mechanisms? I learned that in group and figured I should apply it right away."

"Ah."

"Could you shift over a bit?" I gesture at him to move. "You're in my sun."

"I'm going to be in more than your sun pretty soon," he says, not moving but seeming to get bigger.

"Sounds kinky," I say, and smile.

"Cut that out."

"Am I bugging you, Adam?" In fact, I can't seem to bug him at all, at least not in that way. It's like he's immune to my being female. It's annoying. I reach languorously back with both arms to lift my hair off my neck, and I see his eyes drift, ever so slightly, down my arching body, before snapping back up to my face. That's better—he might be immune, but he's not unaware. "Or is it that I'm not supposed to say the word 'kinky'?"

He mutters a curse then picks up the end of my lounge chair, turns it on its back wheels, and rolls me into the shade.

"Wheeee!"

He sets me down.

"I've been trying to cut you some slack until you calm down, settle in. But there's a limit to the amount of shit I'm willing to put up with."

"I apologized for the coffee episode, Adam, and I—"

"Your therapist is looking for you."

Oh. Uh-oh.

"My what?"

"And I'm starting to wonder why you bothered to come here if you're not going to participate in the program."

I let out an aggrieved sigh and sit up.

"I am participating. I've been up since six o'clock this morning participating."

"You missed your therapy session."

"Are you sure? When was it?"

"Just now."

"Oh. Oops."

"Yeah, *oops.*"

"I lost my schedule, okay?"

"No, not okay. And for the record, I don't believe you. Especially since you haven't been to an AA meeting yet and you didn't go to therapy on Monday, either. I let it pass because I could see how scared you were, and Dr. Owens said to give you a couple of days, some time to come around on your own. But you're running out of chances fast."

"I went to the meeting last night, if you recall. Besides, Talia said I only have to go to, like, three a week."

"Listening to a speaker is not the same as going to an AA meeting."

"Doesn't say that in the rule book."

Adam glowers.

"Hey, at least I've read it. Ever skinny-dip here? It's so sheltered and private, I bet people end up skinny-dipping all the time."

"No, Lola, it's locked for a reason and I—" He breaks off. "These kinds of comments are inappropriate."

I pull my face into a mocking frown, lower my voice, and mimic him, "These kinds of comments are inappropriate."

He closes his eyes and takes what is probably supposed to be a calming breath.

"Okay, I know," I say. "I'm sorry. But you're so serious all the time, you really bring out the worst in me."

"I'm serious for a reason. I'm serious because I know the damage addiction can do—to the addict, to everyone around the addict. I don't think it's something to joke about."

"I think the hardest things are the most important things to joke about," I counter. "Laughter helps."

"Maybe 'make light of' is more what I mean."

"Were you an addict?"

He looks at me like he's going to refuse to answer, then changes his mind. "No. But it's not like I don't have it in me."

"Biologically, you mean?"

"Biologically, genetically, yeah," he says, brows drawing together in a troubled look.

"Your dad?"

"I don't want to talk about it."

"Oh, come on. I'm supposed to share everything but never learn a single thing about you? That seems kind of unbalanced."

He lets out a huge breath, then sits down at the far end of the lounge chair.

"See? How hard was that? Now tell me about your dad."

"He flamed out. You know how it is," he says. "I was really young, but I guess he had a lot of potential. He moved out here and made a good start…"

"Then he didn't make it?"

"Wasn't that, exactly. He was doing well I think—I was little so I don't know exactly—but he got disillusioned. There was a screenplay he wrote that I guess he was really proud of. It got optioned, rewritten, scheduled, preliminary casting, then shuffled, canceled, optioned again, rewritten— that whole cycle."

"Happens."

"Yeah. A lot of ups and downs. My mom says he was partying before that, but at some point it changed from partying to just…nasty shit. Drinking, drugs…and my dad, the guy he'd been, was, like, gone."

I know how that feels. I want to say so, but I don't. Adam slumps, hangs his head, and I reach a hand out to comfort him but pull back at the last second, because where am I supposed to put it—his shoulder? His leg? His hand? Every option feels awkward.

He turns to look at me then, his dark eyes giving me a full blast of everything he's feeling—grief, fury, determination.

"I get it," I say after a few long moments.

"Do you?"

"You have, like, a mission."

"Yeah." He nods.

"So something good came of it."

"I want to help, Lola. I need to. That's why I'm on your case all the time."

"Sure, yeah," I say, hoping to back off from the sudden intensity of this conversation and therefore taking on a teasing tone. "You have to consider, though, Mr. Mentor, that what you think is going to help me and what I think is going to help me might be different…some of the time."

"What *you* have to consider, mentee, is that I actually know a lot more about this shit than you do. For real."

"Here we go again," I say, rolling my eyes and lying back on the chair again as if I'm suntanning, which technically I can't, being that we're in the shade. "I guess our deep moment of sharing is over…"

"Jesus, Lola." He stands up. "You are going to drive me around the fucking bend."

"Aha! I bring out the worst in you, too—admit it."

"Listen: if I report you as noncompliant, you can be kicked out of the program. You realize that?"

"See? That is exactly what I'm talking about." I screw my face up to imitate his frown: "If I report you as noncompliant, you can be kicked out of the program."

"Or you could be transferred to another facility—somewhere less pleasant."

"Ooh, I'm so scared." I continue with the mockery despite the moment of ice-cold panic this particular threat gives me.

"You have to stop doing that," he says.

"Sure. As soon as you stop acting like you swallowed a rule book. Hey—by the way, how'd you find me?"

"Cameras." He points to two places among the vines and I see lenses, one trained on the pool and the other on the wall. "In most of the potentially unsafe areas."

"What?"

"Just because it doesn't look like anyone's watching doesn't mean they're not. Impressive climbing."

"Oh my God. Hello, invasion of privacy?"

"Uh, hello, invasion of the pool area you're not supposed to be in?" he says in a mocking tone. "Are you going to go off about human rights violations again? Am I going to have to change clothes?"

"Well, there's no coffee around, but I could shove you into the pool." I stand up and advance on him.

"I fucking dare you to try," he says, a spark of challenge in his eyes.

"You actually think I would?"

"Are you kidding? I know you would."

I am tempted— so tempted. But he doesn't look easy to move, truth be told, and really it never works to push someone in a pool once he knows you're planning it, so really I'm just inviting a wrestling match, which I would likely lose. And it would be on camera. And just yesterday I promised him I would behave better, and here I am already in trouble again.

Still, he is *so* fun to provoke…

I take a step toward him, then another and another, until I'm close enough that I have to tip my head up to meet his eyes.

"Go for it," he says.

"You don't know everything about me," I say, placing my palms on his chest.

"Likewise."

"To try to push you in now would be so predictable."

"Also predictable? You'd be the one going in, not me."

"And would that be appropriate, Mr. Mentor?" I give him a very small push but do not succeed in moving him.

"Not really," he says, pushing back against my hands for a second. Then he shakes his head, sidesteps away, and heads back to my lounge chair.

"You're tempted, though," I say, following him. "Admit it."

"That's enough, Lola," he says, his change in tone signaling he's not playing anymore.

"Fine," I say. "Another time, then."

"There's not going to be another time because you're not going to be sneaking into the pool again. Right?"

I sigh. "If you say so."

"Promise?"

I make a face.

"I didn't think you liked being in solitary that much…"

"Fine, I promise. No more sneaking into the pool."

"Thank you. By the way, how the hell did you get out of the building in the first place? That part I don't have on camera."

"With my card, of course," I say, and hold it up close to his face. It's the same card, but inside it's been reprogrammed.

"Your card?"

I smile. Adam's eyes narrow.

"Don't tell me," he says. "You got Level Three access."

"Not everyone takes such a dim view of my participation,"

I say, with a tilt of my head and a shrug of one shoulder.

Adam breaks away, takes a few strides from me, and appears to be swearing at the bougainvillea. The words "fuck" and "fucking Koch" are heavily featured.

I'm tempted to say something about triggers and anger management, but decide that might be pushing my luck. Pushing my luck *further*, that is. Instead I pull my beach towel straight on the chair, put my Ray-Ban Fat-Asses on, and lie down.

"I'll be escorting you to therapy on Friday," Adam says, spinning around and coming back.

"Fine by me," I say, stretching my arms up over my head.

"And I mean *all the way in the door* to therapy."

"That's dandy. Very nice of you. Now, would you mind if I catch a few rays before dinner? I'm fragile and I need my vitamin D."

Chapter Thirteen

"'I eagerly surrender to the twelve-step program,'" Adam reads first thing Thursday morning.

"Eager" is a stretch.

As I battle the twelve freaking steps, my rescue effort/love life withers—I have not seen Wade since the meeting Tuesday night.

In addition:

-All the deep thinking and looking inward is getting tedious

-I have yet to see the inside of the spa

-I can't find my canary-feather earrings

-I've decided I don't like exercise—too much work

-And my supposedly mute roommate hates me more than ever

Meanwhile, I swear Adam is tailoring the affirmations

specifically for me.

In group we start an "amends quilt," which requires first making a list of people with whom we need to make amends, then illustrating/sewing/decorating a square of fabric symbolizing each one. When we're done, we'll be stitching them together, and Mary says we can even sign up for a quilting elective on the weekend if we want to do the actual quilting and make it into something we could use.

"Now there's a recipe for sweet dreams," I say. "Who wouldn't want to sleep under the weight of all that guilt?"

"Many people hang quilts on their walls as art," Mary points out.

I look doubtfully at my first two squares, upon which I have used a profusion of glitter glues, sequins, and pompoms. "I guarantee this will not pass the style police at my house. Unless I can prove Angelina Jolie once slept on it or something."

"Regardless," Mary says, her voice weary, and gestures me to get on with it.

"Just being honest."

"Why don't you tell us about your amends list, Lola?"

Faking my way into rehab is actually the worst thing I've ever done, and I can't exactly talk about it.

"If anything, there's a list of people who should be making amends with *me*, not the other way around," I say.

Mary's eyebrows arch up. "Why don't you tell us about that."

One of these days I'll learn to keep my mouth shut. "Kidding."

"Is that so?"

"Yeah, yeah. I mean, of course I stole booze from my moms and I sneaked out of the house and I lied about drinking. Obviously I need to make amends for that. Although I wouldn't say anyone's really upset with me about it. Not too much, anyway."

"What about your dad? You said you were drunk in the bathroom at an event with him. How do you think he's been affected by your drinking?"

"He hasn't."

"Really."

"Yeah, really. Look, I think I caught it early, okay? I was on the brink of some really bad stuff, and sure, his assistant had to cover for me, but he never knew about it. It's not like I went up in flames, you know?"

"Hmm," Mary says. "Let's just everyone pause and close your eyes. I want to do an exercise."

We do it.

"Now," Mary continues, "I want you all to think of the word 'truth.' Just the word."

There's silence as everyone thinks.

Except me. I try not to think, because truth and I have a conflict of interest right now.

"Now ask yourself, *what is my truth?*" She waits a few moments. "Observe. What images come forward? How do you feel?"

La la la la laaaaaa…

"How do you feel, Lola, when you think of the word 'truth' and of your father at the same time?"

"What, just me?" I open my eyes.

"For now. Because I'm sensing something from you about your family, something you may not even be aware of yourself."

LA LA LAAAAAAAAA...

"Close your eyes and tell me what you feel."

"I feel fine."

"*What* you feel, not how. And fine doesn't cut it. Go deeper. Go to your truth and tell us, truly, how you feel your family has been affected by your drinking. Tell us about their pain."

My insides roll over. I open my eyes again. "This is brainwashing. This is ridiculous."

"Are you sure there are no amends you need to make? Nothing you want to say to anyone in your family?"

I see the steely determination in Mary's eyes and feel the rest of the group, all still sitting dutifully with their eyes closed, waiting.

I'm not going to win this.

And anyway, I kind of feel like crying from all the built-up stress, so I may as well use it.

"All right," I say, and blink to let a couple of tears roll down my face, "even by checking in here I've obviously caused them to worry. And probably it's not my dad's proudest moment, having to tell people I'm in rehab. I am sorry about that."

I snuffle, wipe at my tears, and go on a bit more about embarrassing my parents and causing them to worry. I go so deep into it that I actually convince *myself*, and I can tell I've done enough when Mary finally gives me a warm, nurturing smile and then moves on.

Meanwhile, my playacting has left me utterly wrung out, with a sharp headache starting behind my eyes.

Thankfully, after group, Talia and I both have free time and, not knowing I have my own Level Three card, she offers to take me to the beach. I say yes, and it turns out to be the best choice ever because…

Wade is there.

Out in the water trying, not very successfully, to surf.

We walk along the shore until we come to a rock and Talia climbs up onto it with her journal.

"My favorite spot," she says, then pats the surface beside her.

I push myself up and perch at the edge of the rock, eager to escape in order to increase my chances of an encounter with Wade, but trying not to show it.

"You know, I can't stop thinking about my little sister," Talia says.

Crap. "Oh?"

"She's, like, ten. She's little. And she's supposed to look up to me. I mean, she does look up to me and I really— This last time I fell off the wagon, I really messed her up."

"I'm sure she's fine. Kids are resilient."

"No. I lied to her a whole bunch. And I let her smoke with me. I…I stole her allowance money, spent it on drugs."

I can't tell how Talia wants me to react to this, so I give a kind of awkward laugh, then realize she's crying and stop abruptly.

"How shitty is that?"

"Sorry, I..." I reach out and give her shoulders a rub. God, I'm an idiot. I have no idea how to deal with these kinds of conversations. "It's all right," I murmur, though obviously it's the opposite of all right for her at the moment. And then suddenly I've got her head in my lap and she's sobbing and clinging to me. I look around. Obviously I'm not going to leave the poor girl here, but I wish someone more qualified to deal with this would come to the rescue.

"I'm sure she's fine," I say in a soothing voice. "I'm sure she's proud of you for being here now. And you can pay her back, right?"

"I have to tell her, though...tell her I don't want her to turn out like me."

"Okay, so...this is what those amends letters are for, yeah?"

"You're right." Talia slowly pushes herself back up and wipes her eyes. "That and a long list of things not to do."

"Like what?"

"Well, the obvious—don't drink, smoke, do drugs, hook up with strange men..."

I nod.

"And don't lie, steal, manipulate people you love."

"She knows that stuff already, I'll bet," I say softly. "If you want to tell her...well, the interesting thing for all of you—us, I mean—is how it starts. Like, generally as a kid you know what you're supposed to do and not do, and you still know it as you're growing up, so...like for most people, how does it start?"

"We just don't think we'll turn into addicts, I guess," Talia says. "That's part of it. I mean—woo—one minute you're just messing around, having fun, blowing off some steam, no big deal. And then…" She makes an exploding sound.

"Right. So it starts as fun. Or it could start from… boredom, sadness…"

"Loneliness, depression," Talia continues, "escape, thrill-seeking—that's kind of like boredom but not quite the same. Like some people get off on skydiving or race-car driving. Those people need—"

"A lot of stimulation?" I say, cocking one eyebrow and smiling a little.

She smiles back—a big smile. "Uh-huh."

"Your sister fit that profile?" I ask.

"No. I do, though, a little. But I feel like I fit all of them. And wow, that pretty much means I'm doomed."

"No, no. You're a lot of things. I mean, you have a lot of qualities but they're…they're not bad qualities, Talia. I'm saying this wrong, but…you have a lot going for you. You're fun, you're not shy, you're caring. You're a nice person to be around—"

"Stop, you're going to make me cry again."

"No, I mean it," I say, and I realize as awkward as I feel in this conversation, I do mean it. Talia's a little crazy, but she's a genuinely nice, good person. "I'm just saying, don't be down on yourself. I mean, maybe even the things that seem bad to you about yourself, maybe they're actually good things. Like, if you can just get it all working in the right direction."

"Easier said than done."

"I know. One thing at a time, I guess. The amends letter, and the what-not-to-do…maybe you could think about… about how you got on the path. Signs to look for, traps you fell into. Maybe you won't even give it to her. Maybe it would be good for you."

"Roomie, I'm impressed."

I laugh, then feel self-conscious. "Hey, I'm just making shit up. Trying to help."

She opens her journal. "I'm going to start it right now."

"Good," I say. "Want me to sit with you?"

I look around, realizing, wow—I forgot all about Wade.

"No, I'm good. Much better now. I have, like, five meltdowns a day. You go for a walk or whatever—it's your first time on the beach."

"You sure?"

"Positive. And thank you."

"Oh." I start sliding off the rock. "It's all good. Any time. I mean, you're welcome."

"Just remember, you have to stay in sight—don't go past the jetty in the one direction, or those huge rocks in the other. Otherwise the lifeguards freak out."

"Gotcha," I say, then slip off my sandals, tie my ankle-length red cotton sundress up in a knot at the side, and head toward the jetty.

Five minutes later, I hear, "Hey," and look up to see Wade, who had been getting his ass repeatedly kicked by the waves, paddling in my direction.

I turn, smile, and walk a little ways into the water.

"Hi there," Wade says, then floats his board in the shallow water and straddles it.

"Hi," I say, trying not to drool at the sight of him, ridiculously buff and practically godlike with droplets of salt water glistening on his chest and shoulders. He doesn't need to be a good surfer, he could just stand here on the beach looking hot with the board and provide a great service to humanity. "What's up, W.A.D.E.?"

"What's up is I remember you, Carlyle."

My breath hitches. "Yeah?"

"Yeah." He nods and then captures me with a long, intense look that tells me he does remember, that he remembers *everything*. "Yeah, I remember. You look different, but the other day I knew there was something about you…"

"Ah," I say, hoping he means a *good* something and praying the new-and-improved Lola made enough of an impression to override the image of me roaring and lurching around like a zombie, which was about all I had in my flirting arsenal at age thirteen. "Took you long enough."

"Only a couple of days. And it's not like I expected to run into you in *rehab*."

"You either. You especially."

"Why me especially?"

"I dunno. Just because you started out so…grounded and kinda…sweet."

"They eat sweet for breakfast out here in California," he says. "I had to toughen up."

"So, drugs, huh?"

He laughs. Then abruptly stops and looks down at his

board, kicks his leg back and forth in the water. "Yeah, well..."

"Oh, hey, it happens," I say, pained at his suddenly dejected demeanor.

"Actually, I never got too crazy about the recreational stuff, though I haven't been a saint either. I've done all the usuals. You gotta fit in, go with the flow sometimes. But I got hooked by accident after I injured my knee on set."

"Let me guess, doing your own stunt?"

Thrill-seeker...

"Yep. So they prescribed some pills and they worked. Worked so well I said I didn't need to stop shooting. You were the one who taught me never to hold things up, re-member?"

"I meant not holding things up because you can't hit your mark, or forgot your lines, or because you *knocked over the third camera.*"

"Oh man, I still cringe. And the producers were standing there looking like they'd eaten lemons, and your dad was so disappointed. I'll never forget you sneaking us on set the next day and hopping around, running from camera to camera calling all the cues and hollering like a little tyrant until I got used to it. You saved my ass."

"Hey, whatever. It was fun. You just got a little freaked out by the cameras."

"That's a nice way of saying I was a wreck. And your dad's not the most, uh..."

"Patient?"

"Yeah, that's the word. He's not the most patient guy."

Wade looks out at the waves—big ones that would have knocked him flat, to be honest—and clears his throat. "He was going to fire me after that first day, wasn't he? I've always wanted to ask you that."

"He didn't want to, actually. But the producers kept talking to him about Ace Donnely."

"Oh, burn."

"Yeah, I figured it'd be crippling to a person's ego to get replaced by The Donn, especially after only one day on the job. Thing is, he'd have been way too busy looking at himself in the mirror and making stupid requests about people not making eye contact with him to hang out with me."

"You don't think he'd have had time to mess with the walkies or prank his fellow actors between takes?"

"Definitely not. That's the only reason I decided to help you out. Well, and I knew my dad believed in you. We talked about it."

"Wow, that's nice. I owe you. I got a second chance. And now here I am, because of a bunch of stupid painkillers, on the verge of screwing it all up again."

"But you're not going to. You're going to turn it around. Right?"

"I did some bad stuff. And the network basically told me if I don't shape up and finish this program with flying colors, they'll kill off my character. And now that I'm here, I don't know. I've got issues with this whole twelve-step, never-drink-again philosophy. I guess maybe I've got issues, you know, in general."

"Like what?"

"Like I don't like people telling me what to do."

I laugh. "Me neither!"

"And I don't like…I mean, I have to do this, I get it. But I'm off the painkillers already, and besides that, I don't think I have such a problem. The painkillers were the problem because they're addictive. I'm off them. I'm over it. So why am spending my summer here when I could be, hell, I could be anywhere I want?"

"Hmm…"

"And yeah, maybe I seem a little pissy sometimes here, but people—you know how it is—even though I'm doing well in my career, people have fucked with me. There are people who have it in for me. And I have a right to be pissed about that, too."

"I guess…"

"But maybe that's a bad attitude and that's an issue. I've got issues, and issues with them being considered issues. Which is an issue. Maybe."

I stare at him, sitting in knee-deep water on his surfboard and looking like the most perfect, dazzling boy on the planet, and I'm suddenly aware that the Wade Miller I've held in my mind all this time…is not this Wade Miller. My Wade Miller does not have issues— not big ones, anyway. And he doesn't have this angry edge. I mean, even when I heard he was here and in a bad way, I figured all he needed was a few pep talks and love.

He might need more than that. And if he does? Well, look at how awkward I am, just trying to talk with Talia about a simple family problem. I'm going to try, of course, but my normal powers of persuasion might not be up to this task.

"Wade, you just have to remember…who you are. You know?"

"I'm Wade Miller," he says, but I can tell he means, I'm Wade Miller, famous person, star of *Drift*.

"No, you're… You have to live here and survive all the Hollywood BS, but you have to remember that you're you—the you I met all those years ago, Wade from Ohio—not famous, just a good guy with a lot of talent, willing to work hard… You can't start believing what other people say about you, good or bad. You gotta do the work, and then try to be normal. You know? I would hate to see you turn into one of those typical assholes."

"Hey, those are good thoughts." He smiles at me and moves his board closer, then says, "But I didn't mean to get all heavy on you. And you know—I'll toe the line in the end. I'll be a good boy and do my rehab and behave myself. Mostly."

"Mostly?"

"Okay, totally. Don't wanna disappoint Ben Carlyle's daughter," he says, and winks.

"When did you figure it out? That I was me, I mean."

"Oh," he says with a grin. "It was when I saw you doing that bird thing in your drama class—your bird acting reminded me of your zombie acting."

"Oh my God."

"You were the fiercest zombie in the movie."

"Not to mention the shortest."

We both laugh, and water swirls around my ankles.

"But Carlyle, what happened?" he says, his expression getting serious again. "Last I knew, you were a kid and now you're here. What's the deal?"

"Oh," I say with a dismissive wave, "just a bit of a drinking thing. You know how it goes."

"Right…"

"Yeah…"

"I wondered about something," he says, coming closer.

"What?"

"You, ah, you kissed me, Carlyle."

"Oh, you noticed," I say, trying to be nonchalant even as my heart rate increases.

"Yeah, I noticed. Hard to miss."

"Well then, so I did."

"So…? What was that about?"

"Poor impulse control?"

"Really?"

"No." I swallow. "Actually, I always wanted to kiss you. Figured I'd check it off the list."

"Off the list?"

"Yep." I shrug like it's no big deal, even though my legs feel like Play-Doh. "So, now I have."

"And?"

"And it was fun," I say, and then turn and start walking back along the shore toward Talia.

Wade follows, half walking, half paddling in the shallow water.

"Wait, wait! So…you had a crush? During the movie?

Are you saying you had a crush on me?"

"I wanted to kiss you, that's all," I say over my shoulder.

"That's a crush, Carlyle. I call that a crush."

"Maybe."

"Why didn't you say something? I know we lost touch for a bit, but you could've called me. Or friended me on Facebook, followed me on Twitter," he says, all the while struggling to get out of the water and balance his board.

"Followed you on Twitter? Please. I'm not some cheesy fangirl."

I searched Facebook early on, but he wasn't there. By the time I looked again he had three thousand "friends," most of them female. And I do follow him on Twitter, but not as me and not that I'd admit it, ever.

"But you'd have been *my* cheesy fangirl." He comes up beside me, carrying the board by his side. "I'm very fond of cheesy fangirls."

"You have enough of those."

"My loss."

"I'd be a bad cheesy fangirl. I'd get bored. I'm too fickle, I'm crap at the adulation thing, and I wouldn't be caught dead wearing you on a T-shirt."

He howls with laughter.

"Plus, I have trouble sharing."

He stops laughing and looks at me. "Sharing, huh? You sure?"

I feel a moment of eww, but brush it away. "Very."

We get closer to Talia on her rock and the lifeguard station, and our walking slows almost to a stop, as if by silent agreement.

"By the way," Wade says, "I'm sorry about your parents."

"Aw, no big deal."

"Of course it's a big deal. It's your parents."

"Sure, but it happens all the time, right?"

"Not where I'm from. Well, not as much."

"That's why you started out sweet, W.A.D.E."

"Were you surprised? I mean, I was surprised when I heard. Actually I was more surprised that it was your mom who—you know, I was more surprised about that than anything. Although, the way your dad acted…uh, you know, with his own cheesy fangirls, maybe that makes sense."

"It wasn't that bad."

"It affected you."

"Nothing I couldn't handle."

"Listen, I love the guy. I owe him. It's one thing you had to keep his secrets, but he also seemed a little…distant with you." Wade doesn't say it, although obviously he's thinking about my least favorite memory from the zombie movie— the night Dad left set with one of the actresses and forgot I was still there, needing a ride home. Forgot until the next day.

"Let's not…" I don't want him to say it, any of it. *La la la laaaa.*

"I get it. That's fine. Anyway, I haven't seen your dad since…I guess it was at Sundance last year. How is he?"

"He's good. Busy, but we Facetime."

"You get shuffled back and forth a lot? I know that can be a drag."

"Yeah, definitely," I say, but then decide I'd rather not outright lie. Not this time. "Well, actually, no. They're not exactly Chris and Gwyneth."

"That sucks."

"Ah, no biggie," I say with a shrug and a smile.

"If you say so. Anyway, tell him hi for me."

"Sure." I nod and stand looking at him, my insides a tangled mess of exhilaration, nostalgia, confusion, and lust.

"Hour's up!" one of the lifeguards shouts, and then they blow their whistles in tandem. Wade and I both flinch and everyone else starts to head for the steep, winding path that leads back up to the main property.

"I'll bring the stragglers," one of the lifeguards calls out, gesturing to Wade and me, plus a guy who's limping in from the other direction. We're still a few yards away.

Talia, already at the bottom of the path, makes some dramatic faces, presumably about being surrounded by half-naked men, and motions that she'll wait for me at the top.

I wave her off and start toward the steps myself.

"So, Carlyle," Wade says, following, "you gonna kiss me again?"

"What, now?"

"No, not now. Sometime."

"What for?"

"Well…what do people usually kiss for?"

"Oh. That." My pulse is suddenly thundering. I pick up my sandals as we pass Talia's rock and remind myself that the whole idea is to act confident and like I don't care too much. "Probably not."

"Oh."

"Hey, you two okay to walk up?" the remaining lifeguard calls out, looking from us to the top of the path where the rest of the group is arriving. He's still down near the water and he's got an arm around the shoulder of the bedraggled surfer who is either over-exhausted or having a breakdown or both. "We're just going to take a minute."

"No problem." Wade sets his board on the nearby rack.

"Great. Thanks," the lifeguard says.

And then Wade and I reach the bottom of the steps.

"Hey, I was just joking anyway," Wade says, "about you kissing me."

"Oh?"

"Yeah. I mean, we're not really supposed to be..."

"Fraternizing."

"Yeah, that," he says.

"Too bad," I say, as a gust of ocean wind tries to blow the heat from my skin. "Because I was going to say I would probably wait for *you* to kiss *me* next time," I add, and then start up the path.

Chapter Fourteen

Friday brings another opportunity to skip therapy.

Meanwhile, Adam is getting even more pointed with the affirmations, starting with, "I enjoy attending meetings," which means I really might have to show up for the AA meeting tonight, even though I know it's going to make me feel like the biggest liar and worst person in the universe.

Lacking any better options and starting to feel nauseous with dread, I duck out of meditation fifteen minutes early to avoid Adam, who I know is otherwise going to be waiting to escort me to therapy, and head once more to Dr. Koch's office. I can't get in trouble if I'm with the big boss, right?

"Any chance you can be my therapist?" I ask him when he looks up from his desk to where I'm standing in the doorway.

"Miss Carlyle. Come in. Make yourself comfortable."

There's a large high-back leather chair across from Dr. Koch's desk. I close the office door behind me, make my way to the chair, and sit.

Dr. Koch puts down his pen, folds his hands together, and gives me a knowing look. "What's the problem? You don't like your therapist?"

"To be honest…" I say, and then decide *not* to be, "I haven't exactly *connected* with her."

"Therapy is an intrinsic aspect of treatment," Dr. Koch says. "But sometimes the connection is a work in progress."

"I know. That's why I figured maybe you could be my therapist. I mean, *we've* connected. And obviously you're qualified," I say, waving at the framed certifications sitting alongside the celebrity photo ops on his wall.

Actually, regardless of his certifications, I'm sure he's *not* qualified. He seems weak in the intuition department, plus he has the makings of a major fame-whore. Which means he's perfect. I figure it would be much easier to chat with him three times a week than have to contend with the likes of Madam. All I have to do is give him enough juicy tidbits to feel he's getting the inside story of my life without telling him anything of substance. Easier said than done, but I'm up to the challenge.

"You could be my personal doctor—my specialist."

"Well…"

"And I would give you all the credit for my recovery—which of course you'd totally deserve. Has anyone told you you'd be great on TV?"

"I've had a few people say so," he says, sitting up

straighter. "But of course, I'm very busy and fulfilled here at Sunrise."

"Of course."

"It would really have to be the right project, the right situation."

"Absolutely. You wouldn't prostitute yourself out like some people do. But I could see you as the subject of a serious documentary series. Kind of like those ones my dad directed for HBO back in the day."

"Indeed."

"In the meantime, what do you say? Are you my new therapist?"

"I would love to see to your case personally, Miss Carlyle," he says with a sigh. "But ironically, too much of my time is taken up with administration, media inquiries, and so on for me to be anyone's regular therapist. However, I am hoping to be involved when your family comes in. Is there any chance we can get both your mother and father here together?"

I freaking hope not.

"Um…doubtful."

"Let me rephrase that: would it be helpful *for you* to have them both here?"

"I don't see either of them agreeing to that, Dr. Koch."

He studies me for a moment. "Perhaps they need to be made to understand the effect of their behaviors on you? Perhaps they can be persuaded."

"I don't think I can—"

"Not by you. By me."

"Good luck with that."

"I have my ways. And of course you wouldn't be aware, as you're insulated at Sunrise, but the press has been after your father for comments about you being here. So far he has declined, but perhaps he'll want to participate. And your mother is obviously quite willing. You'd be surprised at the progress that can be made when we get a family in a room together. You might also be surprised at how persuasive I can be."

I do *not* need my parents in here, together or separately, and I'm about to say so when the office door flies open, revealing a red-faced Adam standing in the doorway.

Dr. Koch stands up.

"Adam—"

"With all due respect, sir, I need you to reassign me."

"From what?" Dr. Koch says.

"My newest mentor assignment is driving me insane," he says, stalking over to stand in front of Dr. Koch's desk, his back to me. "It's going to send me over the edge. And I can't—I'm afraid I can't remain...detached. I'm not detached enough to do a good job. Please, I need to be reassigned. Ideally to the other wing."

"I see you are upset," Dr. Koch says in a velvety tone. "And I know you care deeply about your work, but that's what makes you so promising. And really, you're only here for the summer."

"But—"

"I'll be finished in a few minutes," Dr. Koch says, with a pointed glance over Adam's shoulder, to me. "Perhaps then we can talk?"

Adam frowns, starts to turn. "Oh, I didn't even realize you had—" And then sees me curled up in the high-back chair and does a double take. "You—!" For a split second he looks embarrassed, but the look quickly turns to aggravation. "Oh, for God's sake, Lola, what are you doing here?"

I bat my eyelashes at him, then smile.

He lets out a strangled, growling sound, then turns back to Dr. Koch.

"I told Miss Carlyle on her first day that she can come to me any time if she needs to talk," Dr. Koch says. "We were just discussing the logistics and possible dynamics of having both her parents here for family therapy, which I would like to oversee."

"I don't see how she's going to do family therapy when she still hasn't made it to regular therapy. When she's doing everything in her power to *avoid* regular therapy."

Dr. Koch turns to me and frowns, but gently. "Is this true, Miss Carlyle?"

"Um…"

"Is it true?" Adam says. "I'm your *staff*, Doctor, and I said it. Of course it's true. She's supposed to be there right now. I was going to escort her."

"Obviously you did not succeed," Dr. Koch says.

"Obviously not," Adam says through his teeth.

"Tsk, tsk," Dr. Koch says, shaking his head, and it's unclear if he's directing it to Adam, me, or both of us.

"I would have an easier time, sir, if I could make her accountable," Adam says. "If she didn't have, for example, expanded privileges on her card that she hasn't earned."

Dr. Koch comes out from behind his desk and makes a mollifying gesture toward Adam. "I know this isn't the way things worked in the, ah, boot-camp environment of your previous placement, but I assure you, we do get the job done for these kids."

"Not all of them."

"I've told you before, the celebrity kids have particular needs. *Unique* needs," Dr. Koch continues, and even though he's theoretically on my side, I feel a little sorry for Adam.

"With respect, I think that's bull," Adam says. "They're addicts and their needs are the same as every other addict."

Dr. Koch backs up, smiles. "We shall have to agree to disagree. But perhaps we could finish discussing Miss Carlyle another time and...in private."

"That's okay," I say from my perch in the chair, "discuss away."

"No, he's right," Adam says. "Dr. Koch and I can talk later."

"Oh, about therapy?" I say, and give an imploring look to Dr. Koch. "I think group and your proposed family therapy thing are sufficient. Especially with all the exercise and meditation and stuff. Honestly, you should see the mountain I imagined myself being this morning. Majestic, grounded, epic."

"She also hasn't been to an AA meeting yet," Adam says pointedly to Dr. Koch.

Dr. Koch presses his fingers together, looks thoughtful.

"Now that does look rather remiss of us," he says. "To have you in rehab and not attending the meetings. The twelve steps form the backbone of nearly every successful recovery program, and I would hate for you to miss out. I believe we are treating you well and giving you ample respect for your...individuality. Do you suppose you could find your way to the meeting tonight, Miss Carlyle? And to most of the evening meetings from here on in?"

"Well, when you put it that way—sure," I say.

Dr. Koch turns to Adam and beams. "You see? Sometimes it's simply a matter of using the right words, in the right way."

Adam looks like he's trying to swallow his tongue to keep from speaking.

I check my watch. Therapy hour is almost over.

"If it's okay," I say as I uncurl from the chair, "I've got music next and I don't want to be late."

Adam scoffs.

Dr. Koch says, "Run along then, and I'll see you tonight."

I wave to them both and head for the door.

"Now," Dr. Koch says to Adam as I'm going, "you wanted to talk about reassignment?"

"Oh, that..." Adam says with a sigh. "Never mind."

Chapter Fifteen

In music, we do a cool thing with drums and a special kind of chanting called "intoning" that we use to create a "continuous voice." It's a trip. Combined with the relief from my successful therapy dodge, my entire body is humming.

When I come out, Adam is there, waiting in the hallway. I brace myself for a lecture, but instead he smiles.

"What?"

"You look, uh, happy," he says.

"I like that class."

"Good."

"Strangely enough, you look happy, too. What's up?"

"I have a surprise for you," he says.

"Really? I thought I was in trouble."

"We're moving on. No trouble."

"So? What is it then?"

"Stop hopping around and come with me and you'll find out. It's in my office."

"I know," I say, falling into step with him, "you're giving me my chocolate back. Or my phone."

"Keep dreaming."

"Or one of my parents sent a care package," I say as we go through the foyer to the east wing of the mansion and down a set of stairs I've never noticed before. "Or, like, lasagna from New York."

"They deliver lasagna from New York?"

"Yep. My mom and Elise get it for us sometimes."

He pauses at the bottom of the stairwell, leaning on the chunky metal rail, and shakes his head. "Seriously, there cannot be a lasagna so amazing I'd be willing to pay to have it sent from New York City. You people are nuts."

"No, it's really good," I say, stopped just above him on the second-to-last step. "Next time we're having it, I'm going to invite you over to try some, and you'll see."

"You think you're going to invite me to your house?"

"Why not? We're kind of…I mean, I annoy you sometimes, but aren't we…friends?"

"*Friends* is not exactly what we're supposed to be when I'm your mentor, Lola."

"Oh. Is that the detachment problem you were talking about when you were trying to ditch me?"

"Lola…"

"Like you're sort of supposed to be the boss of me, and it's not really working?"

"That was supposed to be a private conversation."

"Yes, and I'm a little hurt, actually. And now we're not supposed to be friends. Is it a rule?"

"No, it's not that, exactly. It's about the mentor-mentee relationship dynamic. It's a professional relationship. There are supposed to be lines."

"I'm sure you've noticed, Adam, how I am about lines…"

"Yeah, you like to cross them," he says with a rueful smile.

"If considering you a friend is on the wrong side of some line, I think it's a stupid line. There's no reason for a line like that."

"Yes, there is," he says. "There's a very good reason."

"What is it?"

He gazes at me for a long moment, his eyes parallel with mine for once, because of my being on the steps. Suddenly the stairwell feels just a little bit…small.

"Actually, there's more than one. There are a few. But come on." He breaks away and starts walking. "Let's go."

We head down a long, echoing basement hallway with polished concrete floors and stop at a nondescript door. Adam takes out a key, unlocks and opens the door, and ushers me into a small, windowless office complete with a metal desk and two chairs.

I look for something fun, some nice kind of surprise. Balloons, even. But all I see is a tiny woman in glasses and a navy pantsuit sitting in one of the chairs.

She could practically be my grandmother.

Maybe she's my *long-lost* grandmother come to take me to live with her.

Yeah, she could be my fairy godmother too, come to give me sparkly red shoes and set me on the road to Emerald City.

"Lola, this is Dr. Owens. Dr. Owens, Lola Carlyle."

Yeah, not.

Dr. Owens beams a sweet-quirky-old-lady smile, but the steel in her eyes is unmistakable.

Madam.

"Adam, I'm going to drive you into the desert and feed you to a carnivorous plant."

"I'm simply adjusting to your *unique needs*."

"You? Are not my friend."

"See? I'll be outside."

And with that, he closes the door and is gone.

"Welcome to therapy, Lola," Dr. Owens says. "I believe we have some catching up to do."

I dive into pleasantries and small talk, to no avail.

Then I jump to excuses and justifications; still nothing.

Dr. Owens just blinks at me with her owl eyes and lets me talk until I run out of steam, which happens faster than you'd think. And then she allows for this long, awkward pause that leaves me sweating and shifting in my chair.

Finally, into the excruciating silence, she says, "What are you afraid of?"

"I'm not afraid."

Annoyed, yes. Nervous? Sure. I'm a fake alcoholic in

rehab, and it would be embarrassing—not to mention in-convenient—to be unmasked. And for sure it would subma-rine my forbidden-but-budding rehab romance/rescue with Wade, which is the whole reason I'm here.

The problem with therapy is how to hide that I don't need it, that's all.

I am Lola Carlyle and a celebu-spawn. I am not afraid. Please.

Dr. Owens says, "You're not afraid of anything?"

I say, "Well, sure. War, tornadoes, certain kinds of fish, super viruses, a world without chocolate."

"But not therapy?"

"Nope," I say, shaking my head and looking her directly in the eye.

Dr. Owens whips a large metal bell out of her purse and starts ringing it.

"What the—"

"Bullshit!" she says, ringing and ringing. It's loud. Really, painfully loud. The sound gets under my skin and jangles my insides and I cover my ears, but it doesn't help.

Finally she stops, and I carefully uncover my ears.

"What the hell is that?"

"Why are you so afraid of therapy?" she says, her light blue eyes like lasers.

"I'm not—"

She lifts the bell again, starts ringing it.

"You're insane," I shout.

"Why are you afraid?" she shouts back.

"Stop, stop!"

This time she doesn't answer, just puts the bell right up in my face and rings it harder and harder, rings it until I'd do almost anything to make it stop, and then something wells up, pushes through me, and I go to shout, again, that I am not afraid but instead what comes out is, "Because I shouldn't be here."

The bell stops but I can still hear it. Dr. Owens leans in like she's caught the scent of something.

"Shouldn't be here?" she says.

I nod, swallow, try to get my brain working because obviously I've got to start backpedaling, stat.

"What I mean is…I often feel like I don't belong. And, like what am I doing here? Not in rehab, but *here*, you know, on earth."

Dr. Owens's eyes widen.

"Because sometimes everything seems pointless."

"Ahh…"

The rest of the session chugs along painfully as we dive into my not-entirely-fake existential angst. The whole thing gives me a headache and I hate every second of it.

Afterward, I am shaky in yoga and quiet in group, and only start to feel normal again during the afternoon aquafit class. (Finally the pool! Although one of my bikinis is missing.)

Before Reflection, Adam reminds me I'm expected, no excuses, at AA tonight.

"Yay. I'm having such a good day already."

"Buck up."

"I've had a lot of fantasies about you since you tricked me into that lovely appointment earlier today."

"Fantasies, huh?"

"Oh yes," I continue. "Fantasies about how to cause you bodily harm—the mortal kind."

"Funny, I have similar ones about you. Daily. Sometimes hourly."

"Oh yeah? What happens in yours?"

"You don't want to know," he says.

"Well," I say with an impish smile, "maybe we should wrestle."

"Wrestle?"

"Yeah, like, to get that stuff out."

"No wrestling. Just go to AA tonight, please."

"Fine."

"Do you need an escort?"

"An escort?" I raise my eyebrows.

"Yeah, like a police escort," he says.

"No need. I'll get there."

"Promise?"

I heave a sigh. "What is it with you making me promise things all the time?"

"I don't know—it seems to work."

"Fine. Yes. I promise."

At least Wade will be there.

Back in my room, I'm edgy and anxious and my hair almost ruins everything. I don't want to go to AA. I don't want to *be* in AA. Regardless, I'm in rehab so I guess I'm going. I try deep breathing and finally put the hair in pigtails.

Then I change six times and go crazy trying to find my second-favorite pair of jeans, before finally deciding on a Twenty8Twelve denim dress with orange and blue crinoline peeking out from under the skirt, paired with orange leather flip-flops and a matching belt. It's all very "rehab-upscale."

"Woo!" Talia whistles and then comes to stand beside me in the narrow mirror.

"What?" I say, pointing at her perfectly draped black-and-blue leopard-print top, fitted jeans, and curled eyelashes. "You always dress up for the meetings."

"Sure. But someone's going to want to spank you, just to see up your skirt. I think *I* might want to spank you. What are you wearing under? You should have lace frills on your butt!" Talia says, and proceeds to whip up my skirt and laugh like a maniac.

I shriek and leap away.

Jade, in her usual black everything, rolls her eyes and heads out the door.

"She loves us," I say.

"She doesn't know what she's missing," Talia says.

When we get to the old chapel, I see practically everyone is there—Mary, Clarice, most of the teachers, Dr. Koch in a well-cut white dress shirt with sleeves carefully rolled up, the top three buttons undone and expensive-looking dark blue jeans. And of course Adam, who gives my outfit an amused once-over when he sees me coming in the door.

"I'm here," I tell him.

"Very much so," he says. "Nice, um, dress. That's a dress, right?"

"As opposed to what?"

"I'm not even sure," he says. "A tutu?"

"Don't you kinda want to spank her?" Talia says, holding the back hem.

"Talia!" I give her a warning look—I would not put it past her to whip up my dress again, even here.

"This is the weirdest job," Adam mutters, and then wanders off, and we go to find seats.

"Okay, let me give you the lowdown," Talia says as I try, surreptitiously, to look for Wade.

"Sure. Thanks."

She explains about the blue book and the twelve steps and why she thinks tempeh is better than tofu and the time she was twelve and went to Mexico and drank so much tequila her parents found her passed out in front of the TV with half a quesadilla stuck to her face.

My temples are still throbbing, but I tell myself it's just an AA meeting and can't be worse than therapy.

Wade finally arrives, looking magnetic, healthy, and slightly sunburned in jeans and a long-sleeved T-shirt. I know lots of good-looking people. Usually you get used to them, or you start to find them less attractive over time. Not Wade. He gets more gorgeous every time I see him, and I can't get used to it. Sure, in this circumstance it's partly due to the healthy living, but still it doesn't seem fair. How am I supposed to act normal and chill around him when he sucks all the air out of the room, when a large part of me wants to just grab him and drag him off somewhere and— Crap, I have to stop with this line of thinking.

Stop.

I breathe deeply, really deeply—one helpful skill I've learned here—while he goes to sit nearby. I try not to look at him but I can feel him. I can feel almost every other female in the place looking at him, too, which again makes me want to grab him and—

"Oh my God, Lola," Talia whispers. "*Drift* boy is staring at you. Don't look!"

"Shh."

"Wow. No, he is really staring at you. Did you put a spell on him at the beach yesterday?"

"Very funny." I let my eyes slide over to Wade, who is indeed staring at me. Our eyes meet and I get a full-body heart palpitation.

And then he gives me a two-dimpled smile and waves.

Beside me, Talia gasps.

"He's flirting with you," she says in the loudest whisper ever.

"Shut up," I say under my breath, and wave back.

It might be inappropriate and I know this twelve steps stuff is serious business and I'm sure we're not supposed to be flirting in AA, but suddenly I'm feeling much better.

The meeting begins.

There are rules and regulations, some thanking and sharing, and then a reading from the blue book, then more sharing. The population of Sunrise, and therefore the meeting, is composed of drug addicts, cutters, food addicts, opiate addicts, cross-addicted alcoholics, coke addicts, meth-heads, a huffer…

"What the hell is a huffer?" I whisper to Talia.

"Oh," Talia whispers back, "she inhales nail polish remover, cooking spray, that kind of thing."

"On purpose?"

"Of course on purpose."

"Eww. Jeez."

"Shhh," someone says, obviously meaning us, but I'm not paying attention because something is hitting me. Hitting me again, that is, because it's been hitting me all week in different ways, and suddenly it's coming on like more of a wallop.

These people look normal.

As a group, they look really good, actually. I mean, this is California.

But most of them are wack. They're wack and their *lives* are wack.

Emmy from group, for example, started smoking pot after accidentally witnessing her parents having a threesome. She doesn't sleep and she's angry and paranoid to the point you can't have a conversation with her. And Jenny, the *Barney* girl, got drunk to oblivion and woke up one morning in another city with no idea how she got there. She'd been raped, lost all her belongings, and someone had shaved her head. Now she has this thing where she wears five hundred layers of clothing no matter how hot it is and she has panic attacks every time she's supposed to read for a part, which makes it pretty hard to get work, much less break out of her kids' television persona, which makes her think she'll never work again and die in depressing obscurity. A kid named Stephan found some coke on his dad's dresser when he was eight years old and ate it, thinking it was sugar. He looks about thirteen but he's already been to rehab four times.

Crazy, right?

And all of this adds up to my life looking not so bad.

I may be unlucky in love (so far) and not particularly well understood or *cherished* by my various parents, and I'm pissed off that their divorce made such a mess of my life when it happened, but compared to some of these people, my life has been a model of normalcy and wholesomeness.

"And now"—the chairperson's voice breaks into my thoughts—"this week's new members are invited to share."

My stomach drops. All day I've been walking around feeling confused and messed up and kind of naked (I blame therapy), and now everyone is looking at me and I'm not sure I can do this.

Not today, anyway.

Plus, right before me is Camille—the girl I saw moaning on the floor that first day—and she moved from alcohol to painkillers after her boyfriend and best friend died in a car that she was driving, while drunk. By the time she's done talking, I'm so sad for her I'm ready for some painkillers, too.

Talia propels me to my feet and whispers something in my ear, but I don't hear it.

I shake my head, clear my throat, look at all the faces turned toward me.

"Uh..,"

I can't do this. I shouldn't be here.

"Um, my name is Lola."

I take a breath in. Everyone seems to lean forward in their seats.

"My name is Lola and I'm...I'm..."

I've got Dr. Owens's bullshit bell crashing around in my head, which is throbbing, and I'm a big, fat fake.

"Sorry. Right. My name is Lola and... Oh, damn it...

"My name is Lola and I'm *not* an alcoholic."

Chapter Sixteen

For a beautiful moment, the bell in my head stops ringing and I am a zillion pounds lighter. Floating, almost. If it were a movie, a choir of angels would be singing.

Then, of course, I look at the surprised, puzzled faces around me and magnificent Wade Miller with his brow furrowed in confusion and Talia with wide, wounded eyes and Jade slightly triumphant and Adam standing stock-still and shocked and I think…

No, no, no, no, noooooo…

I open my mouth to take it back.

Nothing comes out. The clarifications and justifications are there in my head and I know they'll work, but I can't get them through the roadblock that is my throat.

I close my mouth. Swallow. Open it again.

"I'm not an alcoholic," I say again.

Shit. My body has turned on me, gone rogue, and it looks like I'm going to be telling the truth whether I like it or not, and then every single person here will hate me. Fun.

"I'm really sorry. I'm not an alcoholic or an addict of any kind, unless you count chocolate. Right, some of you do count chocolate. I guess it's not that funny when people say, 'I'm addicted to such-and-such' when all they mean is they like it a lot, when there are actually people whose lives are being ruined by chocolate, or drugs, or…dish soap…or whatever. Anyway my point is, I shouldn't be here."

"How do you know?" It's Dr. Koch, and despite his velvet demeanor, I have no doubt he's going to be pissed when I confess the rest of it.

"I know because…"

I faked it…

Somehow that part sticks in my throat. I was ready to say it but now it won't come out. Everyone will really hate me if I admit that part because it's premeditation.

Dr. Koch might even sue me or throw me into some kind of juvenile jail when he finds out because he'll be embarrassed. Vengeful. It's possible I *have* committed some kind of fraud-type crime by faking my way in here, and that would mean that my next stop after I leave here is jail! Jail will be like solitary, but so much worse. And the next thing my mom or dad will hear about me is that I need bail, and the charges will be worse because of the premeditation thing.

They'll find Sydney and let's be real: she'll have no compunction about selling me down the river—she'll tell them everything. She won't tell them I did it with the intention of helping Wade, because I never told her that part. Even if I had, it wouldn't have made sense to her, since she's a person essentially without a soul. So, she'll just tell them the really stupid-sounding part—that I faked my way into rehab because of a boy.

Then Mom will kill me for the bad press (there is such a thing) and Dad will feel further justified in cutting me out of his life. Both of them will hate me.

The entire world will think I'm a liar and a fool.

Adam will feel justified for trying to ditch me as a mentee.

Wade Miller will not date a girl with a record—in fact he'll think I'm a cheesy fangirl. Or a stalker! Next thing I know he could be getting a restraining order against me. At best, he's going to think I'm the most desperate, ridiculous, pathetic loser of all time.

I may *be* the most desperate, ridiculous, pathetic loser of all time.

I stand there, momentarily speechless, panic rocking through my blood, shame burning me from the inside out.

One clear thought coalesces: honesty is lovely, but I am not going to ruin my life.

Exactly.

And I can stop lying about things, without telling everything.

Everyone is staring at me, waiting for my answer. I take a few meditational breaths and try in vain to find my quiet place, then face Dr. Koch and go ahead without it.

"How do I know I'm not an addict?" I say. "I just know. I had…some bad experiences with alcohol, uh, one main bad experience, and it freaked me out, and so I kind of maybe… exaggerated…the amount of drinking I've done because I felt like I needed…to be here and…take a break."

Total silence. I keep hurtling forward into it.

"It's not like I don't have it in me to be an addict, but now that I've spent a week surrounded by the real deal, I know I'm not one. You guys are all really brave and you have big stuff to deal with and overcome and, no offense, but most of you are really, really screwed up. Like, I probably shouldn't make a habit of drinking, even once I come of age, but I just am not that screwed up. Which leads me to believe that I shouldn't be here. That I should go."

Big silence, painful scrutiny. I try to avoid the gazes of Adam, Wade, Talia.

"So, that's what I'll do then. I'll go."

But everyone is so still and quiet and some of them are looking at me with…pity? It's creepy.

"Listen, it's not like I had a bad time. The pool is nice and the classes are interesting and if I were an alcoholic I'd be having an amazing time," I say, and then wince. "What I mean is this is obviously a good program and a good place despite the rules and lack of privacy and all the reflecting and contemplating and getting up in the middle of the night and—"

Horse tranquilizers—that's what needs to happen. Someone needs to get some and inject me with them so I can either die, or at least wake up a few days from now when this humiliation is behind me.

"I *mean*…if I meet any teen alcoholics or drug addicts or whatever, or if anyone I know *becomes* one, I will totally send them your way. Right. So, see you later, I guess."

At this, I give what I hope is a friendly-and-confident-but-respectful smile and start backing away. Unfortunately I back into my own chair and almost fall over it and a few people gasp and both Talia and Jade reach out to steady me, making my exit less than smooth. But I manage to stay on my feet and am soon giving a last wave and marching my ridiculous, crinoline-clad self out the door.

And then I'm out.

I'm about to start on the path back to the dorms when the door opens and Adam appears.

"Lola—"

"You know what? Don't even start. I can't deal."

"Okay," he says, right in front of me but surprisingly cool and calm. "What do you need?"

"What do I need? You're actually asking me?"

"Yeah. I'm asking."

"I need to know what has to happen to get me out of here."

"A parent or guardian has to come pick you up."

"I can't just go? Call a limo? Or a taxi, even? I thought the program was voluntary."

"It is voluntary—technically we can't keep you here if

you want to go. But we can only release you directly to a guardian."

"Oh, nice loophole."

"There are good reasons for that, if you think about it. Safety, liability…"

"Yeah, yeah, fine. I need to make a phone call."

"All right, let's go." Adam takes me by the hand, the heat and solidity of his grip sending waves of reassurance through my frazzled body. He leads me into the main building and through the foyer and back downstairs to his office, which is the same room I was in for therapy.

"Any chance I can have some privacy?" I ask as he shuts the door behind us.

"This is privacy."

"I mean, no offense, but from you."

Adam shakes his head.

"Didn't think so."

"Sorry."

He motions me to sit in the chair in front of his desk, then reaches over me, picks up the receiver, and punches in some kind of code.

"There you go," he says, and hands me the phone, then goes to lean against the nearby wall. All of the walls are nearby, actually — it's a really small office. Which means he'll probably be able to hear both sides of the upcoming phone call. Nothing I can do about it, though.

I dial.

After six rings, Mom picks up.

"Yes? Yes? Who is this?" she says, sounding flustered.

"Mom? Hello? It's me."

"Lola? You woke me up."

Why she'd be asleep at nine o'clock on a Friday night, I'm not sure, but Adam is waiting and I'm sure his sympathetic mood won't last, so I need to get to the point.

"Mom, I need you to come get me."

"Come get you?"

"Yes."

"From Sunrise?"

"Yes."

"Darling, you just got there. You can't possibly be cured already."

"Um, no, not cured. That's the thing, Mom. I…I didn't mean to be…ah…I mean, I think I overreacted. About the alcohol. I think I made a mistake and I don't belong here."

"Lola, it's absolutely the best and most luxurious rehabilitation center around. They have an excellent reputation, we've spent a fortune to send you, and everybody knows you're there." From the sound of her voice, she's waking up fast. "You can't just come home after such a short time."

"Everybody knows? Who is everybody?"

"I mean *everybody*, everybody."

I groan.

"Price of fame, honey."

"Mom, the thing is, I know it's kind of embarrassing, but I'm not an alcoholic after all."

"So Monday you were and now you're not?"

"No, I wasn't on Monday either. I just…I maybe got confused, exaggerated a bit. But I'm not. If you'd just come get me, I can explain on the way home."

There is a long sigh on the other end of the phone and then Mom says, "That won't be possible."

"What, you don't believe me?"

"It's not about what I believe," she says. "I don't know what to believe. But for the moment, it doesn't matter."

"It matters to me."

"The point is, Lola, I cannot come to get you regardless."

"Okay, Elise then."

"Elise can't come either."

"Why not?"

"Because, darling, we're in Tokyo."

I stand up fast, gripping the phone.

"You're in …" I glance at Adam, who hasn't taken his eyes off me. "You're what?"

"In Tokyo. Do we have a bad connection?"

"No. Yes. I mean, I can't believe you'd…you just dropped me off in rehab."

"And I'm supposed to…what? Sit by the phone in Malibu in case you need to call, turn down all work opportunities and so on? You're in good hands."

"But…"

"It was very last-minute," she says. "Danny landed me a series of commercials, and Elise came along to keep me company while we shoot."

"What about all your excitement about coming for family therapy?" I shout, even though I was actually dreading it. "That's this weekend. How were you planning to participate *from Tokyo*?"

"You don't actually need me or Elise for that. We know your issues don't come from us."

I try to ignore the series of tiny explosions this statement sets off in my brain.

"Fine. Never mind the family therapy. Or any of it. Maybe you can just give permission for me to take a taxi home." I look at Adam to see if this is true.

He shakes his head and mouths, *No way.*

"Or… Okay, then write a letter of permission for someone else to pick me up?"

Adam's eyes narrow but he doesn't say no.

"Well, Uncle Bruce is at the house looking after the plants and such. I suppose I could scan a letter that says he can come get you."

"Uncle Bruce?" I drop back down into my chair and groan. "That man has never looked after a plant in his life. The best he's probably done is take a piss in one."

"Oh Lola, don't be crass. Besides, Bruce won't bother you."

"Won't bother me? I'm sorry, but Uncle Bruce bothers me just by virtue of being, Mom. He's the Barbie defiler."

"Bruce is just lonely and a little immature, honey."

"Barbie was never the same again," I say through clenched teeth. "She was so traumatized I had to euthanize her."

"Don't be silly."

"I did! I buried her with her favorite ball gowns in the front yard. How could you do this to me?"

"I haven't done anything to you, Lola. You're in rehab,

which you did to yourself. You can go home and be mature enough to deal with Bruce, or you can stay in rehab. Your choice."

"That's not a choice at all!"

"Enough with the hysterics, please."

"Someday I'll show you hysterics for real, Mom."

"I'll be waiting with bated breath."

And then, to show my maturity, I hang up,

Chapter Seventeen

Well, that's great.

I've gone and confessed to everyone here that I'm not an alcoholic, which means I can't stay here, and the defiler has taken over my house, so I can't go home, either.

Adam looks at me. I look back.

"Good chat?"

"Oh, fantastic."

"Yeah, I can tell."

"Don't."

"All right," he says, easing himself down into the other chair in the room, his voice softening. "What about your dad?"

"Yeah, what about him," I say, deflating even further.

"No, I mean, do you want to call him?"

"Yes. I'd love to. I'd really love to."

"O-kay then…" Adam gestures at the phone.

"Nah. Actually, I can't. I mean, I shouldn't. He's…" I keep track of where my dad is most of the time, but I've been distracted, plus I've been without internet so I'm not actually sure right now. "He's directing some crime drama, I think. In New York. I'm not supposed to bug him when he's working."

"This is kind of important, though, wouldn't you say?"

"Look," I say, "if I didn't call him when I was afraid I *was* an alcoholic and might need rehab, I'm certainly not going to call him to tell him I'm not."

"Ah," Adam says, and as I look into his dark brown eyes, I feel like he *knows*, like he can see something I haven't said and he knows about my dad and what I feel way deep down, and all I want to do is curl up into a ball and cry like I am some kind of whiny reject instead of the very smart, strong, resourceful, unsinkable Lola Carlyle I am supposed to be.

Right.

"But hey, whatever. I mean, he sends presents and I have a very nice allowance. Like my diamonds? And how about my dress?"

"Actually, I was thinking earlier that you look cute and sort of eatable—like a cupcake."

"Well, Adam! Are you sure that's an appropriate kind of comment?"

"Not entirely, no," he says, then looks away and abruptly stands up. "Let's go for a walk."

"Do I have a choice?"

"Existentially, yes—we always have a choice."

"I don't mean existentially, Adam."

"Oh. Then, no. Come on."

We leave the office. Adam locks up behind him, takes my hand again, and leads me to the end of the hallway, up a short set of stairs, and outside to a courtyard I've never noticed before, with a labyrinth made of stone in the center.

"Nice," I say.

"Yeah, it's peaceful," he says and then propels me toward a bench. "Now sit."

I shrug and then sit near one end, and Adam straddles the other.

"So, Lola," he says, hands braced in front of him and leaning toward me, watching my every move and expression. "You want to talk?"

"No, not really. You?"

"I'm here to support you for as long as you're at Sunrise."

"I appreciate it," I say, and I do.

"I have a few thoughts for you to consider, if you're up for it."

"Lay it on me," I say, and prepare for a lecture on wasting people's time, waffling about whether one is an alcoholic when for most people it's a very serious disease, and how now I'm going to be sent to some kind of hideous halfway house until some legitimate member of my family can come pick me up.

"You're not the first person to freak out and try to bail at her first AA meeting."

"Well, that's very reassuring, but—"

"Just listen. I know it can be overwhelming, and I can

see from your behavior since you got here that you haven't really come to terms with *why* you're here. Plus, some people's stories are so hard-core, it can make your own experience feel invalid or not serious enough."

"Adam—"

"And you thought rehab would be easier—that much is obvious. Like, you just had to get yourself here and everything would magically fix itself and it didn't. So now you want out. That's your addict talking, Lola, not you."

"My addict. I'm starting to feel like she's my invisible friend." And then what he's saying finally starts to sink in. "Wait. Wait just a second. Are you saying you don't believe me?"

"It's not exactly that I don't believe you, it's just—"

"Oh my God, you don't."

He looks down at the bench, then back up at me, eyes dark, face wiser than his years. Though I guess he's not *that* wise or he'd have figured out I was faking being an alcoholic in the first place, not that I'm faking *not* being an alcoholic now.

"I believe you believe what you said," he continues. "But you need to at least consider that you might be in denial."

I start to laugh, and then I can't stop. I laugh until my shoulders are shaking and I can hardly breathe. And then I'm crying at the same time and Adam is looking at me with a mixture of pity and alarm, which makes me laugh harder, and cry harder. And then he scoots closer to pass me a tissue, clearly not sure how to deal with me, and as I'm swiping at my eyes with the tissue, the crying takes over and I throw my arms around him and bury my head in his shoulder.

He doesn't shush me or really say anything, just holds me, one hand in my hair and the other on my back, until I recover.

"Sorry," I say, once I can speak again. "It's been a heavy day."

"I know."

"So you think I'm in denial."

"Possibly." His hand rubs gentle circles on my back.

I pull away and look him in the eyes. "I've been drunk once, Adam."

"Really?"

"Really, truly, honestly. Not that I never drank any other time, but I exaggerated—lied—about how much. I've only been really drunk once."

"Once might be enough. You arrived with fifty chocolate bars, Lola, and you're as jumpy and edgy as any addict I've ever seen. You skipped therapy to go swimming, you're manipulating people all over the place, and you're very good at avoiding the truth—telling it or hearing it."

"That's…that's not—"

"And you're sad."

"Hey—"

"Not that kind of sad. *Sad*, sad. Like, deep sad."

"I am not sad. Or *sad*, sad. No offense, but piss off."

"I'm just saying if it looks like an addict and smells like an addict…" He shrugs like it's the most obvious thing in the world. "You seem like an addict to me."

"That's…that's… No."

"Listen," he says, shifting so we're sitting side by side but keeping one arm around my shoulders, "regardless of what you believe, there has to be something going on for you to come here in the first place."

I look down at that.

"Why don't you just give yourself a few more days to see how you feel, to see if your perspective changes. I promise you, the program works if you let it."

"Isn't it, 'It works if you work it'?" I say.

"That, too."

"If I stay, will you promise to be more fun?"

Adam laughs, then says, "Nope."

"Damn."

"Besides, you don't exactly have a choice. For now, you're staying. My advice is, get your shit together and make the best of it."

"Right. Goody."

"One thing you might think about is the attitude," he says. "It doesn't help."

"*Au contraire*," I say. "My attitude usually helps me quite a bit."

CHAPTER EIGHTEEN

The truth does not exactly set me free.

I soon discover it's done the opposite.

Thanks to my supposed state of denial, when I go back to the room, our balcony door is locked and we are put on half-hourly room checks throughout the night. Jade and Talia are uniformly unimpressed.

And then on Saturday morning, just when I'm getting ready to bail early from Contemplation so I can go try to find Wade to tell him I'm still here, they descend.

Dr. Koch, Mary, and Dr. Owens show up in the lounge and "invite" me to come with them. Adam gives the affirmation (*I am rigorously honest with myself and continue to make an inventory of my shortcomings*) and then he comes along, too.

"What's the deal?" I say as we enter Dr. Koch's office. "I

don't get to Contemplate?"

Adam points to a chair.

"No coffee even?"

Dr. Owens and Dr. Koch sit across from me on the couch and Mary sits in another chair.

Adam hovers.

"We're concerned about you," Mary says. "And we also want to show you our support."

"Yes," says Dr. Koch. "We've seen this type of crisis before, and we are equipped to help you through it."

"But I'm not—"

"Mary is planning a special process group this afternoon with the other female patients to talk about what happened last night, Adam has been pulled off all other files and has committed to accompanying you throughout each day, and Dr. Owens here has come in voluntarily on her weekend to do an emergency therapy session."

"Look, I can see this denial idea has taken hold with you all, but I'm really not—"

"I have also heard from your mother, who is adamant that you stay in the program."

"What happened to the whole *voluntary* aspect?"

Koch ignores this question, which actually kind of answers it, and continues. "She wishes me to convey that your sobriety is her utmost concern, and she has requested and paid for you to have therapy daily from now on."

I put my head in my hands and groan.

Ten minutes later, I'm walking into Dr. Owens's office. She shuts the door behind us with a *thud* that vibrates in my bones.

"So, a rather rough night last night?" she says.

"I guess."

"And how are you this morning?"

"Uh, fine. And you?"

Out comes the bullshit bell, *ding, ding, ding, ding, ding…*

"I haven't even sat down yet," I shout over the sound of the bell.

"I want you to be honest," she shouts back.

"Everyone says 'fine' when someone asks how are you. I was being polite. Stop that. *Please.* Fine, I'm miserable. Happy?"

She stops.

I sit.

"Your psychological test shows you're depressed, and now you're trying to leave the program," she says. "I don't want you to be polite; I want you to be honest."

"Yeah, I tried that. Yesterday."

"You're referring to your statement that you are not, in fact, an addict?"

"Of course. All it did was convince everyone I'm in denial. My own mother doesn't believe me."

"Hmm."

"Kind of shitty, don't you think?"

"You're feeling as though you can't depend on her."

"I'm feeling like Sunrise has become the most expensive babysitting service on the planet."

"And your mother is not here for you."

"I guess not."

"And neither is your father."

"Well…in the sense that he's not *here* here, no."

"What about in other senses?"

"Do we have to talk about this? My parents are fine. Leave them out of it."

"I find it interesting, though, that you are here and protesting that all is well and you have no problems with your parents. And in the meantime, your supposedly concerned parents are nowhere to be found and/or refusing to come get you. Which means they either feel strongly that you need help or…"

"Or?" I say, even though I know I'm falling into her trap.

"Why don't you tell me?"

"Give me the bell." I stand up and grab for it, but Dr. Owens pulls it onto her lap.

"What do you want it for?"

"I want to ring it. I should be able to ring it, too, when you're bullshitting me."

"How am I bullshitting you?"

"Well, you're using bullshit techniques. You're trying to trick me."

"Trick you into what?"

"Into saying my parents don't love me, into saying I'm an alcoholic. Or something."

"Do your parents not love you?"

"Fuck off."

"Why are you so defensive?"

"I'm not defensive, I'm just not doing this."

"Why not?"

"I don't need therapy and I don't enjoy being badgered by a wack job whose sole purpose in life is to make people break down and cry. I'm not into it. Plus I'm not going to tell you anything about my family."

"You know I'm legally bound to keep our sessions private, don't you?"

"Yeah, like that ever stops anybody."

"There's an opportunity here, Lola," she says after a pause. "An opportunity to get things off your chest, to know yourself better, to find ways to deal with the things that are bothering you."

"Why are you so sure anything is bothering me?"

"Besides the things I already mentioned?"

"Yeah, besides those."

"Because you're human, and because you're here."

CHAPTER NINETEEN

Therapy is bad, but the next thing is almost worse.

It's group family therapy ("therapy" and "group" being two of my least favorite words, I like them even less when combined with "family"), and since Adam is now apparently glued to my side for eternity, there's no chance of skipping it.

The only good thing turns out to be that it's not *my* family. Otherwise, it's excruciating.

First up is Camille, the one who killed her boyfriend and best friend while driving drunk. They give her a seat at the front, lead her parents plus a brother and an aunt to sit across from her, and then each family member gets a turn to list and describe every bad thing Camille ever said or did to them in service to her addictions, and how it made them feel.

Like she doesn't already want to annihilate herself.

The aunt goes right into a story about taking Camille in after a family fight, only to have Camille steal money from her purse and disappear.

Camille's brother tells her that at school he's embarrassed to admit he's related to her.

Camille's mom cries.

Her dad yells at her and then cries. The massacre continues. Camille cries so hard it looks like she's going to break into pieces.

I bleed for her. I have the urge to run up to the front and put my arms around her and shout at these people who are putting her through this to stop. Of course I can see they're in pain too, that they have legitimate cause for their pain, but still.

It goes on.

Three hours, four families, more agony than I ever wanted to see.

There's nothing to distract from what's happening in the room or lessen the intensity, and the anguish and drama are impossible to turn away from. What this means is that every person who talks yanks us all (or me anyway) into their shoes, into their issues, their agony.

For some bizarre reason, no one gets to defend themselves; they just have to sit there and take it.

Midway through, Jade gets up, goes to the back of the room, and starts to slowly, rhythmically, bang her forehead against the wall. One of the staff stands nearby watching, but he doesn't stop her.

Messed. Up.

At the same time? I get it because I feel like throwing up, like I've been poisoned by all the sad/bad/gross/horrifying stories from this session, and at this point I'm starting to think banging my head against the wall might help.

After, I practically limp to the dining hall, where I eat my lunch with Adam beside me.

Talia is nowhere to be found, and I also haven't seen Wade since last night.

I've been trying to ignore Adam since I realized he turned me over to Koch. He went from being a comforting presence last night to a betrayer this morning, in my opinion. But finally I have to ask: "Okay, where is everybody? I mean, the ones who weren't in Family Flogging."

"They're on a sober outing," he says, with nothing but a lifted eyebrow at my other comment.

"A sober what?"

"Outing. As in, going out. Sober. You have to be Level Three—"

"I'm Level Three."

"*Real* Level Three. Plus you need permission from your group leader, your therapist, and"—he grins—"me."

"Sounds a little overly wholesome anyway. Obviously they're lawn bowling, or attending a G-rated movie with all the lights on. Or drinking wheatgrass lattes."

"They're hiking Topanga Canyon."

"Exactly. But still…"

"No chance we'd let you go," Adam says. "Even Dr. Koch agrees you're high risk for a runner right now."

"A what?"

"Taking a runner—running away."

"Oh, sure," I say. "Because homelessness or living with a perv are great options."

"Well hey, next Saturday is Disneyland. Maybe by then you'll be approved. You ready for the process group this afternoon?"

"Okay, you know what? I'm not impressed."

"About?"

"You led me to believe if I stayed I'd be given some time and space to figure out…you know…whether I really need to be here. But instead you're letting everyone gang up on me."

"We're here to s—"

"Support me?"

"Yes."

"Yeah, right."

"And you do have a free period right after this. You can lie by the pool, read a book or some magazines…"

"Or work on my list of shortcomings."

"Sure. Absolutely," he says, but he has the decency to look embarrassed.

"While you sit on my freaking shoulder."

"I will be accompanying you," he says stiffly, "if that's what you mean."

"Well, thanks for the suggestions, *Cupcake*," I say and his mouth opens, then snaps shut. "But I think I'll go hang myself instead. That was a joke."

"I—I know."

"Good."

"You can *not* call me Cupcake."

"You're right—you're more of a bran muffin anyway."

We're walking by the lounge on the way back to the dorm when I pull away.

"Where are you going?" Adam says.

"Duh," I say, and head toward the lounge.

"But…"

"It's *my* free time. I'm going to make a phone call."

"You can't—"

I take out my Level Three card, wave it in his face, then pass it to the tech on duty.

Adam rolls his eyes and goes out to the balcony, leaving me with the lounge to myself.

Once I'm settled on the couch, I try Sydney on her cell. It rings and rings, the voicemail picks up and says her mailbox is full, and I hang up, try again, get the same result. I sit for a few frustrated moments, then decide to try the cell one last time because, well, I don't know any of her other numbers and damn it, I need some answers from that girl. Just when I'm about to hang up, she answers.

"Sydney? It's me—it's Lola."

"Holy shit, Lola," she shouts, her voice, combined with the background noise, so loud I have to hold the phone away from my ear. "Where are you?"

"Where do you think I am? You know exactly where I

am." I want to shout, but am too aware of Adam just outside. "My question is where are *you*?"

She laughs.

"No, seriously. You're laughing about this? What the hell?"

"Oh honey, I didn't think you'd really do it." She's still laughing, not sorry in the least, obviously. "Then I saw you and your moms all over the internet and I heard my clean-cut friend is actually a badass boozer. I almost fell over from shock. WATCH THE DRINK, BUDDY. Hang on, let me go somewhere quieter…"

"Sure," I say, and listen to what sounds like a huge party going on in the background, then hear the noise receding and the click of high-heeled shoes.

"Ah, that's better," Sydney says.

"Where are you?" I say.

"Oh my God, the craziest pool party—that action flick with whatsherface in it—they're having a party. Like a wrap party but they haven't actually wrapped. I have the best dress, you won't believe it, and a Real House-husband just hit on me. Who let him in, I can't imagine because he's obviously not in the film. The script is supposed to suck but whatever—they hired circus performers for the party and I heard Drake was going to do a surprise concert this afternoon and you won't believe—"

"*Sydney.*"

"What?"

"When I said where are you, I actually meant where are you because you're supposed to be *here*. And I am not supposed to be stuck here *without* you. You knew I was going to do it. What happened? And why didn't you tell me you'd left?"

"Oh, that. Well, I guess my parents freaked. Too much information or whatever. Too much work. And the thing is I don't want to be a meth face but come on, a girl's gotta be able to have a drink sometimes. Plus, no iPhone. And sharing a bathroom? Please. My mom asked me if I really wanted to stick it out, I said no, she sprung me."

"But you knew I was coming. You're the one who said it was so great—practically a spa, you said. Remember that?"

"I honestly really never thought you'd do it."

"Bullshit."

"What do you need me for, anyway?"

"Nothing at all, apparently," I say, feeling, for a moment, like I might cry, like I am going to hang up on her and never speak to her again. But then the horror stories of my fellow patients rise up in my mind and I'm filled with a gut clenching worry about her. She just got out of rehab without completing the program and she's at a *party*. Being a shitty friend might be the least of her issues.

"So tell me, have you made any progress with Mr. Miller yet?"

"Wait, Syd. Look, I'm pissed. Really, really pissed, like I might never believe anything you say again. But are you okay? This addiction thing is worse than I realized."

"I'm good, I'm good. No need to call sexy Dr. Koch on me. I'm not going to take any drugs. And you know I can handle drinking. I'm totally fine."

"Really?"

"Do I sound drunk to you?"

"A little, actually."

"No, no. Anyway, alcohol I can handle. And I have your clutch ready in a gift bag when you get out, by the way. How long are you staying? Who're your roommates? Tell me about Wade Miller. Is he as perfect and sweet and dreamy as you remember him?"

"He's here," I say quietly, giving up on the idea that I can be of any help to her at the moment. "And we've hung out a bit. But you also misled me about how much I'd be able to see him. Not to mention the rules about fraternizing."

"Oh, no one cares about that. They just have to put that in there for liability."

I'm pretty sure Adam would care.

"So? Progress?"

"Y-yes…" I realize I don't know what to say about Wade. I still have a crush on him, but I can't rescue him. The chemistry is good, looks promising, but I can't get enough time with him to find out more, and I can't really tell how much of his old self is still in there. "The thing is—"

"Just a sec—I'LL BE RIGHT THERE, LOVER BOY— oh my God, I forgot to tell you, I've been partying with your dad."

All other thoughts and concerns fly out the window. "What?"

"Oh don't worry, that's not who I was calling Lover Boy—your dad's cute for his age but I'd never do that to you; it would be way too weird. Can you *imagine* me as your stepmother?"

"No. God. That's…" I shudder and shake my head. "He's there? Right now?"

"Earth to Lola—that's what I said. He's in fine form, I must say. I told him I can't believe how much you two look alike these days. You don't see it as much in pictures as you do in person."

"So you told him…I mean, he remembered you?"

"Duh. Well, I've grown up a bit so I had to remind him, but of course. How many freaking sleepovers did we have?"

"Right. Well. Did he…does he…" I stop, thoroughly flustered at the hurricane of emotions I'm experiencing and the list of things I want to know but cannot ask.

Does he care that I'm in rehab, for example?

"I'M COMING, DON'T START WITHOUT ME! You know what, Lo? I can't wait to hear everything, but I have to go."

"Oh."

"I'll say hi to Ben for you."

"Oh, I… No, that's—"

"Or wait, it might be loud but let me see if I can find him again. I mean what a coincidence, hang on…"

"Hang on. *Wait*," I say, but either she's not listening or she can't hear.

There's clinking, laughing, splashing, and a deep, thumping bass and lots of rustling as Sydney goes back inside the party.

"BEN? BEN!" I hear her shouting over the noise.

My heart is in my throat, which means I won't be able to

speak and what the hell will I say anyway? I can't do this. I should hang up.

"OVER HERE, BEN, I (rustle, rustle) SURPRISE (rustle, thump) YOU…"

Holy shit. I'm going to have a stroke. I'm going to pass out. My thumb is hovering over the end button and I'm going to push it because there's no way this can go well. Except I might hear his voice at least and he would hear mine and maybe…

"Hello? Who's this?" It's him. My dad.

My mouth moves but no sound comes out.

"Hello? Someone just shoved a phone in my face, who is this?"

Fucking *speak*, Lola.

"D-Dad…" I manage to croak.

"What? Can't hear a thing. Call back tomorrow… (thump, rustle, dial tone…)."

Afterward, I sit for a long time, listening to the dial tone and staring into space until Adam comes back in to get me.

I'm not hearing bells or looking for the deeper why or pondering the meaning of life.

I'm not even looking for the quiet place…just a less painful one.

CHAPTER TWENTY

Saturday evenings are mercifully free of programming, even for those in denial.

Instead there's a movie night and I am actually allowed to attend, albeit with Velcro Adam by my side. But at least it's a break from the scrutiny and self-defense that now fill my every waking moment and a distraction from the ache that's been expanding in my chest since I heard my dad's voice this afternoon.

We all crowd into the chapel where there are snacks — bags of popcorn, fruit slices, baked chips, veggies with dip — and pillows on the floor. Wade is there, and I am suddenly overcome with feelings of dorkishness. The intensity of the day has me exhausted and off my game, so instead of being cool when our eyes meet, I break into the biggest, happiest, most ridiculous smile that probably broadcasts to the entire world, including him, that I have a crush on him.

It's hideous.

But…he smiles back. And then I kind of freeze, standing there smiling like an idiot and causing a backup in the snack line until Talia finally gives me a gentle shove.

I stumble forward. Need to get a grip.

Talia and I, with Adam in tow, head to the back, away from Wade, who's looking for a seat near the front. Talia sits on one side of me and Adam plops down on the other.

I look at him. "Okay, really?"

"What?"

"Don't you have other patients to liaise with?"

To my surprise, he looks a little hurt. Just for a second.

"Or are we on a date all of a sudden?" I say, trying to turn it into a joke.

Talia giggles.

"I mean, you're actually lovely, Adam. Most of the time. And you're a one hundred percent cute enough to date. But as you so clearly pointed out to me a few days ago, this is a professional relationship. Right? So could I not have, like, a five-foot radius? I mean, you must be sick of me by now, too."

He grunts and then moves so he's directly behind me instead.

"Better?"

"Perfect. Now you can *literally* breathe down my neck."

He puts a handful of popcorn in his mouth and crunches loudly, probably on purpose.

The movie is just about to start when I look up to see Wade standing over me.

"Anyone sitting here?" he asks, pointing to the spot Adam vacated.

"Yes," Adam says, just as I say, "No."

"I'm asking her, not you, dude," Wade says to Adam, then looks back at me. "Well?"

"Have a seat," I say to Wade, then glare over my shoulder at Adam, who glares back.

Wade sits down beside me.

"When you made that big speech at AA, I thought we'd lost you, Carlyle."

"Yeah, well, apparently I'm still here," I say with a roll of my eyes.

"Hey, we all freak out sometimes. Don't feel bad about it."

"Let me guess, you think I'm in denial?"

"You tell me."

"As a matter of fact, I'm —"

"You two know each other?" It's Adam, and he's actually physically poked his head in between us from behind.

I say, "No."

Wade says, "Yes."

Adam says, "I see."

"I worked on a film with her dad."

"Years ago," I add, mention of Dad giving me a little hoof in the solar plexus. "I was in it, too."

"Yeah, her dad got tired of her causing trouble on set and put her to work."

"I didn't actually cause any trouble, he was just afraid I might."

"You? I can't imagine why," Adam says.

"I did once use Channing Tatum's trailer to play hide-and-seek and kind of scared the crap out of him. But I was only, like, ten and Channing wasn't mad. Not that mad."

Wade chuckles and Adam snorts.

"Anyway," I say with a hard look at Adam before turning back to Wade, "no, I don't think I'm in denial. But it appears not to matter what I think."

The overhead lights dim.

Wade opens his mouth to say something and Adam makes a shushing sound and moves in closer behind me.

"What's the movie?" I whisper.

"Don't know," Wade whispers back, and Adam gives me a nudge from behind.

I turn, glare at him. "Am I not allowed to have a conversation?"

"Watch the movie," he says.

The movie turns out to be *Leaving Las Vegas*, all about Nicolas Cage's character drinking himself to death. Nice. Here I thought we were getting a chance to relax, maybe watching an action flick or something funny, but no. After being tortured all day long with therapy and group family therapy, not to mention the almost-conversation with my dad, now I have to watch one of the saddest movies of all time.

I sigh from the bottom of my soul and brace myself for the agony.

The only bright spot is Wade sitting next to me. I am hyperaware of him, but also of Adam, which is weird and makes me self-conscious. A few minutes in, Wade's knee touches mine, and I hold myself very still so as not to lose the connection. It's like every nerve ending in my body has gone to my knee, like my entire being is there, waiting breathless in that one circular inch of contact.

Then Adam gets up for a popcorn refill and Wade leans over to whisper in my ear.

"Carlyle…"

"Yes?"

"When?"

"When what?"

"When can we hang out?"

"We're hanging out now."

"You know what I mean."

"Okay, yeah I do. But I don't know. Apparently I have a freaking bodyguard now because everyone thinks I'm 'high risk' for running away or something."

"You are at high risk of my kissing you."

"Now?"

"Yeah, now."

"That's insane," I say, but he's leaning in closer and I'm not moving away. "You wouldn't."

"I would. I will." His hand slides up my arm and he's inches away, but it's not nearly dark enough and there are people all around us. "You chicken?"

"To get kissed? Hardly."

Wade's lips are milliseconds from mine and I'm about to let him do it, consequences be damned, when at the last second his mouth veers away and instead his voice is in my ear. "Next time, Carlyle. I promise."

And behind us, Adam's knees crack as he sits down with his fresh bag of very loud popcorn.

Later, Adam insists on walking—more like stomping—back to the dorms with me.

"What's the matter with you?" I ask him finally, and he stops so abruptly I almost trip over him.

"Me? More like what's the matter with you?"

"What?"

"Whatever you're doing," he says, bringing his angry face close to mine, "you have to stop."

"I'm not doing anything."

"I'm not blind, Lola."

"I never said you were. What is it you think I'm doing?"

"If I say it, then I have to do something about it."

"Do something—what does that mean? What do you think you're going to do?"

"Just don't make me say it," he growls.

"Okay."

"And don't be doing it."

"I can assure you, I'm not *doing*—"

"Stop it; I'm not stupid. Just stay out of trouble."

"All right, all right. You don't have to be such a dick about it."

"I'm a dick?"

"I'm not saying you—"

"Oh no, you know who's a dick? That guy. That guy is a total dick. And I don't want him anywhere near you."

"Oh...so it *was* supposed to be a date," I say. "And now

you're jealous."

"Jesus, Lola, you never stop, do you?"

"Do you really want me to?"

For an answer, he swears and stomps off.

CHAPTER TWENTY-ONE

The anti-denial campaign continues on Sunday.

Most people have visitors, but since I don't, I get yet another bonus therapy session where, against my will, I begin to tell Dr. Owens my life story.

I am spared group, but there's no letup in the intensity. Presumably because the barrage of verbal/emotional tactics failed to extract a re-confession from me yesterday, Adam and Dr. Koch are trying something different. My day is now "enriched" with hot yoga, a drumming class, one-on-one meditation, one-on-one Vision, and lots of bickering with Adam in between.

Lunch is a tad depressing, what with the truckloads of visitors and everybody all excited. I eat quickly, then push back from the table.

"Where are you going?" Adam says. "I'm not finished."

"Not my problem."

He bites back a swear word, leaves his half-eaten lunch, and follows me out of the dining hall, up the stairs, and to the door of the lounge where I once again present my card, then go to the phone and pace back and forth in front of it.

"You gonna use that phone or just stare at it?"

"Feel free to go back and finish your lunch."

"I would love to," he says, not moving.

"Could you go outside, then? Like you did yesterday?"

"No," he says grumpily. "I don't think I will."

"Fine." I shrug and then, in one swift movement, plop down into the corner of the couch, grab the receiver, and dial.

I wait, shivering with nerves.

And then a click and a computerized voice, "This number is no longer in service."

I hit end. Try another number.

Reach a confused-sounding Hispanic man.

Hit end. Try the first number again, just in case.

Nope.

Classic. All that effort to get my courage up, all these months thinking I could, potentially, pick up the phone and reach him at any time. Like I had the power. And all that time I didn't even have his number anymore.

Of course, there is one more number, and no one in showbiz takes the weekend off...

I press grim lips together and dial.

"Ben Carlyle's office."

Bingo.

"Jo-Ellen?"

"That's me. Who's calling?"

"It's, um—"

"Oh, hold please."

I hold. Breathe through my nostrils. Watch the clock and the lounge-room door and avoid looking at Adam. After a full three minutes, she comes back on.

"All right now, who's calling?"

"It's Lola."

"Lola?"

"Carlyle."

"Good Lord. Well, this is a surprise."

"Um, yeah. How are you these days?"

We make uncomfortable small talk, followed by an awkward pause. There's no way she doesn't know my dad and I haven't been speaking and there's also no way I'm talking to her about it. It's bad enough that I need to have this conversation in front of Adam.

"So, I seem to have the wrong number for Dad's cell. Probably one of those things where I've got the numbers reversed, or, you know, just typed it in wrong…"

"Is that so?" she says.

She's going to make me ask. Worse, she might not give it to me.

"So, could you…"

"You want me to tell him you called?"

"No. I mean, sure, but…could you just give me the correct number?"

A pause. She may have to be polite, but Jo-Ellen hates

me. Or thinks I'm a ridiculous, spoiled brat, anyway. And possibly in the past I may have been a bit rude to her, which was shortsighted, considering.

"Please, Jo-Ellen? He won't be able to call me back here and I don't have my cell."

"He's working."

"It's important."

"Listen," she says, her tone warming up slightly. "I heard about...where you are. It explains a lot. And you're doing a brave thing."

"Oh. Well, thank you."

"You have a pen?"

"No, but my memory's good."

I'm about to dial when Jade and Emmy come into the lounge. Emmy ignores me and Jade gives me her usual glare. I glance at Adam and then wait while they grab bottles of water from the fridge.

Finally they leave, and then before I can chicken out and with hands shaking, I dial.

"Ben Carlyle here."

"Dad?"

A pause.

"Dad, it's me."

"Yep. No one else calls me Dad. Hello, Lola."

"Uh, how are you?"

"I'm all right."

"Me, too."

"Pardon?"

"Me, too. I'm all right, too."

"Of course. Sure. Good. That's good, Lola."

"I guess you've heard…"

"Yes, I heard. How's it going?"

"Um, it's interesting, I guess. But Dad, are you…are we…"

"Are we what?"

"Are we okay?"

"Sure, we're okay. Sometimes people need to take some space."

"I… Sure." I swallow. "Space. Ha ha. Well, we definitely have that."

"You didn't say how you're doing there."

"Oh, I'm fine. It's nice, I guess. Hey, you know who's here? Wade Miller. From the zombie thing. Remember him?"

"Of course I remember him—he cost me a fortune on his first day. Never had an actor bleed a production so hard and fast as on that day. But he pulled it together."

"Sometimes people just need a chance. Another chance, I mean."

"Well, everyone loved him in the film. He's a great kid. Hope he's okay."

I press my ear into the phone as we weather another awkward pause.

"That was a fun time, wasn't it?" I say. And I know in this moment that I would go back to being twelve, take the braces and the short, skinny body and the gawkiness and all of it, just to go back. It wasn't perfect by a long shot, but I'd give up almost anything to go back. Even Wade.

"It was."

"It was the last…kind of the last good time before—" I stop. "Well, it was an easier time, anyway."

"Is there something you want to talk about? Something you need to say?"

"Say? Oh. Well…yes. I mean…now that you mention it, I was kind of hoping…"

"Yes?"

That you would come see me, that you would come back into my life and be my dad again and forgive me…that you would love me again.

"That you could come and get me," I say instead, though it wasn't my plan.

Adam's head snaps up.

"Please, Dad? I need to get out of here."

"What?"

"Mom is in Tokyo and she's not listening to me at all and I really am in the wrong place. I'm not supposed to be here. And the program is voluntary but they need a parent or guardian or they won't release me so I thought—"

"That's why you're calling me?"

"Well…it's not the *only* reason."

"That's why you're calling me."

"No. I mean, sort of."

"Let me get this straight," he says in a low, measured voice. "A year ago you throw a fit—"

"I did not—"

"*You throw a fit* and call me a bunch of names and tell

me to…let me see if I can remember the exact wording…oh yes, tell me to get the hell out of your life."

"I was upset."

"To fuck off and get the hell out of your life."

"Listen," I say, feeling myself start to boil and suddenly not caring anymore if Adam's listening. "I was sitting in Arrivals at LaGuardia for eight freaking hours."

"You could easily have hopped in a limo, Lola."

"You weren't even *in* New York, Dad."

"I said I was sorry, and I'm not going to rehash it. Regardless, I'm a busy man, and I won't have my daughter telling me to fuck off. I told you if you were going to say things like that you'd better mean it, and you said you did mean it. And then three months later you show up drunk and whining at my gate, no apology and no evidence of any change in your attitude, and now you're calling me because you need someone to spring you from rehab. Have I got it right?"

"I, no. I mean, I'm not…I'm really not an alcoholic, Dad."

"Could've fooled me."

"I didn't mean it, Dad. What I said. I didn't mean it."

"Well, what did you mean, exactly?"

"I…I…"

"You're exactly where you need to be, Lola," he says, and then hangs up.

Tears pool in my eyes as I stare at the disconnected phone.

"I meant try harder," I whisper.

I said *fuck off*, but I meant *try harder*.

Chapter Twenty-Two

I grit my teeth and attempt some deep breaths, though the two actions kind of cancel each other out, and try to take the mass of pain, shrink it down to a manageable size, and swallow it.

And then, with it still there, burning in my belly and threatening to come back up, I stand up, smile brightly at Adam, and force myself to say, "What's next? I can't wait."

"Hang on, hang on," he says, coming forward with his best concerned face on. "What happened?"

"Not much." I push past him and head out the door. "Good news for you, though; my dad's not coming to get me."

"None of that sounded like good news—for anyone. You keep telling me how close you and your dad are but—"

"You never fight with someone you're close to?" I say,

voice cracking slightly and avoiding his eyes.

"Of course I have."

"See? No big. Now, come on, what's next?" I grab the schedule out of his hands and look. "Massage. Really?"

"Give me that." He takes it. "But yeah, really."

"Awesome."

"Lola, wait…talk to me."

"Not happening." I put up a hand and swallow convulsively. "Seriously."

"Fine. Maybe later."

"Awesome. Take me to the spa, dahling."

A dmittedly, it takes me a while to relax into the massage. In fact, it would be a stretch to say I relax at all.

And then to make things worse, the massage therapist, Rose, sticks her elbow into this spot near my shoulder blade and suddenly it feels like all my limbs are going to fly off.

I gasp and practically jump off the table.

"All right," Rose says in a singsongy voice, "let's check that out."

"Right," I say. "Sure. Check it out."

I drop my head back down on the doughnut hole thingy and tell myself to chill. Meanwhile, Rose proceeds to dig right back into the same spot.

To my chagrin, I start to cry.

"Okay, so we've released something…" she murmurs.

"Un-release it, then. Put it back."

"You don't want that."

"Yes, I do."

"You know, addicts store pain in the body. It can be a shock to—"

"No, no." I sit up on my heels and pull the sheet around me. "It's not stored pain, it's *pain* pain. And I'm not an addict." (This assertion is no doubt undermined by my being naked and crying over a massage…and being in rehab, of course.)

"Why don't we talk through—"

"I don't think so." I slide off the table. My entire body is starting to shake and I'm hearing my dad's voice and clearly about to lose my marbles in front of a complete stranger, which is just not happening. "I thought this was s-supposed to be relaxing."

"Lola, please. Let me call your—"

"No!" I find my clothes, sweep them up into a ball in my arms, and edge toward the door. "Don't call anyone, I'm f-fine. I just d-don't like m-massage, that's all."

Rose backs up, gives a placating gesture with her arms.

I wrap the sheet tighter around me, find my shoes and slide my feet into them, push the door open, and rush through the empty waiting room and into the corridor where I turn left, run to the end, turn right, and hurl myself through another door and into the labyrinth courtyard where hopefully I can find two precious minutes of solitude so I can get my act together, because there's no reason for me to be freaking out like this.

But of course, I'm not alone.

Talia is there, along with her two sisters and her mom. And I see Adam and a few other patients, all of them standing around chatting like it's a perfectly normal day. Wade is there, too. Standing there flirting with two very pretty girls.

Talia notices me first, breaks off midsentence and shushes the group. Soon everyone is quiet and staring at the freak show also known as me.

"Oh, hey guys," I say, as if it's totally normal and apropos for me to be wandering around crying, limbs shaking, and wearing nothing but a sheet.

Talia's eyes widen, her mom looks away, and her sisters stare.

Adam stands up and starts toward me. So does Wade.

"Don't mind me." I put up a hand, force a smile, and find myself speaking an octave higher than usual. "I'm just… looking for the toga party. Ha ha ha."

Adam glares at Wade, stopping him in his tracks, and keeps coming.

"Lola, are you all right?"

"Perfect! Great! By the way, my massage was just totally, totally relaxing."

"You were only in there for ten minutes."

"Well, I reached such a deep level of relaxation that I cut it short. I figured any more relaxed and I'd be dead. Now, I just need…" I wipe at my face, almost lose the sheet, cast about for an escape route.

Adam reaches me, puts a hand on my arm, and I yelp.

"Don't touch me! There's nothing wrong with me."

"I didn't say there was."

Wade hovers nearby like he kind of wants to help but kind of also thinks I'm a freak. This whole get-to-know-each-other-in-rehab idea was terrible, obviously. First I make the most asinine AA speech ever and now this. He's never going to fall in love with me.

"I'm perfectly fine," I insist again. "I just didn't like the massage."

Now Talia's on her feet, coming toward us, but Adam, who can't see her but obviously has some kind of Spidey sense, puts a hand behind him and waves her back.

"Talia, Wade—maybe you'd like to show your friends and families the dining hall," he says. "Or the vegetable garden."

"Yes!" I say as they're leaving. "Because that's what we do when the crazy people get loose around here. Pick vegetables."

There are approximately two seconds of quiet before the door behind me opens and Rose steps out.

I recoil.

Adam looks from one of us to the other, then she reaches out her hand, palm open. In it is my Daddy's Girl bracelet.

"You left this," she says.

I snatch it from her.

"If you'd just come back, maybe we could..."

I never hear the rest of her sentence because I'm pushing past her, back through the door she's left open, and running. I find a stairwell and dash up three flights of stairs and stop at the top, out of breath and hoping not to pass out.

I lean my bare upper back against the wall, enjoying the

cold, then let the ball of clothing in my arms drop to the floor in front of me. I bend over and hunch with my hands on my knees, trying to still the shaking and hold back the new crop of tears that wants to come.

But it's the thoughts I can't stop.

I am an idiot. Again. Still.

I know better than to need things from people or to put myself in such a vulnerable position with my dad. Normally I know better. But hearing his voice in combination with everything being so intense here—I let it get to me. And now I'm letting it get to me again when what I'm supposed to be doing is… Well, I'm not even sure anymore.

Regardless, I need to get a grip.

"Lola? Lola!" Adam comes sprinting up the stairs and looks very relieved when he rounds the final corner and sees me huddled against the wall. "Why didn't you answer?"

"You were coming anyway."

Adam lowers himself onto the step across from me, never taking his eyes off my face.

"Talk to me."

"I don't need to talk. I need to get a life."

"Lola…you should go back to the spa and talk with Rose."

"I'm not going."

"You will if I make you."

"Yeah? I'm practically naked under this sheet. You try that and it's going to get awkward."

"I have to carry you naked through the mansion, it's going to get really awkward."

"You would not."

"You don't think?"

"No way," I say, but actually I'm not sure. "Look, I don't know her and I'm not interested in lying around crying with my face in a freaking doughnut hole. I just need to use all my new coping skills to prevent stupid things from getting to me."

"Is it the fight with your dad?"

"I don't want to talk about it."

"All right…" he says, then thinks for a minute. "I have an idea."

"No offense, Adam, but I don't always like your ideas."

He smiles. "No, this one is totally… Well, you'll like it because it could get me in a lot of trouble."

I look at him, feel a little spark of humor coming back.

"Really?"

"Trust me."

"All right. Don't make me regret it."

"Excellent," he says, and gets to his feet. "First, I'll go down one flight, you…ahem…get dressed."

"Then what?"

"Then I'm taking you somewhere."

Chapter Twenty-Three

Five minutes later, we're leaving from the staff door and heading to Adam's car.

Fifteen minutes after that, we're sitting at the open window in a tiny beachside café, looking at the chalkboard menu.

"Did you just break me out of rehab?" I say.

"Koch told me you have unique needs," he says with a devilish smile I've never seen before. "I'm just trying to meet them."

"As my mentor."

"As your very dedicated mentor," he says. "Look, I know it's been a rough few days. I felt like you needed to get out of there. And I figure I can handle you."

"Is that so? You don't think I'm going to go wild and, like, do a stick-'em-up on this place demanding all their coffee and dark chocolate, and then take off down the coast?"

"No." He gives me a half grin. "Not that it wouldn't be interesting to witness and not that I would put anything past you. But I don't think you will."

"Why not?"

"Because I'm choosing to trust you."

"Oh." Sudden, un-asked-for tears well up in my eyes, and I look away, blinking them back as fast as I can. "I'll keep that in mind, then."

"Speaking of unique needs, what's the coffee concoction you find so lacking in the Sunrise lounge?"

"All of them, but especially the lattes. That machine is crap at making them."

"I'm an espresso guy myself. But I think the lattes are good here, too," he says, pointing to the open kitchen and bar area. "See, they have a real machine with a human doing the foam."

My latte, when it comes, is steaming hot and perfectly foamy with a little design in the foam, and I sigh with pleasure at the normalcy of just sitting in a café.

"Thank you," I say.

"You're welcome."

"How old are you, Adam?"

He tilts his head sideways and gives me a funny look.

"What? It's a normal question, isn't it?"

"I'm twenty," he says. "If you must know."

"I'll be eighteen in September," I say.

"I know," he says.

And then there's kind of a long moment where we're

just looking at each other. It's not comfortable, but it's… not unpleasant, either. In fact, I would say it's pleasantly uncomfortable, if that makes any sense.

"Hey," I say, looking for something to talk about before things go from pleasantly uncomfortable to *un*pleasantly uncomfortable. "I've been meaning to ask you—about your dad and that screenplay. Did it ever get made?"

"Oh yeah," Adam says with a bitter chuckle. "It got made. And my dad got paid and his name was on it."

"Well that's good, at least."

"Yes and no. What got made…was unrecognizable from his original script. Honestly, I hate to say it, but it was a piece of shit."

"Oh." I wince. "And it tanked?"

"As a matter of fact, no." He shakes his head. "It was a hit."

"No way."

"Oh yeah, box office hit."

"Freaking Hollywood."

"Seriously."

"Okay, you have to tell me what it was," I say. "I've probably seen it. I probably know people who're in it."

He gives me a squirmy look, then shakes his head.

"You won't tell me?"

"Lola, it was so bad…"

"Come on. What is it—some kind of family shame?"

"No, but…" He trails off, the look on his face confirming what his words are denying—he's embarrassed.

"Adam, it's not your film. It sounds like it's not even your dad's film. Have I not told you an extraordinary amount of crap about my life? I mean, I'll have you know I've told you more about my life than I've told anyone, probably."

He grimaces, then takes both my hands in his and says, "Okay. I'm trusting you."

"Wow." I squeeze his hands back. "You're making that a habit."

"*Forth Shot*," he says. "It's called *Forth Shot*."

"*Forth Shot*? Holy shit, Adam."

"I know. Craptastic. You saw it?"

"Sure I saw it. You're being modest—it was huge. Not...a great work of art or anything, but it was fun."

"Not for my family, it wasn't. Critics hated it, and yet everybody still wanted him to write a sequel. He was done, though. How could he write a sequel to that?"

"Mm. I see your point. Especially if it didn't turn out anything like his original concept. But he was... He'd have had the cred to write something else, wouldn't he? Or was it too late?"

"Too late. Took his money and started drinking it. Et cetera."

"Et cetera being...?"

"Shooting it, smoking it, snorting it."

"Damn."

"Yeah."

"So he had an artist crisis."

"Is that a thing?"

"Are you kidding?" I say. "Artists do crises better than anyone. It should be a thing. You could, like, do a PhD on that and make it a thing."

"I'm not going to stay in school that long."

"I'm just saying you could. Anyway…Hollywood is a rough place."

"I can't blame Hollywood," Adam says. "I used to blame him. Like, why did he have to be such an idealist? Why did he have to be an idealist but also so weak? Now, though, I get how so much of it is the disease. He could have been in any career. I do think he cared too much about what people thought. Critics, his peers, complete strangers. I try not to do that."

"Care what people think?"

"Strangers especially. Like why leave your measure of self-worth up to a bunch of people who don't even know you? I'm never going to do that."

"Never?"

"It's wasted energy. Think about it. And it's not just strangers—I try not to care what people think of me in general."

"How can you not care? How does that produce…a positive result, even, if you don't care what other people think?"

"I don't mean I don't care at all," he says. "I mean if I'm making decisions from just knowing what's right and wrong, or knowing what's right for me to do in the moment, then the rest should hopefully…fall into place. Like this—I sneak you out of rehab—yeah, it's against the rules. Someone might judge me for it, I might get in shit. It's not that I don't care, it's just that…" He gazes out the window, then shrugs.

"They weren't there when I made the decision. They're not in my shoes and they don't get it. But I do. So if I get in trouble or whatever, I can live with it."

"But if you made a decision you weren't so sure about?"

Faking your way into rehab, for example…?

"Well…then you do end up curing, because there's doubt involved. Hopefully that's the moment to admit you were wrong and apologize."

"Such a mature vision of the world you have for a twenty-year-old," I say, with a grimace. "All good decisions and taking responsibility and apologizing…"

"My mom says I was born an old man."

"You *totally* were. You are."

"Oh yeah? How old, then? Old-old?"

"Yeah, like a grandpa."

"Oh, no." His look of dismay is almost comical.

"No, I'm kidding," I say, laughing. "More…old like some friend's older brother I'm not supposed to have a crush on who tries to pretend I don't exist."

"You have a crush on a friend's older brother?"

"No, I'm just trying to give you a pertinent example," I say, and then feel myself starting to blush as I realize I just made it sound like I have a crush on *him*. "Although that's not quite right…uh…as a comparison. My point…my point is more that you seem my age sometimes, and then you turn into…you know, the bran muffin."

"Nice."

"From the cupcake. And that's what tempts me to try to provoke you all the time."

"I see," he says with a quirky half smile. "Well, consider me provoked."

"I'm a pain in the ass, I know."

"It's all good."

"I should be better."

"Probably." He nods, but he's smiling at least.

"I guess maybe I—wait—is this some kind of stealth therapy?"

He laughs, his brown eyes warm. "Nah. Just two people out for coffee, talking about life."

"You know what I like? And that I'm surprised I like?"

"What?"

"That this isn't just any old bullshit conversation that I might have with one of my friends. It's about something."

"I kinda suck at bullshit conversations, so that's good," he says. "Although I can talk music and pop culture all day long, and I don't think that's bullshit, necessarily."

"Agreed. We should do that sometime," I say, leaning forward.

"Sure," he says.

"Okay," I say.

"Good…" he says, and then just sips his espresso and waits.

"So," I say when the silence has gone on too long. "Back to this not caring thing of yours… Don't you think our survival—whether we thrive or not—is based on whether people like us? Or approve of us? Both my parents—their careers wouldn't exist without people wanting to see their work, and people have to like their work to want to see it, and people have to like them to want to see their work in the first place. That's true about a lot of jobs, not just in the arts."

"But if they're thinking about people liking them while they're doing the work—how do you think that affects the work?" Adam says. "Particularly in the arts?"

"Hmm… By the way, I love you for this latte."

"Oh, now you love me? Don't you hate me most of the time?"

"I'm taking a break from hating you, Adam."

"It's that good?"

"Yes. But you don't really think I hate you, do you?"

"No," he says, and then we have another one of those pleasantly uncomfortable moments.

"About what you were saying earlier." I clear my throat. "When you think about it, every artist of any kind has to live with that I-don't-give-a-shit-what-you-think-but-I-need-you-to-love-me paradox."

"Hence…" Adam holds his hands palms up. "Addiction. Lots of dead actors, addicted or dead-too-young musicians, writers, painters. Not everyone can live with that paradox."

"No, I guess not…"

We get quiet again, finishing our drinks, and I think about my parents from the perspective of all of this. They're not awesome parents, but both of them are, consciously or not, living with a lot of psychological stress, and you need to be strong to handle it. And maybe in your fight to handle it, you lose sight of other things. Like your kids.

After, Adam says we have a little more time before he thinks we'll be missed, so we walk out to the cove. It's windy and overcast, but because of that, it's deserted. We leave our shoes behind, walk along the waterline for a bit, and then I follow him onto a rocky outcrop that stretches into the ocean. Midway out is a larger, flat-ish rock, and Adam sits down on it. I join him.

"I wanted to ask…" Adam says tentatively.

"Yes?"

"I don't want to upset you again, and I really don't mean it as stealth therapy as you called it, but I have this feeling you might need to talk…"

"About earlier?"

He nods. "Something really got to you today."

I look away, then back to meet his eyes. "I just got needy," I admit. "It was neediness and loneliness and wishing things were different."

"On the phone, I didn't mean to eavesdrop—"

"Sure you did; you were standing right there," I say, but without rancor.

"All right, I was listening," he admits. "In case you forgot, I'm supposed to be looking out for you."

"I know."

"You said something about being stuck in the airport?"

"Oh…" I look down, feeling a stab of shame. No one needs to know, not even Adam, about how I'm such a loser that my own father forgets me on a regular basis. No one needs to know he'd forget me overnight on an empty studio set and then again, years later, when I've flown across the country to see him. No one needs to know how scared I was sitting in the airport all those hours or how humiliating it was to call Jo-Ellen only to have her inform me Dad was actually on vacation in Cabo.

I never talk about it. I'm not going to talk about it now.

I lift my head and tell Adam the fake, happier version of the story—the one I tell everyone, if I have to tell it at all—about how Jo-Ellen messed up his flights and it wasn't his fault, but how I flipped on my dad anyway, causing a big argument.

"I'd have flipped, too," Adam says sympathetically.

"It's not like he wasn't excited I was coming," I say, inwardly cringing because I feel like my desperation, my pathetic-ness, is just oozing out of me, like the lie must be so obvious. "He just had the dates wrong. Because of her."

"Of course," Adam says.

And then, even though this is when I'm supposed to continue the story, I stop. Because I can't do it.

"Shit," I say, and hang my head.

"What is it?"

"You and your stuff about feeling what's right," I mumble. "You're messing with my head."

"What? Lola." He leans in, puts his fingers under my chin, and lifts it so I have to look at him. "Talk to me."

"Fine. Okay. I just told you my 'official' version of that story. The spun version," I say.

"I see," he says quietly. "Why?"

I want to look away, but I can't—partly because his hand is still cupped under my chin. I want to keep lying but somehow can't do that, either. Because after everything he's done and the day we've had, it feels like total shit to lie to Adam. It feels poisonous. "It's not that I wanted to lie to you; it's more like I want to lie to myself about it. I like the 'official' version better than what actually happened."

"What did happen?"

"Dad's assistant didn't mess up the dates. He just plain forgot about me. Forgot I was coming. Went on vacation."

"Oh, Lola," he says, and puts his arm over my shoulders and hugs me to his side. "Damn."

"It's so humiliating," I whisper.

"Humiliating? If anyone should be humiliated, or embarrassed, anyway, it's him, not you."

"Intellectually, I can see that, but emotionally… somehow I feel like I'm, you know, like it's something about me."

"There is nothing wrong with you. That's bullshit."

"Please don't tell anyone," I say. "I mean, it's not a major trauma compared to some of the stories I've heard the last few days, but I don't want people to know."

"I won't say anything. But forget comparing your hardships. It flat-out sucks, and you're allowed to think it sucks. In my opinion, anyway."

"Thanks, Cupcake."

We talk a bit more about it, and what's nice is how pissed off he is on my behalf. I can hear it in his voice and I can feel it in the way his arm has tightened around my shoulders, keeping me close at his side. After a few minutes, we both go quiet and I relax against him, the parts where our bodies meet humming with warmth, the silence comfortable.

"Do you feel better?" he says finally. "From talking about it?"

"I do, actually," I say. "Physically and everything—I feel much better."

"Good," he says.

"That was nicely done, by the way." I glance up at him with one eyebrow cocked.

"Huh?"

"You know, getting me to talk—first the sneaky escape, the great chats, the perfect latte, and this…" I indicate the cove, the ocean, the sky, with a sweep of my arm.

"I wasn't trying to manipulate you, Lola," he says, looking concerned.

"I didn't mean it like that," I say. "I just mean—this is nice. It's all been really nice."

"Oh. Okay."

"Is this, like, your spot?"

"My spot? Kind of. One of them. I love to explore all these kinds of coves, up and down the coast."

"So," I say, thinking to lighten the mood, "you bring all the girls here?"

"I'm not going to dignify that with an answer," he says, stiffening and taking his arm off me.

"Wait…what?"

"I'm offended." He moves away from me.

"Hold on, what just happened? You're offended at what? At my suggestion that you would romance girls on beautiful beaches, like I'm saying you're some kind of greasy ladies' man? 'Cause I didn't mean it like that. Or are you offended at me putting myself in the category of 'girl' when I am a rehab patient and you would never in a million years think of me as a 'girl'?"

"Forget it—"

"And by the way, I think I just caught you caring what I think of you."

"Damn it."

"So?"

He turns to face me. "Fine," he says, eyes locking on mine. "Offended, maybe stupidly, because yes, it is one of my favorite places, and no, I haven't brought anyone else here."

"Okay…" I study his expression, trying to shake the feeling that I am suddenly in territory I have no idea how to navigate.

"And concerned about what you think…yes. Unfortunately."

I frown. "Why unfortunately?"

"Because I care about you, and because…"

"Yes?" I say, still confused.

"I guess because despite what I said earlier, as this day goes on, I'm not sure my bringing you here was completely, um, grounded in what I…think I should be doing."

He finishes and then watches me, like I'm now supposed to know what the hell he's talking about and make some kind of response.

"I… Is this… Do you mean you're mad at yourself all of a sudden for breaking the rules? Or you thought this would be good for me but now you don't think so…even though it so obviously has been? Help me out here because honestly, I'm having the best day. One of the best days in…I don't know how long. So what's the problem?"

"The problem," he says, then exhales forcefully, "is that I *have* been thinking of you…as a girl. Sometimes. More than occasionally. Despite my best efforts not to."

"As a girl…?"

"Yes. Is that clear enough?"

"You…" I stare at him, willing my brain to catch up to what the rest of me already knows. "Really?"

"Yes," he says and rolls his eyes in exasperation. "Really."

"Holy shit" is all I can manage to say at the moment. Everything has gone into a simultaneous slow-motion/fast-motion state—slow-motion in the present where we are sitting facing each other on this pile of rocks out on the ocean, and every tiny changing expression on his face suddenly has to be translated inside me to mean something new, and all the sensations in my body stretch out from one heartbeat to the next—the places he was touching me only a minute ago so much colder than they should be, my lungs not quite getting enough air, the deep-down pull to get closer to him. Meanwhile the fast-motion swirls in another part of me, where my mind is replaying all my moments with Adam since I arrived at Sunrise—the sparring, the provocations, the banter, the push and pull of will and emotion and intellect, the between-moment moments—this film plays in my mind and I see, for the first time, that there is something there, has been something there all along.

Not like the thing with Wade—something totally different.

"Holy shit," I say again, shaken. "You like me."

"Yeah." He gives a cute, weird, almost helpless sort of laugh. "Yeah, you could say that."

"So..." The wind picks up. I swallow, eyes still locked with his. "You brought me here to do something about it?"

"No," he says, "that was definitely not my plan."

"But now you're going to do something about it?"

"Other than telling you? No. No way."

"What?"

"Oh my God, I shouldn't have even told you. We need to go." He scrambles to his feet, breaking the moment, then reaches a hand out to help me to mine, and once I'm up, starts off ahead of me for the shoreline.

"Wait—Adam..."

He has to have heard me, but he doesn't turn back. In fact, he's practically running away.

"Listen, you chickenshit," I shout, huffing and scrambling as I try to catch up. "What the hell?"

By the time I get to the beach, he is up at the top, putting his shoes on, and I have no choice but to jog after him, slide into my flip-flops, and then follow him to the parking lot.

In the car, we get our belts on and he puts the key in the ignition.

"Wait," I say, putting a hand out to stop him from turning it. "Please could you just hold on a minute?"

"Yes," he says with a heavy sigh, refusing to look at me.

"Don't you even want to know if I'm...if I would be into it?"

"No," he says. "Because whether you would or not, neither answer is going to make me happy."

"Well, that's too bad, because maybe I would be."

He groans and puts his head in his hands.

"Seriously, right now, Adam? Okay, my mind is a little bit blown and it took me a second to…uh, adjust, but guess what? I think I would be."

"No, no, no," he says.

"Why not?"

"Because." He raises his head to look at me. "As I have told you over and over, there is a line. Our relationship is supposed to be professional. We shouldn't even really be friends, much less…the other things I'd like us to be."

"Other things, huh?"

"Don't."

"I can't help it, Adam. We're talking about it, so I'm thinking about it. We're alone in a locked car in a mostly deserted parking lot where no one knows us," I point out. "We could do *other things* right now and no one would have a clue."

"No." Adam turns and presses his forehead against the driver's side window. "And besides, this isn't about just wanting to mess around in a parking lot."

"Fine."

"Which would be a huge mistake."

"I said fine," I repeat, voice sharp because now I'm feeling embarrassed.

"Okay," he says.

"So…are we talking never?"

"Not while I'm working at Sunrise and you're a patient,

or even an outpatient. And you'll be an outpatient for a long time, ideally."

"You do realize it's still true, however effed up I may seem sometimes, that I don't need to be in rehab? That I'm only still in rehab because there's no parental unit willing to get me out?"

"Doesn't change anything."

Now I'm the one to put my head in my hands and groan in frustration.

"Lola," he says softly, putting a hand on my back, which sends sizzling pangs up and down my spine, "not doing something you really want to do because you know it's the wrong thing, or the wrong time—doing the hard thing—that builds strength. That's what character is about."

"Blah, blah, blah…"

"I'm sorry. I was stupid to tell you. Regardless, I can't be a good mentor to you if I'm trying to be something else at the same time. And you? Admit it—you have no idea what you want. Maybe you're vulnerable. Lonely. Maybe you're just flattered. Maybe you didn't even think of me like that until five minutes ago."

"Maybe I'm going to punch you in the nose for making assumptions about what I do or do not feel, or what I do or do not want," I say, though he has an extremely valid point about my not having thought about this until five minutes ago. I'd felt it, yes, but I hadn't thought about it. "Let's just forget it."

"Please don't be mad."

"Mad? Mad is the least of it, Adam."

CHAPTER TWENTY-FOUR

To my frustration and discomfort, Adam accompanies me to dinner and for the rest of the evening until I return to the dorms. It's his job, I get it. But I can't clear my head with him so close all the time, and I need to clear it because now that I've clued in, I am suddenly insanely attracted to him. Not only that, but since we've agreed not to talk about the "other things" subject and that's all I can think about, it leaves me with nothing to say to him, which is awkward, which makes me grumpy.

He doesn't have much to say either, probably for similar reasons, plus the fact that he's beating himself up for all of it. Still, he refuses to ditch me.

And then, when he finally leaves me and I head into the dorms, I miss him.

It's infuriating, frustrating, confusing, insane.

I go to bed early, exhausted, but only sleep fitfully. Around midnight, Talia climbs into my bed.

"You're awake," she whispers.

"I am now."

"You were already. I could tell by your breathing. And you're giving off some crazy energy. Don't worry, I brought my own pillow," she says, and snuggles down under the duvet. It's such an odd thing, I'm not sure how to respond.

"So you kind of wigged out today, huh?"

It takes me a second to realize she's talking about the post-massage, running-around-in-a-sheet-acting-hysterical episode. That was this morning, but it feels like it happened a week ago.

"I guess I did," I say.

"One time last year we were down in San Diego—my mom had a conference. Anyway, I got into the minibar and somehow ended up running naked through the streets of San Diego with nothing but a knockoff Prada bag to cover me."

"Seriously?"

"Yeah. I know if it were you, you'd have a real one. Anyway. For some reason I always end up stripping naked when I'm high. And, you know, you tend to meet people really easily that way—when you're naked."

"I'm sure you do."

"So then I met up with this band and we did coke and then I had sex with one of their roadies who was this freak- ishly over-endowed ex–circus performer. Unfortunately he thought it was fun to try to strangle me in the middle of it and I tried to fight and it…didn't end too well. Lot of bruises."

I manage to breathe, "Jeez, Talia," all the while battling the visual imagery and trying not to be shocked.

"Anyway, I thought that might make you feel better."

"Feel better?"

"You know, about today and running all over the place in a sheet."

"How…how was that supposed to make me feel better?"

"Just that it could have been worse."

"Ahhh."

She wriggles closer so she's right next to me. "I hope I'm not making you feel weird."

"Your feet are freezing."

"Oh, sorry." She moves them away. "I'm not trying to get sexy with you or anything. Anyway, I like guys. But I miss my sisters and I feel so…I'm cold all the time, you know? I think sometimes that's why I have sex."

"Because you're cold?"

"Yeah."

"Talia, that's the worst reason to have sex I've ever heard."

"I know, I know."

"Try clothing, you know?"

She giggles.

"Seriously. You run around naked all the time, you're going to get cold. Invest in some layers—a wool sweater, some leg warmers. Talk to Jenny, our *Barney* girl; she's got that down."

"Sure. Problem solved. Who needs rehab, huh?"

"Exactly."

"So…you running around in a sheet…breakthrough? Break*down*?"

"I don't know, I was just feeling a little crazed. I called my dad and we had a fight."

"Really? About what?"

"Oh, you know, he can be kind of…overprotective," I say.

After that, I am awake for hours, thinking about Dad, Mom, about Wade and the fact that I forgot he existed for much of yesterday—the entire time I was with Adam, basically. I think a lot about Adam and how I don't really know what to think about my attraction to Adam, but how the result of that last part of our outing yesterday is that yet again, I've been rejected.

Monday morning, Talia is back in her own bed. I feel horrible—from being awake most of the night, and maybe cumulatively, from all the drama. I feel like a truck fell on me.

Of course there is no chance in hell anyone will let me stay in bed, not with such a momentous "breakthrough" going on.

And…I want to see Adam. Well, I do and I don't…but more do than don't.

I emerge slowly and pull on ripped boyfriend jeans and

a hooded light blue T-shirt with a Warhol banana on it. I put my hood up and tie it tight under my chin so none of my hair shows and then put on my bracelet.

As part of my rehab-chic line I'm going to create "get a real boyfriend" jeans, "get your own boyfriend" jeans, and indoor sunglasses—sunglasses with big, lightly tinted lenses that you can wear inside and hide your eyes but still be able to see perfectly.

And maybe some armor for these crappy days when it feels like regular clothing is not enough because the whole world can see through it and under your skin.

Anyway.

A few minutes later, I sink into one of the chairs in the lounge and start on the two cups of (craptastic) coffee I've poured myself, which makes me think of Adam, who is not there yet.

Adam arrives, freshly showered and shaved by the look of him, but a little puffy around the eyes, like maybe he didn't sleep well, either. He glances quickly at me, then away, and all my hopes of my attraction to him being a one-day thing go down the drain. I want to run my fingers up the back of his neck, where his hair is just long enough that it starts to curl. I want to drag him off, somewhere away from here, and talk to him for hours. I want to know what his mouth feels like on mine.

I'm in deep trouble, in other words.

Up in front of the group, he opens his binder, looks down to find the affirmation. "'My intuition tells me the right thing to do, moment to moment. I trust myself.'"

I see it work on him—see him, as he says it, letting the thought settle in, like he always tells us to do. I see how he is decided, how he actually, no matter what he might feel for me, does trust himself—it comes off him in waves.

And I think, *Yay for you.*

And I think, *Screw you.*

And I think, *Maybe it's time to refocus my energy on Wade.*

And another part of me thinks, *Who…?*

Wade Miller. Gorgeous, sweet, needs-to-be-rescued, has-fewer-scruples Wade Miller. Yes. That will help.

I take myself back in time and see him like he was when we first met, back in time to that feeling—thirteen and crazy about someone for the very first time.

It helps, but only for a little while.

don't mean to be a shit, but I'm already in a bad mood and drama therapy pisses me off.

First it's a bunch of rolling around on the floor in order to "warm up," and then everyone presents her "worst memory ever" story—that we're supposed to have scripted and rehearsed.

Let me tell you, seeing everyone's tragic and tawdry secrets made into poorly acted dramas is a total drag. Worse than a drag—it's hell. There are things I don't want to know about people, things that are just too awful, too pathetic, too sad.

When my turn comes I say, "I don't have one."

"One what? A memory?" Clarice says.

"I mean I don't have anything prepared. I couldn't think of anything."

"Are you saying you don't have a single bad memory?" Clarice asks, her voice rising. "Maybe you have amnesia?"

"I don't remember."

This earns me a few guffaws and a killing look from Clarice.

"What exactly is the problem, Lola?"

"The problem is I think this is crap. Sorry. But I think it's crap and I'm not doing it. I don't believe airing my dirty laundry is going to benefit me in any way. Maybe for some of you this is therapeutic or whatever, but I think it's gross and intrusive and I refuse to do it."

"Young lady, your attitude is—"

"Hey, I'm being honest here. I could have made up a bunch of bull or done some kind of weird abstract number everyone would have pretended to understand and thought was deep and meaningful even though it was a crock of shit. And then you wouldn't have been mad at me but it would have been a waste of time. Instead I'm just telling you the real deal."

We were all sitting on the grass, but I'm standing now and so is Clarice. I can see her taking deep breaths and trying to commune with her spirit guides or whatever to keep herself from losing her shit.

"More than anyone I've ever met, you need to face your dark side, confront your memories, and start being true to who you are," she says.

"That's actually what I'm doing," I say. "Believe me, I'm totally in touch with my memories. I'm just not sharing them with you. Or *OK* magazine or the *National Enquirer* for that matter. So you may as well forget it."

"One of these days you're going to discover the power of surrender."

"Didn't you get the memo? I can't surrender—I'm in denial."

N ext is therapy.
Don't ask.
Okay, well…

Dr. Owens notices my strange mood and I tell her why—not including the part about Adam, which admittedly is a huge part of it. There isn't a single part of that I can tell her. This means, because I'm avoiding that subject, I end up telling her more about my massage-inspired meltdown than I normally would have, and then she badgers me to death with her bullshit bell until I cave and tell her all about the night I fell asleep and woke up to see my dad charging out of the bedroom he shared with my mom, where he'd discovered her presumably in some state of nudity with Elise and was now totally freaking out.

I tell her about how he stopped to yell at me, demanding whether I knew about them, which I did but which I denied and which he did not believe, and that was *before* my mom came out and yelled at me for falling asleep at my post (thanks, Mom). It was pretty unfair, considering he wasn't exactly a saint of a husband and I'd kept all of his secrets, too—secrets just as sordid if not quite as dramatic as Mom sleeping with a female porn-star-turned-stuntwoman.

I don't tell Dr. Owens that last part, though—about Dad.

"It sounds like they took a lot of their pain and anger out on you," Dr. Owens observes.

"Uh, yeah," I say, thinking it doesn't take a psychologist to figure that out. "It got kind of funny after that, though. Elise came running out with her boobs all spilling out of her leopard-skin bustier and an actual drawer full of socks and started throwing them at my dad, one at a time. His own socks. So Elise is whipping socks over the banister and my mom is yelling and crying and my dad is yelling and the whole thing was so freaking out of control."

"But painful, yes?"

"Sure. Yeah. I mean, it's obviously not a great memory. But come on, it's not like anyone took out the golf clubs, right? By the way, if any of this ever gets out, I'll know exactly who to sue."

"You've never shared this with anyone else, you mean," she says, as usual giving everything more significance than it actually has.

"I mean I will sue you."

"I'm honored that you shared it with me."

"Don't be."

"So while all this was going on, what did you do, Lola?"

"Me?"

"Yes, you."

I shrug. "I stood there watching and trying to melt into the walls. What else was I supposed to do?"

"But your own emotions, despite your determination to dismiss them, your own emotions must have been overwhelming."

"People cheat and have fights and get divorced all the time. Nothing I couldn't handle."

Dr. Owens rings the bell like a maniac.

I cover my ears.

"Okay, okay, I admit, it sucked. It really sucked. Would you fucking stop?"

She stops.

"Now, when you say it sucked…could you be a bit more descriptive? Could you tell me how it felt?"

"Like a seeping, infected wound that dragged me to an abyss of sharp knives covered in salt that I could only neutralize if I drowned myself in tequila," I say with a dramatic eye roll. "Like death."

Dr. Owens holds the bell, poised to ring it, and studies me.

"Go ahead, ring it."

"Do you have any idea, Miss Carlyle, how much you tell me when you're trying not to tell me anything?"

Chapter Twenty-Five

So, Monday I am back in the shit, and Tuesday and Wednesday, I remain there. Yes, there was the half day of freedom with Adam, but it was only a brief (and dubious in terms of leaving me relaxed) reprieve from the anti-denial boot camp Dr. Koch has set up for me. Between trying to repress/ignore/forget my feelings for Adam, and dealing with all the people trying to delve into my psyche, I am overwhelmed. By Wednesday, I would gladly pick up a real addiction if one were available.

Anything to ease the stress of everyone on my case and all the emotional drama, not to mention I have not had a single second to myself since my idiotic move at AA on Friday night.

Meanwhile, Adam has retreated to full bran-muffin, perfect-ethics, goody-two-shoes mode, to the point that I'm starting to think I imagined Sunday afternoon. Except if I had imagined it, I would have imagined it going differently. And now I can't stop imagining it going differently, which results in my being, in addition to stressed, irritated, et cetera, almost painfully drawn to this person who doesn't want me anywhere near him.

In addition, I keep losing track of my stuff, which makes me feel like I'm going crazy. I have now lost my favorite pair of jeans, a bikini, some earrings, one of my new pairs of sunglasses, a lip gloss, and my Warhol T-shirt; the only person I really like (Talia) is overly intense, clingy, prone to breakdowns and TMI; and my other roommate is an increasingly malevolent presence with a rapidly intensifying head-banging habit. Seriously. And finally, Dr. Koch has slapped me back to Level One status so I can barely take a pee without someone making note of it.

And then things get worse.

It happens in group, where we're making sock puppet self-portraits.

I've got my head down and I'm trying my best to stay out of trouble. Except I'm sitting there as silent as Jade and I keep catching her staring at me with her nasty emo glower and it's annoying. I mean, here everyone's been pestering me to death and we have this massively-talented-but-screwed-up hypocrite among us and everyone's just ignoring her.

And there she sits, all *edgy* with her black, leather-haired, marble-eyed puppet wearing a freaking dog collar around its neck.

"What, Jade, no mouth?" I say.

Her head snaps up.

"How long you going to keep that up?"

She looks at me. I look back at her. The rest of the group is quiet, either studiously ignoring us or watching. Finally Jade shrugs and reaches for a red marker and draws a jagged scar of a mouth on the white tube sock.

"Gorgeous," I say. "Almost looks like she might burst into song…"

Jade's eyes go wide and her mouth hardens.

I smile at her, then go back to gluing silver beads onto the right wrist of my puppet.

And then an unfamiliar voice says, "Fuck you."

I look up.

"Fuck you, Lola Carlyle."

It's Jade, standing with the puppet on her hand, holding it in front of her face so we can't see her mouth moving behind it.

"Okay, you are so weird," I say.

"Jade," Mary pipes up in her counselor voice, "is there something you'd like to say?"

"Uh, I think she already said it," I reply.

Mary ignores me and looks expectantly at Jade.

"Oh, come on. She's swearing at me and you're going to encourage her? That's bullshit."

"Lola, this is not about you."

"Fuck you, fuck you, fuck you…"

"Why do people always say that? It's *happening* to me."

Mary goes to Jade and puts a hand on her back. "Jade, honey?"

Jade shoves her off and takes a step toward me, puppet in front of her mouth, eyes like throwing knives.

"FUCKYOUFUCKYOUFUCKYOU…"

Now would probably be a good time for me to say something calming, or else walk away. Problem is I'm not so good with backing down.

"Fuck you, too, Jade."

And that's when she lunges for me. Fortunately, Mary is fast and, dreads flying, gets to Jade before Jade gets to me.

"Stop. Stop it *now*," she shouts, holding Jade in something between a hug and a headlock.

"What, you're going to kill me with a *tube sock*?"

"You are such a fucking bitch," she screeches.

"I never did anything to you. I even kept your pathetic little singing secret until now. So what is your problem?"

"My problem is you never shut up," Jade shouts. "You never shut up about your clothes and your fucking jewelry and your fucking lifestyle. You sit here every fucking day acting like you're better than us and don't need rehab, like you just happen to be here because you need a vacation. And you're *full of shit*."

"What the hell are you talking about? You don't even know me."

"Oh, I know you. I know you better than you think."

"What's that supposed to mean?" I say.

"You don't want to find out," she says.

"Oh, I'm scared. By the way, you forgot to use 'fuck' in that sentence."

"Guess what, you spoiled little bitch, I could—"

"Come on, Jade, stop," Talia says, coming forward. "You don't need to do this."

Jade pivots toward her, still straining against Mary. "I don't have to listen to you, Miss Kiss-Ass. I'm sick to death of listening to you."

Talia puts her hands up. "Hey, I'm only—"

"You want to be all cozy and climbing into her bed whispering secrets at night and acting like you're her best friend, go ahead. Wait until she finds your little stash of stolen treasures."

Talia's mouth opens and her chest seems to crumple like she's been hit.

"That's right. Her clothes, her jewelry, what else have you got squirreled away?"

Talia looks from me, to Jade, and back. Tears come streaming down her cheeks and drip off her chin. "Lola, it's not... I didn't... Well, I did but not... I can't explain but it's not how it looks."

I hold myself very still, trying to take this in, while Jade gloats and everyone else stands frozen.

Talia starts toward me. "Please, let me—"

I step back toward the door, palms out in front of me like I'm pushing it all away. "For fuck's sake, is there not a single person on this planet I can trust?"

Thirty seconds later, I nearly flatten Adam in the hallway.

"Whoa, whoa. Where's the fire?" Then he sees my

face and grabs me by the shoulders. "What's wrong?"

"Nothing. I need to talk to Dr. Koch," I say, trying unsuccessfully to disengage and go around him.

"About what?"

"Nothing! I need to talk, that's all."

"Come on, it's me."

"Oh, like that helps. You don't want anything to do with me."

"Lola—okay, we need to talk," he says, taking me by the arm and propelling me down the hallway where he pulls out his keys, unlocks a classroom door, and pulls me inside, closing the door behind us.

"What?"

"Look," he says, walking into the center of the room. "Maybe I didn't explain it well Sunday because I was… confused. And now you're upset."

"I'm upset? You're the one who's acting like we're total strangers."

"I am trying to put some…distance back, that's all. Meanwhile you keep looking at me like you want to punch me."

"You're really reading me wrong, if that's what you think I want."

"But you're hurt."

I look down, wishing, too late, that I'd hidden that fact a bit better.

"You're hurt and you're pissed. Because maybe I didn't explain it very well. I wasn't thinking."

"But you're thinking now?"

"Yes. Can you listen?"

"I've got a few other problems right now, but fine. Yes."

He leans back on a desk and looks at me intently. "I don't want to be selfish about you," he says, slowly and clearly like he wants to make sure I hear it. "I don't want to complicate your already complicated situation here. I want to do the right thing, and the overall worldview right thing, at the moment, is also the right thing for you because we need to have trust. How're you going to trust me if you think all I'm trying to do is…hook up with you? Not to mention how do I stay objective at all about your care, your program, your headspace, if I'm spending all my time thinking about you like that? I can't. Not to mention, how would I trust any feelings you think you have for me when they might be transference? When you're—no offense—so volatile? When every chance you get you're flirting with that Miller dude? Don't you get that at all? I'm not doing it."

"So you're just…not thinking about me, is that it? You just flipped a switch and shut it off?"

"It's an attraction," he says, totally matter-of-fact. "They happen. It'll pass."

"Oh, that's really nice. Now I'm a passing attraction. In that case why do you care who I flirt with?"

"Honestly?" He pushes himself away from the desk. "Because I think you use that kind of thing to distract yourself from the real work you're doing here. And because I don't like that guy. And because, as I keep saying, you're vulnerable right now."

"What if…" I say, coming close to him, but in a furious,

up-in-his-face kind of way, and then stalking him through the classroom as I rant. "What if I am actually just a regular, moderately messed-up human being and not an addict and don't actually belong here, and half the issues I'm dealing with actually have to do with being locked up with a bunch of lunatics and liars and thieves, which is what I keep telling you? What business, in that case, do you have making all these judgments about what I do and don't need?"

"You're here, so it's irrelevant," he says, finally backing into a wall of vision boards.

"And if we were out in the real world instead?"

"I would still want to strangle you half the time," he says. "Most of the time, in fact. But that question, too, is irrelevant. We're here. We're not doing this."

"No?"

"No."

"Okay, fine. Is it passing yet?" I ask, stepping even closer into his space. "The attraction? Has it passed?"

"I'm sure it will," he says, and swallows. "Any minute now."

"Right," I say, putting both my hands on his chest. "Fine. From here on in, I will try to play by your awesome principles." My hands slide up to his shoulders and he shudders. "But if you want to keep this all professional and everything, I suggest you stop dragging me into empty classrooms because it makes me very…" I'm right up against him, hands on the back of his neck, and I can feel how shallow his breathing is.

"Lola—" he says in a low, warning voice.

And then, because I can't help it, I kiss him.

At first he lets me. Then he grunts, swears, pulls away, but my arms are still around him and his are around me, too, and with an insanely sexy moan and another muttered curse, he pulls me closer and kisses me back, deep and hard and surprisingly sweet.

It is beyond good or great. It's dazzling, sizzling, bring you to your knees hot.

It's bells ringing, birds chirping, insides melting, clothes falling off by themselves hot.

Except our clothes do not fall off because while my little bit of a conscious brain is thinking about dragging him onto the floor and yanking his shirt off, his little bit of conscious brain is telling him...

"*Stop.*"

He drags his lips from mine, then puts his hands on my shoulders and straight-arms me.

"Shit, shit, shit," he says, then shoves me away. "No! Haven't you listened to a single thing I've said?"

"I—" I am so breathless and stunned from the kiss, and simultaneously furious and humiliated by being shoved away, that I don't know what to say.

"We have to get out of here," he mutters, looking around, then finding his set of keys on a desk just inside the door. I notice he's breathing just as hard as I am, and he's also flustered as hell.

"Wait, Adam..." I reach out to touch his face, but he catches my hand, holding it but pushing me away at the same time. "Please, can't we take a minute? To, uh, calm down?"

"I am not going to calm down while I'm alone in here with you," he says in a harsh voice. "Let's go," he says, and then stomps his way to the door and opens it for me. "And by the way, this subject is closed."

"You don't get to go all Mr. Authority Figure when you just kissed me like that."

"Shh!"

"Fine," I say, passing him to get into the hallway and feeling the pressure of fresh tears forming behind my eyes. "I still need to see Dr. Koch."

"That's the thing: you should be talking to me," he says, like we're just continuing the argument from before, and no kiss happened at all, although he still looks flustered and flushed.

"Well," I say, trying to do the same, "the fact is, you have a tendency to be a lot less helpful than Dr. Koch."

"Because I'm actually aware that what you want isn't always what you need—"

"Don't even talk to me about what I need."

"—and because I actually give a shit."

"And Dr. Koch doesn't?"

"Are you really asking me that question?"

I look away. Dr. Koch cares about Dr. Koch. We both know that.

"I understand what makes Dr. Koch tick," I say, jaw clenched, body still buzzing, every part of me wishing we were back in the classroom, making out, and yet so mad at myself for being so weak. "The fact is, it's what I'm used to and I know how to deal with it and I know how to get what

I need from…that kind of person. And that's who I'm going to right now."

"Damn it, don't you hear how that sounds?"

"Like the truth?"

"Fine. We'll go together."

"Dr. Koch, you have to get me out of here," I say before I've even crossed the threshold of his office.

"Miss Carlyle, Adam. What a pleasant surprise."

"Please. My one roommate, Jade, is a psychotic bitch, and it turns out the other one—the one I liked—has been stealing my stuff. Plus I have no privacy, my therapist is a nightmare, and everyone is discriminating against me"—I shoot a look at Adam—"because I'm not actually an addict."

"What is it you expect me to do?"

"What I said—let me the hell out of here! Talk to my mother and convince her she needs to get back here to take me out. And in the meantime I'll…I'll stay at a hotel or something. Or you could just give me a private room and excuse me from the program until she comes back. I promise I won't make any trouble."

Behind me, Adam makes a choking sound.

"Shut up, Adam."

"You wish."

I turn back to Dr. Koch. "Even if my mom can't come back…I've got this *lovely* uncle who's house-sitting for us right now and I'm sure if you and my mom both signed off on it—I mean, you're the one with the power, right?—then it would be okay for him to come get me."

"As her mentor, I do not advise this course of action, sir," Adam says, coming up beside me, but not so close that we're touching—not that it matters, because I can feel him anyway.

"You stay out of it," I say, turning to glare at him.

"Dr. Koch—" Adam starts forward, and then cuts off as Koch holds up a hand.

"I will speak with Miss Carlyle alone."

Adam lets out a frustrated sigh and turns to lock eyes with me. "I'll be waiting," he says, and then leaves and shuts the door behind him.

There's a moment of quiet after the *thunk* of the door when it feels like all the energy has gone out of the room.

Then I turn back and my eyes meet Koch's and I get a sudden shiver.

"Sit," he orders.

I sit, he smiles, almost erasing the chill I just felt. Maybe I imagined it.

"Believe it or not," he says smoothly, "roommate issues are not uncommon, particularly among the female patients. Have you asked yourself what life lessons and personal growth might be gleaned from facing up to these problems and resolving them, rather than running away?"

"Are you serious?"

"Indeed I am."

"Jade is a nutcase. I don't think it can be *resolved*, it just *is*. And it's got nothing to do with me. Ditto with someone stealing from me."

"But perhaps there is something in you, some unconscious behavior, that is sparking these reactions in others."

I surge up out of my chair. "This is not helpful, Dr. Koch."

"Sit down."

Yikes. Coldness not imagined. I sit.

"I have been good to you so far, have I not?" he says,
now in a smooth but dangerously low voice.

"You have."

"And I believe your outlook would improve if you had
your privileges restored and were also approved for the
sober outings? This Saturday, for example, everyone with
Level Three status is going to Disneyland."

"Yeah, of course I'd love to go to that, if I'm still here.
But—"

"Let me be clear," he says, coming to stand in front of
his desk and giving me a gross smile. "You are not going
anywhere. You are an addict and you are going to be cured.
Period."

"But—"

"No buts. Sunrise is my project, Miss Carlyle. Mine. It is
the fruition of a great deal of work, and I am on the brink of
realizing some of my greatest dreams. The timing is rather
delicate right now. The entire world—the one that concerns
us, anyway—knows you're here, and I can't have you leaving
the program without completing it. I need success stories,
do you understand?"

"The thing is, Dr. Koch, I'm really not—"

"Success stories!" he bellows, and for a moment I see

his real face—the ugly, angry, grasping face that lies beneath his usual charming one. I knew it was there, but it's scarier than I expected.

I shut my mouth.

"You came to be treated and you will be treated, Miss Carlyle. You can do it the hard way, and I assure you, you haven't even *begun* to experience the hard way, or you can do it the easy way," he says, charming smile back in place. "The easy way, you'll have noticed, can be much more pleasant and offers many *perquisites* for those who are cooperative. The quality of your experience is up to you, but you will complete this program and you will do it successfully."

"So…you're not letting me out."

"Of course not. And if I don't start seeing some commitment and personal growth from you, be assured your stay here will not only *not* be shortened, it will be prolonged. Now," he says, propelling me out of my chair and toward the exit, "of course my door remains open to you should you need anything, but I suggest you move along— you have a great deal of work to do."

Chapter Twenty-Six

"You have to give me my chocolate back," I say, marching past Adam and away from Dr. Koch's now-closed door.

"What?" He follows me along the hall to the main foyer, where I stop and face him.

"My chocolate. I need it. Come on, I really am going to have a breakdown."

"Break*through*."

"Yeah, I got that from Talia, too." I'm so frustrated—from being shot down by Dr. Koch, from being deliciously, painfully scorched from the best kiss of my life, and then pushed away, from the roommate drama, the family drama, all of it. It's not all on Adam, but he's the one in front of me, and so I look at him and just want to shake him. Take him by the shoulders and shake him, or shove him into the nearby fountain, or throw him to the ground and make him kiss me again.

"Talia's a smart girl sometimes," Adam says, all mentor-ish, which is to say disgustingly cool and calm, like he didn't feel anything, or doesn't feel it now, anyway.

"Oh, sure. Talia who's been stealing my stuff. Witnessed by Jade, who attacked me. She's been a great help."

"What?"

"Last class. Yup."

"Physically?"

"Yes, and verbally, and emotionally."

"Why didn't you tell me?"

I glance at him and raise my eyebrows.

"I was busy with the *closed subject*."

"You see?" he says. "That's why it's closed."

"Fine."

"Good."

"Point being, I am feeling vulnerable and unsafe, Adam. Not to mention very frustrated and confused and aggravated."

"Chocolate's not going to help that."

"Not true. Chocolate always helps. It soothes me, it gives me energy…and I need energy to get through all the drama I apparently bring upon myself and all the breaking through I'm supposedly doing."

"No."

"Your favorite word," I say, and he turns red. "Come on. You could just bring some of it to your office and I'll eat it there. It's not even like I'm going to gobble it. With dark choc-olate you have to eat it really slowly; you lick it, sort of. So you don't need much. You could watch me the whole time."

For a second he looks pained. "That is so many terrible

ideas in one, I can't even believe it," he says. "So many, and on so many levels."

"Oh," I say, suddenly feeling a tiny bit better, because getting to Adam almost always makes me feel better, I realize. "Are you saying you'd find that..."

"Inappropriate? A bad idea? Yes."

"But no one needs to know," I say. "I'll even give you some. You can leave the office door open..."

"Do you have any idea how you sound? No. No way, no chance. I can't believe we're even having this conversation."

My head is pounding and I feel...needy and lonely and every kind of hungry. I feel like I'm going to lose it if I don't get...something. Like there is a void, an achy, sad, unsatisfied place inside me that needs to be fed, taken care of, fixed. Freedom from Sunrise might fix it, a drive in a really fast car with the top down might fix it, Adam in a dark place with his mouth on mine would definitely fix it.

Chocolate won't fix it, but it would help temporarily.

"I need it, Adam. I'm not addicted to it, I just need it. I'm telling you, there are studies about women and...and hormones and chocolate. A girl has to have some chocolate when she's going through all these crises. I have not one but two lunatic roommates to deal with, as you know, and I'm starving and stressed out and exhausted."

"You seem pretty energetic to me."

"Are you kidding? I feel like my limbs are made of Silly Putty. Nothing is working."

"Except your mouth," he observes as we stop in front of the dining hall doors.

"Oh, you should talk!"

Bam, there it is—I got to him again. He turns abruptly, walks away three steps, mutters to himself, comes back.

"Look," he says determinedly, "I've got something I need to deal with, but I'll be back soon. No chocolate. Have some lunch instead. And I suggest you discuss this habit with Dr. Owens."

"Fine, but just so you know? If I'm addicted to chocolate, I plan to keep using."

He goes—a relief and a loss at the same time. I head into the dining hall, where I march past Talia and send powerful celebu-spawn piss-off vibes to everyone else.

Jade is nowhere to be seen. I hope she's enjoying *her* breakthrough as much as I'm enjoying mine.

I eat four large bowls of plain yogurt with multiple tablespoons of honey. After that I am still hungry, sick-hungry like I have a bottomless pit instead of a stomach, sick-hungry with a need that feels hot, desperate, needy, and clawing.

It takes two grilled mozzarella sandwiches followed by a cup of steamed cauliflower covered in ranch dressing and two and a half dinner rolls before I finally hit the zone where I feel floaty and somewhat relaxed, but nothing will completely make the world go away, which is what I need.

Then Talia is standing in front of me trying to apologize and I can barely hear the words.

"I need your card," I say, interrupting her.

"What?"

"Your card. Will you give it to me? On loan?"

"W-why?"

"Because, as I'm sure you know, I'm having a very shitty day," I say in a low voice. "I have five seconds of Adam-free time and I'd like to go outside."

"Sure, but I could take y—"

"Alone."

"You're not going to—"

"I'm just going for a walk."

"Okay," she says, nodding, and then does a surreptitious look around and slides it over to me. "I'll just…say I lost it. Or something. Or maybe I won't need it."

"Thank you."

"Can we talk, though? Later?"

"When I can talk to anyone, I promise I'll talk with you."

Outside, I choose a path, take off at a run, and run hard, run until my lungs are bursting, and then I collapse onto a rock that overlooks the path down to the ocean, throw up over the side, and then lie there facedown, forehead balanced on the rock.

Lying there with the heat of the rock under me and the sound of the ocean below, it occurs to me that running wasn't the best plan after the massive amount of food I just had… and that what I did with the food was the epitome of addictive behavior.

And then my brain starts replaying the things Jade said about me, imagining myself in her eyes, and I feel my insides starting to heave again.

"That you, Carlyle?"

Oh shit.

"No," I say into the rock.

Wade chuckles.

"Really, it's not."

"You don't look too good."

"Thanks."

I feel him sitting down next to me, and then his hand is on my back.

Wade. Wow, I keep forgetting about him.

"What's wrong?" he asks.

"Oh, just everything."

"Aww." His hand moves, rubbing in circles. At first this makes me tense, but then I start to relax, because it's nice. And it's Wade, who, regardless of my crush (do I still have one?) and his extreme, irrefutable hotness, used to be my friend. A nice guy. And here he is, being a nice guy again.

We stay like that for a couple of minutes, not talking, me facedown.

"So…you ever going to sit up? Or turn over so I can see you at least?" He tugs at my arm. I slowly sit up, wondering whether I'm about to get the same contact high at the sight of him I usually do, or if this thing with Adam has caused it to go away.

He surveys my face, and I survey his. He remains so decadently handsome, it's sick. I'm still affected; I think maybe you would have to be dead not to be. And yet it's not a full-body palpitation or a slow burn, either. It's not sneaky and irritating and thought-provoking like the thing with Adam; it's a flash, a heat wave, cotton candy versus cheesecake or…I don't know.

But given the state of my insides (recently heaving), I

should probably stop with the food comparisons and focus on him as what he is for certain—an old friend.

"I'm all fucked up," I say.

"Yeah?"

"Yeah. My mute roommate just attacked me in group— said a bunch of shitty things about me. Some of them, upon reflection, might even be true. And I've got problems with the other roommate, too. Plus, Dr. Koch just gave me some serious carrot and stick—you know, good-cop-bad-cop, but all in one person, and Adam...well, never mind him. It's basically that overall I feel like I'm losing it. And I don't like people seeing me like this. Especially you."

"Hey, I'm the one whose trailer you slept in that night your dad left you on set, remember? I've got your back."

"Thanks."

"And I'd take your front, too," he says, the side of his mouth quirking. "If you'd let me."

"Wade. Oh my God, you did not just make that joke."

"What?" he says. "I'm just trying to lighten the mood."

I wrinkle my nose. "Have you ever seen what happens to cotton candy if you leave it out in the heat?"

"Huh?"

"Never mind."

"Okay, it was a bad joke," he says. "Thing is, Carlyle, I've never said a word about that, or the stuff we both know your dad was up to that night. And I won't."

"Thanks."

"I hope you're not still thinking of leaving."

"Well..."

"Because I think you'd miss out. I mean, you have a chance to figure things out — why not take it?"

"I know. I guess…I don't know, I might. I don't like being bossed around, though. I don't respond well."

"Well, selfishly, I want you to stay. Not just because of… you know, that I want to jump your bones, which I do."

This statement does not cause me to feel like it would have a few days ago. It's not that it has zero effect — it makes me feel good, i.e. attractive and wanted. And it gives me a bit of a flutter, but not a massive one. I almost wish it did, since Wade remains charming and beautiful, and Adam doesn't want to be with me anyway.

"The thing is, Carlyle, you remind me of a better me. Less jaded, all that stuff. Plus I have this fantasy of being with you at Disneyland."

"Ha. That was the carrot. One of them anyway."

"What about me?"

"What do you mean, what about me?"

"Am I a carrot?"

"That's a good question," I say. But I'm more worried that he's cotton candy, which if left in the heat deflates, shrinking into just a plain sticky ball of sugar.

CHAPTER TWENTY-SEVEN

It takes me the afternoon to come to the conclusion that I need to survive this rehab thing with my sanity intact, and I can't do that with the denial police breathing down my neck and Adam glued to my side when it's obviously going to be…difficult. Even I can see it's not a healthy situation for us to be together all day, every day, how having him constantly by my side, even if I'm annoyed with him half the time, could become an addiction.

Lust, even frustrated lust, it turns out, is seductive.

I need to turn things around, get Adam off full-time Lola duty. I need to cooperate, in other words.

And frankly, even if I'm not, strictly speaking, an addict, I've learned that I do have an addictive personality. Plus there are a few other problematic areas in my life that might benefit from being addressed—my friendships, my family issues, my coping mechanisms, my habit of alienating the very people I want to bring closer, my being so ridiculously screwed up that I thought it was a great idea to fake my way into rehab…to give a few examples.

I have work to do and I either have to start pretending to do it, or I need to bite the bullet and actually do it. Based on my experience so far, pretending is just as hard as the real thing—maybe harder.

Plus…I really want to go to Disneyland. I mean, I am a kid who lives in California who, despite numerous parental promises, has never been to Disneyland. It's practically traumatizing.

Finally, I really, really need my roommates to settle down and the people in this place to start trusting me so I can stop going through all this extra drama.

After dinner and Reflection, I notice that Talia's left my missing stuff in a neat pile on my bed. I put on jeans and a thin gray T-shirt with a giant floppy gray flower on the chest, and silver sandals.

Then I go to the AA meeting where I stand up…and reconfess.

It's not my proudest moment, but Dr. Koch made his expectations abundantly clear, and anyway, a girl's got to be practical.

Besides, my confession isn't even really a lie.

It goes something like this: "My name is Lola and I *might* actually be…an addict…of some kind. And I am certainly as flawed and messed up and confused as anyone else here and could use some life lessons and coping mechanisms and so on. So   I thank you all for your support and patience as I…as I work this out and work…*on* it. And, uh, I'm sorry if I've been a pain in anyone's ass."

The reaction is awesome.

People cheer.

Dr. Koch gives me a wink and a thumbs-up.

Adam claps, though his expression remains serious, almost puzzled.

Talia cries, though that is her first response to almost everything.

Jade studies me instead of glaring.

Wade smiles a super high-voltage smile.

It's a big moment, and when the meeting is over, I'm practically mobbed with people coming up to embrace me or thump me on the back, to offer their time if I want to talk, and so on. They're happy for me, supportive and sweet.

Except Adam. He's the only one I still can't read. I thought he'd be happy—proud of me, or at least relieved. Of all the people in the room, he's the one I most want to come congratulate me, ideally with a long, tight hug, which would be okay (right?) because everyone is all about the hugs here and it would be public and therefore aboveboard and yet still get me nice and close to him, at least for a few seconds. But he doesn't come over. Instead, he leaves. And as the door thuds closed behind him, I am disappointed, confused, hurt.

After all, I'm only trying to do what he does and follow what feels like the right thing.

But fine. Screw him. It's not my fault he decided to

confess his feelings for me and that now we're both all messed up about it—he did that. And now he doesn't want to do it. Like, ever. So, fine.

Meanwhile, Wade is standing at the back of the mob, waiting his turn and never taking his eyes off me until finally there are only a few of us left in the chapel.

"Carlyle," he says, finally coming over and wrapping me in a big, more-than-friendly hug—tight and warm and just a little bit sexy, the exact kind I wanted from Adam. "Nice job."

"Well, I'm not totally comfortable about it all yet, but it felt…good, I guess."

"Excellent. Now, I just have one question for you."

"Yes?"

"How do you feel about roller coasters, Carlyle?"

I gaze at him, purposely summoning up the old feelings, giving him a sly smile. I know I can't rescue the guy, and the old feelings, while easy to recall, aren't necessarily as strong as they could be. But a little flirtation can't hurt, and might even help. "Same way I feel about carrots, Miller."

I enter my room that night with a mix of dread and determination. It may be that I've recommitted myself to rehab, but I've still got Talia (thief) and Jade (psycho) to deal with and there has to be some way to make peace. When it comes to Jade I'm even willing to eat a bit of crow to make it happen.

"Okay," I say to Talia as soon as I'm in the door, "you first. Let's talk."

"I think it should be me first," Jade says.

Meanwhile, Talia kind of shrinks into her pillow.

"Making up for lost time with the talking, huh, Jade?" I say.

"Fuck," she says. "Why do you do that?"

"Why does it bother you?"

"Because it's so…just so…"

"It's my sense of humor, that's all," I say, and move to stand in front of my dresser so I can see them both. "I'm trying to survive and get through the day like everyone else. And yeah, I'm not too into showing my vulnerable side so I make a lot of jokes. You're not exactly an open book yourself."

"But I'm not bothering anybody."

"You don't think so?"

"No. And I don't spend all my time bragging about my fabulous life either."

"I don't…I'm not…"

"I hate to say it because I love you and all," Talia pipes up from the depths of her bed, "but Jade has a point."

"Look, my life isn't that fabulous," I admit. "I talk about the good parts because that's what I want to focus on. What's wrong with that?"

What's wrong with it is I'm full of shit, just as Jade said when she freaked on me earlier, and it looks like maybe I'm working a little too hard at hiding the things I don't want people to know about.

"What's wrong is nobody wants to hear it," Jade says,

almost spitting. "Because some of us are in pain."

"How do you know I'm not?"

"How would I know you are?" she counters.

"Just because I'm not playing the my-life-is-worse-than-yours game some of you people seem to be into, doesn't mean there aren't incredibly shitty things happening in my life sometimes."

"Actually, I don't really care if there are."

"Fine. That works just fine for me. I don't need you to care. But we have to live together for the next few weeks, and I don't want to be worrying you're going to stab me in the middle of the night, so I'm going to try to annoy you less. Okay?"

"There you go again with the jokes."

"It's not really a joke. You're scary sometimes. You're like some kind of psycho-goth-ninja. I never know what you might do."

At this, she chuckles. Progress.

"Okay, what else? You don't like me talking about my family. Right?"

"My parents just died."

"Holy shit."

"Don't get sympathetic," she snaps. "I can't handle it."

"Fine," I say, schooling my emotions and trying to present a blank face. "Fine, no sympathy."

"And Talia told you the very first day what an ass her dad is and yet you go on about what great buddies you and your dad are. Get a fucking clue."

I breathe in slowly through my nostrils and out through my mouth, reminding myself my job is not to delve into any of this or, conversely, to pick any more fights. "I won't talk about them, then. Unless I have to in class or whatever."

"All right," Jade says, and I can see her relaxing. A bit.

"I can't promise not to annoy you, though. You know, just in general. But I'll try to cut down."

She rolls her eyes.

"But *you* have to stop doing that. And giving me the finger all the time because that's rude, not to mention it provokes me."

"Fine. I'll try," she says.

"All right. Me too."

"But I don't want to be your friend."

"Yeah, I got that. Ditto."

"Done." And with that, Jade gets off her bed, grabs her cigarettes, and goes out to the freshly unlocked balcony, leaving me alone with Talia.

I push away from the dresser and sit on the edge of my bed, facing her.

She pulls her duvet over her and closes her eyes.

"Look, Talia, if you can't explain…whatever. I mean, I'm not happy you stole from me, but if you could just assure me it won't happen again, I guess that'll do."

"It's not because I don't like you," she says in a small voice. "It's more because I do."

"I… Okay, I don't get it."

"I know. It's weird. It's complicated."

"Well…if you want to borrow something, just tell me. I don't care. You can keep some of the stuff, even. I mean, I have tons of clothes. I can just order new ones."

Talia gives me a look, and suddenly I get it.

"Oh," I say. "That was one of those moments, right?"

She nods.

"I don't mean it… I don't really mean it to… Okay, but I'll work on it. And you can tell me when I'm doing it. Yes?"

"Hey, I know this time you were actually trying to be nice," she says.

I nod. "But…"

She nods. "Yeah. Oh, you know, your jeans didn't even fit me, by the way."

"Sorry to hear it."

"And I could never pull off those feather earrings."

"Sure you could."

"Matter of opinion."

"Or the Ray-Bans—the Fat-Asses—you should keep those. I have two pair, exactly the same."

"Fat Asses…?"

"Yeah, my mom told me they make me look fat."

"What…?"

"So I bought two pairs just to piss her off and I call then the Fat-Asses. See? There's a nice little tidbit from my less than fabulous life. Here, take them," I say, handing them to her.

"We can be twin fat-asses, then," Talia says with a pleased smile.

"But back to the reason," I say. "I still don't understand why you took them in the first place."

"I just…I kept thinking you were going to leave. I don't like it when people leave me."

I stare at her, trying to see behind the words to something that makes sense.

"So…taking my stuff was supposed to stop me from going?"

"No. It's just…objects are permanent. And sometimes you just need something. It doesn't make sense but you need it."

"Oh wow, I know that. I know that feeling. I had that feeling today. I…I think I have it all the time but I just never was aware of it before. It's like you just…" I reach out my hands in a grasping motion, trying to demonstrate. "It's like hunger, but…more. Worse."

"Yes," she says. "Oh my God."

"All right. So I get that part   you needed something."

"I did. That's how I felt. I would have returned it all, though, I swear."

"I still can't say I completely get it," I tell her. "But, I mean, did it help?"

"Temporarily."

"Ah. Yeah. Like everything."

She nods.

I sit down beside her, wrap an arm around her shoulders, and squeeze her to me. "I feel better that it wasn't malicious. That makes a big difference."

"Never," she says, leaning her head against mine. "But I'm really sorry."

I nod. "Me, too."

Thursday morning, I am in the lounge before Adam. I see him in my peripheral vision when he arrives—as always with slightly damp hair, face clean-shaven and wearing his no-nonsense T-shirt and jeans. I don't look up. He doesn't stop to greet me, either. He just goes to the front of the room and opens the binder.

"'I know a new freedom,'" he says, and then finally meets my eyes, almost as if he's giving me a challenge.

Then Dr. Koch arrives and hands me a new Level Three card.

Apropos, as Talia would say.

As we're dispersing to our Contemplations, I can't help drifting to where he still stands, near the door to the balcony.

"So," I say, "happy?"

"About what?"

"Your new freedom? Or," I continue when he frowns, "my new freedom?"

"My freedom's irrelevant," he says, eyes boring into me. "As for yours…"

"Yes?"

He shrugs. "I just want you to use it wisely."

"But…why are you acting so weird? I thought you'd be proud of me. I thought you'd be happy."

"Lola…" He closes his eyes for a second, lets out a sharp sigh, opens them. "Everything's fine, okay? I'm fine, you're fine, you're ready to do the work and that does make me happy. It's all good."

"But I just…" One of my hands reaches out, almost of its own volition, to touch his forearm. He looks down at it, then back to me, and steps away with a quick shake of his head.

"Oh for fuck's sake," I say, pissed off but whispering, just in case anyone is close enough to hear me. "I can't touch your arm?"

"Go," he says, his voice harsher and deeper than usual. "Go Contemplate. I'll see you later."

I only see Adam a couple more times that day, and only in passing. It's weird, but a relief, I guess, since we apparently can't have even the simplest of interactions without things going sideways. His demeanor is friendly, if a little formal, and for a while I follow his lead because really, what else can I do?

Friday, though, he shows up to escort me to therapy, still obviously not trusting I'll go.

We walk there in silence.

I survive the session and hate it a little bit less.

To my surprise, he's there when I come out.

"Am I in trouble?" I say, trying unsuccessfully not to sound sarcastic.

"Not that I know of," he says. "Let's go. I'll walk you."

"I have a free period," I say, following him down the long corridor overlooking the ocean where I tried to charm him that first day. "I don't think you need to worry about my attending it."

"You're doing well, Lola. I'm impressed with your compliance," he says stiffly.

"Adam." I stop walking.

"Yes?" he says.

"Can you…do you want to hang out with me?"

He hesitates, not quite meeting my eyes.

"You're mad," I say. "You seem mad."

"No," he says. "I'm really not."

"Listen, it affects my mental health if my mentor isn't on his game, you know. Or if he's bullshitting me. You're lucky I don't have Dr. Owens's bell."

"I'm not mad at you," he says, more convincingly this time.

"All right then, come on," I say, and point to the courtyards below. "Let's go sit. You're my mentor and I want to talk."

"All right," he says, and we head down the stairs and to the door.

"Your card or mine?" I say, holding up my Level card and cocking an eyebrow.

"Go ahead," he says, shaking his head and trying not to smile.

I hide my own smile at this hint of progress, and use my card to take us outside to one of the many peaceful, empty courtyards, which may or may not stay empty, but hopefully will.

He looks around, chooses a bench in the shade, and sits.

"Okay, spill," I say, swinging my denim-clad leg across the bench so I can sit straddled, facing him, but not too close, even though at the moment he's facing dutifully forward, so it's only the side of his face I'm looking at. "Clarice would say your energy is heavy."

"Ha," he says, not really laughing, but smiling a little.

"What's wrong?"

"I'm just mad at myself."

"Right. So, Adam, I know the subject is technically closed, but—"

"It's okay," he says. "We can open it. For a short time."

"Really?"

"A *short* time."

"Awesome. I can do short. Because while you've been learning lots of things about me, I've also been learning about you, and I think I can sum it up—the problem you're having. Then it'll be out in the open, which might help. And then we can just…close the subject back up. Deal?"

"Go for it," he says, glancing sideways at me, both amused and skeptical at the same time.

"You regret it," I say matter-of-factly, but in a low enough voice that no passerby would hear me. "Telling me, kissing me back when I kissed you, all of it. And now you're having a crisis because you don't know if you can trust yourself to do this job—so you're questioning your entire future."

"Huh," he says, turning to face me finally, drawing one knee onto the bench and dropping it down on the other side. "Impressive."

"Am I right?"

"On some of it. I am having a bit of a crisis, especially about this career—the future, as you said. But I've put two years of school in already and it's still what I want."

I nod, and gesture him to continue.

"Regarding us—no, I shouldn't have let anything happen."

The word "us" sounds so good it makes me ache. Lame, short-term boyfriends like Trevor of the smushed-bug-on-the-windshield kisses aside, I've never been part of an *us*, even a not-happening *us*.

"But?" I say.

"But I don't regret it."

At this, I let go of a breath I didn't know I was holding.

"I'm supposed to," he continues, looking at me in that super-honest and direct way he has that used to make me nervous and now makes me feel weak in the knees, "but I can't make myself, and it would be such a lie to say I did. I don't."

"I'm so..." I look down for a moment, worried he's going to see all the mess of emotion I'm trying to keep in check. "I don't either," I say, then look back up again. "I'm so happy, so relieved; I mean, it shouldn't make a difference, but I...I don't want you to regret it."

Though we're a few feet apart and clearly nothing is going to happen, we are both very still, very still and staring at each other, and in my case hardly breathing. It feels like my stomach is full of tiny, tumbling acrobats, maybe an aerial act or two.

Someone has to say something or the tension might kill us both.

"You know I wish... I mean, it feels like..." I stop.

"What?"

"Oh shit. No, what I was about to say...uh, it wouldn't help."

"Tell me," he says.

"While the subject is still open?"

He nods.

"It's inappropriate," I warn him.

"Yeah, I figured." He stretches out his legs just far enough that both his ankles tuck inside mine. Of course it's just our ankles so it shouldn't feel like a big deal, and no one who saw us could accuse us of anything…but knowing he's been trying not to touch me at all makes this intensely personal and ridiculously sexy. Yep, ankles touching and I might pass out.

"Tell me," he says again.

"I wish we could just lock ourselves away somewhere private for a couple of days and, you know, try to get it out of our systems."

"I don't suppose you mean talking it out…?"

"Nope."

"Lola…" he says, his voice a deep rumble.

"I know it's not a real option. But the thing is, all of this…" I make a churning motion with my hand in the air between us. "I don't know what to do with it. How to…get rid of it."

"You ever tried the getting it out of your system method before?"

"No." Heat rises up my neck and onto my cheeks. "I've never, ah, needed to."

Or even really wanted to—not like this.

"I don't think it would work," he says. "I'm pretty sure it would make things worse."

God, I want to make things worse.

"But it would be fun."

"I don't think I can handle worse," he says, almost like he's in pain.

I slip my feet out of my sandals and, without ever losing eye contact with him, slide one foot, and then the other, up the sides of his legs to rest them on the tops of his thighs, my denim on his. He looks down, then back up at me.

"Inappropriate?"

"Yes," he says, but gently places his hands on my shins. "Completely."

"Sorry."

"No, you're not."

"You're right, I'm not."

Neither of us moves. The distance between our bodies, all the parts that aren't touching, which is most of them, feels huge. And yet we could close that space in no time at all.

"I just want to point out," I say finally, "that people don't come out to this courtyard very often."

"I know," he says, hands gripping my shins, then sliding upward, toward my knees.

"Please can we just—"

"We have to stop this."

"Uh-huh." I look down at his hands, now on my thighs. "I see how you're stopping."

"I will, I swear. Any second," he says, then his hands go behind my knees, gripping like he wants to pull me forward—up and onto his lap. It would be so easy, so fast. And if he does it I will wrap my legs and arms around him so tightly he won't be able to get rid of me. I'll run my hands up under his shirt, up his back, bury my face in his neck and inhale the scent of him, kiss him till he doesn't even know his own name anymore.

Into these delicious, tempting thoughts come…

Voices.

Not our voices—voices of people who are approaching, and fast.

Shit.

It's a split-second decision. We're not in a horribly compromising position and we could probably get out of it and back to "normal" in time, but in that moment I am certain there must be a visible, smoking cloud of lust surrounding us. Not to mention, I would be hard-pressed to have even a semi-intelligent conversation right now. No matter what we do, they'll know, and then we'll be in deep trouble. Par for the course for me, sure, but I don't want it for him.

And so, in a dazed, panicked move that feels to be in both fast and slow motion, I leap away from him, scramble off the bench, then start tugging him by the arm toward a thick clump of bushes nearby.

"What the—'?" he whispers, following me but looking over his shoulder at the same time.

"We look guilty as hell," I hiss. "Hide!"

"You're insane," he says, but he follows me as I scramble under the bushes, squirming tight to the wall to make room for him. He pulls himself in beside me, swearing under his breath.

"Shh," I say.

He goes still, and none too soon because Clarice and

Mary enter the courtyard, chatting intensely about some protocol or something—honestly I'm so focused on not getting caught I don't take it in. It sounds like they're just going to walk through, but there's a long, torturous moment where they pause near our bench, which would mean we'd be stuck five feet away from them, for as long as they wanted to chat.

Adam and I are side by side on our backs, chests heaving, trying to stay silent. I am terrified his feet might be sticking out of the clump of bushes, and also afraid they might look too closely and see us. It's not like we're behind a hedge. And it's not like there would be any chance of anyone thinking we were innocent now, if we got caught like this.

And still, I am tempted to roll on top of him, or maybe nibble on his earlobe.

Instead, I reach for his hand, but he moves it away.

After an excruciatingly long couple of minutes, Mary and Clarice move away from the bench and then, finally, out of our courtyard.

To be safe, we wait until their voices are very faint.

And then I start laughing. It's a silent laugh, a silent, shaking laugh that starts in my chest and shoulders and spreads to my belly. I put my hand over my mouth, but I can't stop.

"You think this is funny?" Adam croaks.

I'm unable to respond.

"I don't think it's funny at all, Lola," he says, and starts pushing his way out of the bushes. "Come on."

I follow him, still laughing because I can't control it and can't explain it, either, and then we're back standing on the path, looking the worse for wear. He has sticks and leaves in his hair and streaks of dirt on his shirt and jeans. I've got scratches on my hands and arms, and dirt on my jeans and tank, and Adam points to my hair—almost reaching out to touch it, then changing his mind—where I find leaves.

"Why the hell did you dive in there?" he demands. "We could have just…moved apart."

"Well, you didn't have to follow me," I say, the laughter finally easing.

"Oh, and stand there trying to explain why my mentee is hiding in the bushes?"

"Well, I just—"

"Never mind. Fuck, that took five years off my life, I swear. And you sat there laughing. This is exactly why—"

"Why are you shouting?"

"Because I'm upset," he shouts. "What the fuck am I doing?"

"You didn't *do* anything. We did nothing wrong."

"Oh, seriously. If they hadn't come along? We were about to be doing something, Lola."

"Were we?" My breath hitches and I tilt my head flirtatiously.

"Cut it out. Shit. I have to get my head out of my ass."

"I don't think that's where it was."

"Lola, I'm not kidding, we have to stop—" He comes toward me like he's going to grab me, then backs away instead, holding his arms out from his sides. "I have to get reassigned. To freaking China or something. The North Pole."

"You think all that ice might help? Send me some when

you get there."

"I don't know." He shakes his head grimly. "Maybe if I got entombed in it."

I laugh, but again, he doesn't.

"You know what I really hate about this?" he says.

"What?"

"All this…" He gestures to the bench, to the bushes, then from himself to me. "All this garbage, and having to hide, and having it be that we just are both repressing all this…"

"Mm-hm?"

"It makes it… I don't want to have this kind of *sordid thing*…with you."

"You think it's sordid?"

"Yes. No. I mean, God, I shouldn't talk about it anymore. We can't do any of it. But also, I wouldn't want to, like this. Hiding in bushes, feeling guilty. You're not just some girl I want to get naked with. That's not enough. That's not good enough."

I'm tempted to say I thought the bushes thing was fun, and ditto the classroom kisses, and all the insane, built-up tension between us. But I know what he means and am both confused and moved by it.

"You would want to take long walks and talk about philosophy and see art films…"

"And wander deserted beaches and hold your hand and sit around talking about nothing, and learn about your favorite things, and listen to music, and not be a secret or a broken rule," he says.

"That sounds really good," I say after a long, painful

moment.

"Fuck," he says.

After that we spend a couple of minutes making sure we look somewhat normal, and start walking, keeping our distance from each other.

"Please don't get reassigned," I say to him as we approach the mansion. "I would…I would really miss you. Even fighting with you, I would miss. I promise, pinkie-promise, cross my heart, I will behave."

He snorts.

"I will."

"It's not just you," he admits.

"I know, but I won't make it worse," I say, then flush, remembering our earlier conversation about making things worse. "Not any kind of worse. I'll stay away. I mean, I'm still me, so realistically I might still be a bit of a handful for you. But not about this, I promise. I won't so much as flirt with you. I won't get you into any trouble."

"I'm in trouble already," he says.

"Adam, please. You are the only person I trust in this place."

A long moment passes, then finally he says, "I'll think about it."

I break into a huge smile.

He doesn't smile back.

Chapter Twenty-Eight

Saturday morning, I put on my slip dress and some capri leggings and get ready to go to Disneyland.

Also along for the sober outing are Talia, Jade, Emmy, and a few fellow patients I don't know very well.

And Wade.

And Adam as chaperone. His look is almost festive in shorts and a bright shirt with crazy graphics all over it, but one glance at him and I can tell he's not in the best mood.

"You, huh?" I say, coming up beside him as we gather in the drive.

"Yeah, me." His eyes slide over to mine, then away. "I drew the short straw."

"Are you kidding? Disneyland wouldn't be considered the short straw by most people."

"I'm not most people. Not right now, I'm not."

"So, you don't like it in general, or you just don't want to go…today?"

"There's no point talking about this, Lola."

"I'm not talking about—"

"You promised."

"Sure, but—"

"Lola," he says in a warning voice.

"Okay, fine," I grumble. "I was just…making conversation. You don't have to read something into everything. I'm going to keep my promise, but you need to chill out."

His shoulders slump, and he swears under his breath.

"I'm sorry," he says after a few tense, silent moments. "I mean it. This is just…challenging."

"It's all right. I know. I'll just…" I back away, eyes on his. "I'll do my own thing today, okay? That work for you?"

"Yeah," he says with a sad smile. "You do that."

I join Talia and listen to her chatter while waiting for the bus, but I'm not really hearing a word she says because I'm thinking about how this thing with Adam feels like a breakup. All the pain of a breakup but with none of the fun of ever having the relationship. How much does that suck?

But the fact is, he means business. The thing we have, or could have—he's not doing it.

Mr. Irritating Principles.

Mr. Freaking Nobility.

So what's left for me is to jettison the crappy, woeful, pathetic thoughts, forget about him, and have a good time today.

Because I am going to Disneyland and nothing is allowed

to ruin that.

Exactly.

Dr. Koch arrives and announces himself as the second chaperone, which seems odd. I'd have thought being a chaperone was far outside his job description and it's not like he's hands-on normally. Not to mention he's far too busy a man to be able to drop everything to spend the day at Disneyland.

But whatever. Maybe he's a Disney fanatic and this is his excuse to go.

Not my business.

We get on the small bus and I follow Talia to the back. Wade's hand brushes my bare leg as I pass and what I feel… is the urge to look at Adam to see if he noticed.

Wade touches me and I think of Adam.

Not good.

Especially not good since my chances with Wade currently look much better than my chances with Adam.

"You are going to get somewhere alone with that boy today," Talia murmurs.

"What boy?"

"Oh, don't pretend."

"I have no idea what you're talking about," I say, although of course I do, because she's looking right at him.

Despite the various romantic tensions, once we get to Disneyland, I'm thrilled. We wander Main Street and then take a carriage ride, the earthy smell of horses mixing with the scents of popcorn, candy, marigolds, and hopeful morning air.

I breathe it all in and let myself feel like a kid again. Even Adam seems to relax a bit, though I feel him watching any time Wade comes near me, which is often.

It doesn't piss me off—his being rather obviously jealous of Wade—in fact, I like it.

Of course it doesn't take long before someone recognizes Wade, even though he's in a baseball hat and sunglasses, and the next thing I know, he and Dr. Koch are posing for giggling tween girls and a couple of families in front of Walt Disney's old apartment. Then some guy in head-to-toe khaki recognizes me, which doesn't happen all that often unless I'm with one of my parents or at an event, and I get pulled into the photo op, too. The three of us stand smiling for strangers while the rest of the group wait, looking bored and annoyed, and I think of Dr. Koch and all those photos on his wall and realize this is probably a good part of the reason he's along as a chaperone today—the freaking photo op. And it makes him feel famous.

Any second I'm expecting him to whip out his own camera and start taking selfies, but he restrains himself, and soon Adam comes to help move everybody along. After that, Wade uses a bit of the pocket money we've all been allowed to bring for the day, and he buys a Mickey Mouse hat and bigger sunglasses, which disguise him better. But clearly Disneyland isn't an easy place to try to be anonymous.

Finally, we make our way to the rides, and soon we've blasted through Space Mountain, the Matterhorn, Astro Orbitor, Alice in Wonderland, and a bunch of others. We get soaked on Splash Mountain and then dry off while watching the lunchtime parade. We switch who we sit with constantly so I end up riding with everyone, except Adam, because we are mutually avoiding each other.

There are tourists, characters, princesses large and small. Talia gets a kiss on the cheek from Peter Pan and Jade buys (and puts on!) a pair of purple fairy wings.

Later, Wade wins a tiny elephant and gives it to me.

Adam gives me a look as I tuck it into my purse.

"What?" I say.

"Nothing." He shrugs. "Didn't know you liked elephants."

"It's just a stuffed animal."

"I know."

"It's not an inpatient, not an outpatient, not anybody's mentor..."

"Lola."

"So I can keep it if I want to. Sleep with it in my bed, even..."

He shakes his head and walks away.

"I'm just making a joke," I call after him.

"Oh, I'm laughing," he says.

In the afternoon we split up briefly, with Wade, Talia, and me going with Dr. Koch and some others to It's A Small World, and everyone else going with Adam to yet another roller coaster. The next thing I know, Wade has accidentally-on-purpose gotten us on a different boat from the rest of the group.

We grab the backseat, and right away he takes my hand. At first I let it happen because I'm surprised. And then I continue to let it happen because, well, it's not like I'm immune to him. He is sexy and charming and sweet. His hand feels warm and solid and weirdly comforting. He smells good. He's Wade Miller. He's my first crush, someone I thought I loved, maybe did love, maybe could still love, once I purge myself of this Adam business. So I let him hold my hand.

I listen to the music and watch the animated dolls singing and dancing and feel him there beside me in the semi-darkness.

"Carlyle?" he murmurs as we pass mermaids gurgling a wordless version of the famous song.

"Yes?"

"Come closer."

"Closer?" I say, trying not to sound panicked. "Dr. Koch is right in front of us."

"I know," he says, sliding over so his side is right up against mine.

Ahead, Dr. Koch and Talia's boat turns a corner. The second they are out of sight, Wade seizes me by the shoulders. Crap, he's going to kiss me. What flashes through my mind as it's about to happen is how ironic this is, how sad, how ridiculous it is that Wade Miller is about to kiss me right at the moment when all I can think about is someone else. Such a waste. And yet if it could lessen the ache of knowing I can never have Adam, maybe it wouldn't be a waste, not a total one.

He bends in and I know it's coming, and I let it happen. He leans in and kisses me like he means business, and I kiss him back.

God, I always, always wanted to be kissed by this boy— really kissed.

And now I am.

In the background, there are Polynesian steel drums playing, and it's dark and perfect and romantic, and he's a good kisser, not too aggressive, not dead-fish-smooshy like Trevor, just enough of the good things and none of the bad.

It's all perfect, except...

He's not Adam.

It doesn't feel bad; it just doesn't feel good, or right.

I pull away just as we round the corner back to North America.

"You are so hot," he says into my ear, still sitting as close to me as he possibly can.

"You are too, Wade. Undeniably. But, um...this might not be a great idea right now. I mean, we really shouldn't be—"

The conversation is cut off because the ride ends and we immediately rejoin the rest of the group. I don't get the sense that Wade understood, or even heard what I said, because he doesn't back off at all. Instead he stays right next to me, or behind me, constantly finding what he thinks are subtle ways to touch me—on my arm, my leg, the small of my back. I try moving away, but every time, he follows. I can't even look at Adam, and it seems that in order to shake Wade I'm going to have to tell him more forcefully, more directly, which needs to happen in a private conversation—I don't want to humiliate the guy, much less risk anyone, especially Adam, finding out I just let him kiss me.

More rides. More Wade. I'm not having a good time anymore.

"Wade, don't," I whisper/hiss at him as we're getting belted into a roller coaster and he's putting a hand on my thigh and squeezing. "We signed papers saying we wouldn't fraternize, and I don't want either of us to get in trouble."

Wade laughs. It's almost a nasty laugh. And then he says, "You think Koch is going to care if we get involved? He won't. He's a yes-man. World is full of 'em. He'll probably be delighted by two famous people getting together at his rehab center...as long as we promise him an invite to our wedding."

"Wedding?" I push his hand away.

"I'm just illustrating a point—no ring yet, Carlyle." He puts his hand back.

"I'm not really famous. But even if that's the case about Dr. Koch, I think we should...at least wait until we're both out of the program to—"

"I didn't think you were such a worrier. Come on," he says, and slides his hand farther up my thigh as we go on a huge ramp to a terrifying height, from which the roller coaster is about to drop us. The rest of that conversation is lost in screaming and yelling, and Wade removes his hand to hang on to the seat bar instead.

Finally, we all get coffees and then find a grassy hill to sit on. I wait to see where Wade is sitting and then sit with Talia instead. Then I meet Adam's eyes and wish I hadn't. He's, well, his expression is a lot of things, but pleasant isn't one of them. Wade gets up from his spot and comes to sit as close as he can get to me, and Adam turns away.

I can't get rid of him and I can't explain to Adam that I

am, in fact, trying to get rid of him. I want to scream.

Meanwhile Dr. Koch, who has been texting constantly and isn't the most engaged of chaperones, wanders off to take a phone call.

That leaves Adam with ten of us. Then one of the guys urgently has to go to the bathroom, which is a problem because no one is allowed to go unchaperoned, even to the bathroom, lest they run off and try to score some drugs or whatever. (As if.)

"Adam, dude, I'm going to shit my pants!"

Adam looks from him to us, then makes a decision.

"Can I trust you guys?"

We all nod.

"Dr. Koch is around the corner and I'll be right back. All of you stay right here."

We all nod. They go. Everyone is chill, lying on the grass and chatting, drinking their lattes, looking at the sky or whatever.

Wade nudges me, points up the hill a bit, where no one else is sitting.

I shake my head.

He gets up and goes anyway. Talia kicks me and hisses, "Go—when will you have a better chance?"

I'm about to enlighten her on the real situation when I realize it *is* a good chance—a good chance to tell Wade I'm not into it. I'll tell him gently but firmly, and we can go back to being friends and he'll hopefully stop trying to feel me up at every opportunity.

I join him on the hill.

"Listen," I say as I'm sitting down, "I want to talk to you—"

"I know," he says, and now he's all boyish and excited. "We've found each other after all this time, and I'm crazy about you and I can't believe it."

"Well, I—"

"I know—maybe we should talk in private," he says, then jerks his head to the rise of the hill. We could be over it and out of sight in about three seconds.

"I don't know…"

"Just for a couple of minutes. No one will even notice." He starts sliding backward up the hill, then does a very athletic back roll kind of thing, landing on his feet and managing to keep his Mickey hat on at the same time, then sprinting to the top of the hill and vanishing.

"Shit," I mutter, then follow him over the hill and down into a small copse of trees where he grabs me, pulls me close, and then backs me into a tree.

"I'm all yours, baby," he says. "The situation sucks and I know we haven't spent a lot of time together, but you are the perfect girl for me, I can tell."

He lunges in to kiss me again, and I turn my head away.

"Wade, wait."

"I know, I know, we'll go back in a minute."

"No! I mean, yes, we should, but…I'm trying to say this nicely—I don't want to do this."

"What?"

"I don't want to do this with you. It doesn't…feel right."

"Like from a moralistic perspective? You get religion all

of a sudden, or what? I seem to remember you kissing me the very first time I saw you here. You weren't too worried about the rules then. Besides, I thought you liked me. I know you did."

"I do. I did. I still do, but not…I had a crush on you for a long time, Wade, and I always cared about you, but…I'm not sure this feels right, now that it's happening."

"Too fast?"

"Maybe…?"

"We can go slower."

"No, I don't think we should 'go' at all."

"Are you…not attracted to me?"

"You're completely attractive, Wade. I just don't want to do it. It might have seemed like a good idea to me at one point, but it doesn't anymore."

"Okay," he says, raising his hands, palms forward, and backing away. "You know you're missing out, right? I might not be so willing when you change your mind…"

"I'll take the risk."

"Because it's not like I can't get a girl. I can get almost any girl," he says, and in that moment I see how little there is left of the Wade I used to know.

"Well, then you should be fine," I say.

Though I'm really not sure he will be.

"Right. See ya then, Carlyle," he says…and takes off.

Chapter Twenty-Nine

For a few moments, I'm frozen with indecision—Wade is an addict, he's upset, he can't be allowed to run off by himself. But I might not catch him anyway—I should go back, get Adam, even Dr. Koch.

With one last look at Wade's retreating form, I run back over the hill to the group.

But there's no group there. They're all gone.

"Holy shit." I look around, can't see any of them, look back toward the hill. There's no rendezvous plan, and no one has cells except Adam and Dr. Koch. Did they all take off, too, or are they somewhere looking for us? If so, I'm in super deep trouble.

I am in super deep trouble no matter what.

Maybe I can at least catch up with Wade...

And so I take off at a run, back up the hill and through

the copse of trees and out onto the roadway...where he's waiting for me, a smug smile on his face.

"Change your mind?"

"Pardon me?"

"I knew you wouldn't be able to let me go."

"No, that's not why I'm here. We have to go back."

"I don't have to do anything," he says.

"Listen! I went back and everyone was gone."

He frowns. "That's weird."

"Well, either they're looking for us, or they also took off, or somehow they decided to leave and no one noticed we were missing."

"So," he says, "that means we're free. Let's go."

"No, we should go back to the hill and wait for them to come back."

"Oh, fine," he says with a heavy sigh. "You're kind of a wet blanket, you know that?"

We go back.

Thirty minutes—thirty uncomfortable minutes at that, since we just got together and broke up all in one day—and no one from our group appears.

I am starting to feel panicked.

Wade wants to go on some more rides—ideally the big ones again. He does, then he doesn't. I'm noticing, the more time I spend with him, how his personality kind of flips around—one minute he's sweet and funny and normal and reasonable, the next he's slightly aggressive, devil-may-care, unreasonable. It's like he has a Jekyll-and-Hyde battle going on inside him, and I never noticed it before because I was never with him for a whole day.

"Fine," he says, "you're right—it might look bad if we went on rides. But we should at least walk around and see if we can find anyone, or go to an information booth."

"Actually, an information booth is a good plan."

Of course, there are still fans recognizing Wade, and we are waylaid multiple times for autographs and photos. Eventually we duck into a store where he buys himself a Mad Hatter costume, complete with hat.

"Now everyone's just going to think you're Johnny Depp," I say, although this ensemble does disguise him much better. He laughs, acting more like his normal self, and hands me his Mickey Mouse hat and we slip out a different entrance and into the crowd.

A few minutes later, we find ourselves face-to-face with Talia and Jade.

Talia and Jade without the rest of the group and with two random guys in tow.

"Heyyyyy!" Talia says. "Check it out—this is Ricky and Sam and they are awesome. Ricky, Sam, our friends Lola and Wade."

The guys, older, overly buff, and tanned the old-fashioned way, shift from side to side and give us both the thumbs-up.

"Thank God we found you!" I say, looking from Talia to Jade and back. "Where's the rest of the group?"

Jade, although she does talk these days, just shrugs.

"Are you kidding?" Talia says. "You think you two get to be the only ones to have any fun today? Screw that, we took off. Ditched the rest of them before Adam came back. And guess what, we went *crazy* and flashed our boobs on Splash Mountain. Did you know its nickname is Flash Mountain? It's right there in the photos they take — Jade, we have to go buy the photo! Two copies because our boobs look *so good*. And that's how we met these sweetie pies."

"But Talia…where's Adam? Where's everyone else?"

"Don't worry, we left a note."

"A note?"

"Yeah. On a napkin under a rock on the hill," Talia says, and then she grabs on to one of the guys (maybe Sam?) and starts swaying against him and humming. He grabs hold of her ass with two hands, squeezes hard, and she gives a flirtatious squeal.

"Uh-oh," Wade says under his breath.

"Oh my God," I say and start trying to pull Talia away from him.

"No, no, no! You are not going to ruin my day," she says, and then before I have a chance to do anything else, she grabs him and runs off.

I move to follow but suddenly the other guy is in my path. "Yo, get lost," he says.

"Uh, Sam?" I say.

"Ricky."

"Right. Sorry, Ricky, but you don't understand. My friend is very…fragile and she cannot be running around Disneyland with your ass-grabbing buddy."

"She doesn't look fragile to me," he says with a definite leer. "She looks like she can handle herself just fine."

I close my eyes. "Oh my God."

"Look, man, get out of the way," Wade says.

"Or what?"

"Or nothing. Just get out of the way."

I glance over at Jade, who has sat down at the edge of a shallow pond and looks far too relaxed for the situation.

"Jade?" I say. "You okay?"

"All good," she says. "Just leave her be."

I march over, lift her sunglasses up, and stare into her eyes.

"Crap, Wade," I say, turning to him, "I think she's high."

Ricky starts laughing and ambles over to us, all the while making scaredy-cat squeals and going, "Oohh nooo, she's high! Oh, oh, it's the big bad wolf," in a mocking falsetto voice.

"You think it's funny, huh?" I say.

In response he makes a particularly obscene gesture at me and then reaches for Jade.

And that's when I kind of lose my temper...and use both hands to shove him from behind and into the fountain. He flies over the side, landing headfirst in the shallow water.

"Holy shit," Wade shouts, and beside me, Jade giggles.

Nearby, some kind of alarm goes off. Ricky surfaces, swearing and with blood on his forehead, and from a distance I see security guards starting to run in our direction.

"Time to go," Wade says, pulling Jade to her feet.

"I agree."

And with that, we start running in the direction Talia went.

The next two hours are a nightmare.

Wade and I chase after Talia, who's stoned enough that she's not doing the greatest job hiding but still managing to disappear every time we start to get close. Meanwhile we're still dodging security and dragging an unwilling and very slow Jade along with us.

I can't imagine what is happening with the rest of the group—where they are, what they think has happened to us. And it keeps running in my mind, how I told Adam I wouldn't cause any trouble. Of course I didn't mean this, because how would I have even imagined it? But he is not going to be impressed. Not to mention, he is probably in a panic and making terrible assumptions about the kind of person I am.

By 5:00 p.m. we are sweaty, thirsty, hungry, sore, and completely stressed out. We've lost Talia again somewhere on Tom Sawyer Island and decide to pause and regroup. Wade and I slump on a bench and Jade sits down on the grass a few feet away, looking like she'd rather not be seen with us.

Suddenly two security guards jog in front of us, talking into walkie-talkies and looking toward the woods. They continue around and out of sight, and then we hear a distinctly Talia-like hoot coming from the same woods.

"That's her," I say, standing up, all exhaustion forgotten.

Wade is on his feet and running already. I dash over to Jade and pull her up.

"Come on! I think we found her."

"Yeah, well you can all jusfuckofffff…"

"No, Jade, it's Talia. Come on."

I tug at her arm and she comes, but not easily. Nevertheless, we're soon on the path after Wade.

"Know about you," Jade mutters.

"What?"

"Knowallaboutyou...fucking fake," she slurs. "Fuckingrichbitchfake."

"I thought we were over this."

"Fuckingruinmydaybitch."

"Focus, Jade. You can call me names later." I hear shouting erupt ahead and pick up the pace—as much as I can with Jade the deadweight along for the ride.

"She said...youwerecoming," Jade continues, still slurring but words clear.

I stop cold. Turn to Jade.

"What?"

She squints at me and then laughs.

"What did you say? Who said I was coming?"

"You know, your"   she puts her fingers up in air quotes and says—"friend."

"My friend?" *Please no.*

"Ssssydnnneyyyy. Hahahahahaaaaaaaa . Sydneyyourshittyfriend...s'true you can'trustanyone."

I'm standing there, jaw hanging open and watching Jade sway in front of me, and I feel like someone has stuck his hands into my insides and pulled them out.

And then we hear a screech and I remember why we're here.

"Shit—Talia! Come on, Jade."

"No," she says, and plops down on the ground. "I'll wait…here. I'mgoodhere."

"Fine. I think I've looked after you enough for one day," I say, and, though the events of the day should make me know better, I leave her there.

I arrive in time to find Wade, who has lost his disguise hat, rolling in the dirt with Sam and Ricky. He's outnumbered but they're wrecked, which means nobody's winning the fight.

Talia huddles nearby, shaking and—surprise, surprise—naked.

I'm trying to decide whether to go to Talia or enter the fray when one of the security guards bursts into the clearing, bellows, and jumps into the fight.

I run to Talia, casting about for her clothes, and another security guard comes running through the trees followed by Adam (I have never been so happy to see him) who is, in turn, followed by some guy with a camera. The fighting intensifies and then abruptly stops. The security guys have Ricky, Sam, and Wade pinned in the dirt and Adam is helping Wade to his feet.

With Wade standing, Adam's eyes land on me, and he rushes over.

"Jesus, Lola," he says, and for a second it looks like he's going to hug me. The relief in his eyes is intense, but it's soon replaced by fury. "You're okay?" he asks with a clenched jaw.

"Yes, but—"

"Not now."

"Right."

The guy with the camera is taking millions of pictures and suddenly I realize he's the same head-to-toe khaki guy from this morning, which means he must be a paparazzo and he might have been on us all day. Crap. He's all over Ricky, Sam, and Wade, but it'll only be a matter of time before he spots the *naked girl*, and I haven't been able to find any of her clothes.

If I had a T-shirt I'd gladly whip it off to cover her, but all I've got is my slip dress, which would leave *me* almost naked. Instead I opt for basically sitting behind her and wrapping my arms and legs strategically, trying to cover her, warm her up, and hide both our faces at the same time.

"Get that guy out of here," I scream at the security guards. "Get his camera and then get him the hell out."

The guard is busy handcuffing Ricky and Sam and ignores me. But Wade and Adam both hear and start toward the paparazzo, who takes one last shot of Wade and bolts into the trees and out of sight.

"Fuck," Adam says.

"Should we chase him down?" Wade asks.

"That's only going to make things worse at this point," Adam says. "Like things could get any worse."

"You have a point," Wade says.

Adam shakes his head and turns back toward Talia and me, then averts his eyes and swears again. I want so badly to talk to him, to explain, but it's not the time and maybe there won't ever be a time. This may just be too big of a disaster for us to get over, even as friends.

Meanwhile, one of the guards is unlocking another set

of cuffs and coming toward Talia.

"Are you kidding me?" I say. "You're cuffing her?"

"She's violated a number of park rules," the guard says. "And clearly she's been using drugs."

"But you don't—"

He ignores me, hauls her to her feet, and starts putting the cuffs on her.

"At least let me find her clothing," I say, and at that moment Adam barks out from behind us.

"Here. Got 'em."

They let Talia get dressed as Wade and Adam stand by, looking embarrassed and horrified at the same time.

Actually, Adam doesn't look embarrassed and horrified, he looks *furious* and horrified.

"Um, so where's everyone else?" Wade asks Adam as the security guards talk on their walkie-talkies and Talia and I stand side-by-side, my arm around her waist.

"Unlike you, they stayed together. Dr. Koch took them home to Sunrise." And then Adam's head snaps up and he looks at me. "Hang on, where's Jade? I heard she was with Talia."

"Oh, sorry to scare you, she's just down the path a bit," I say, and my stomach clenches as I remember what she was saying to me right before all of this happened.

"This path?" Adam says.

"Uh, yeah. She's not in the best shape, but she wasn't going anywhere. Rather the opposite, actually."

"All right," says the first security guard, interrupting us. "Security van's picking us up in five. Time to go."

They haul Ricky and Sam to their feet and inform us that Talia, Wade, and I have to go to their holding cells, too.

"You're under park arrest and I've got one more set of cuffs," he says, and puts them on Wade.

"Great," Adam mutters. "Fucking great."

We take the path back toward Jade. One look at her dilated pupils and they're going to arrest her, too, just to make sure our "sober outing" is a complete and utter disaster. And let's not forget there's a paparazzo sneaking around somewhere looking for a big payday. Wade Miller in handcuffs at Disneyland should do it.

But right then, we've got a bigger concern.

Because when we find Jade, she's lying face-first in a pile of blood and vomit.

And she's not breathing.

Chapter Thirty

The setting sun blazes orange and red in the sky. Cameras flash from beyond the barrier the Disney security team has put up. They tried at first to stop the picture taking, but there are too many people, too many cameras. Wade, Talia, and I stand side-by-side in handcuffs, each of us sick, pale, and terrified as the unconscious Jade is wheeled into the back of the ambulance. Adam is beside her and looks out at us with haunted eyes. The doors close with a double *thump* and I gasp.

Life is fragile.

The flashing lights and the wail of the siren fill the air as the Disney security guys take us inside to holding cells until someone from Sunrise can come to collect us.

Back at the center, we are each tested for drugs and then sent to solitary and given a plate of soggy food for dinner.

My dress is filthy, I'm sunburned, I've got scratches on my arms and legs, and the inside of my mouth feels like glue.

None of it matters.

I lie awake thinking about how my day went from fun and freedom to vomit and sirens.

And how every bit of it is my fault.

You are in the deepest of shit.

   You might have killed your roommate.

You've lost the trust of the best person you know.

You will never sleep again.

Those are my personal affirmations on Sunday morning.

But there is no actual affirmation.

Instead, an uncharacteristically silent Talia and I are escorted back to our room by a tech who refuses to tell us anything, given fifteen minutes to shower and dress, and finally taken to Dr. Koch's office.

The only person there is Adam, and my heart lurches at the sight of him. He's sitting on a high-backed wooden chair with his head in his hands, wearing the same clothes he had on yesterday. He has to have heard us enter, but he doesn't look up.

Talia's hand closes around my arm like a frozen claw, and the fear I've been fighting since we found Jade yesterday coalesces into a ball of chewed-up nails in my gut.

She's dead. Oh God, she must be dead.

Talia and I sit gingerly at the edge of the couch.

The door opens and Dr. Koch enters, followed by a pale and hollow-eyed Wade.

He gives me a wan smile and I try to return it, all the while remembering the moment yesterday when we thought we could sneak away for two minutes and get away with it, no big deal.

It's a pretty big deal if Jade is dead.

Even if she isn't.

After all, by now there are pictures of him splashed all over the internet—DRIFT STAR ARRESTED AT DISNEYLAND, DRIFT STAR IN FISTFIGHT OVER NAKED GIRL, DRIFT STAR IMPLICATED IN DISNEYLAND DRUG SCANDAL—and he's lucky if his show hasn't cut him loose. No one will have bothered to find out the truth before posting the pictures. They don't have to.

Dr. Koch and Wade both sit so the five of us are now in a rough circle.

"Please," I say finally, unable to contain myself, "how is… What's happened to…with…Jade?"

Adam finally looks up. His eyes are bloodshot and his skin has a grayish tinge.

I want to throw myself across the circle and hold him, be held by him. I want to be facing this—whatever it is we're about to face—together. But the gap that was between us is now more like an abyss.

Dr. Koch gestures to him, giving him the okay to speak.

He clears his throat. "I spent the night in the hospital and just left an hour ago."

Oh God. Oh, please God, I'll give up everything, anything. I'll be honest and responsible and stop pining after stupid things. I'll take my life as it is and just be grateful. I will become a proper fake alcoholic. Or a non-fake alcoholic. Or whatever it is I'm supposed to be.

I will become something better.

Better than I am.

"It was a very difficult night," Adam continues. "But as of an hour ago, Jade is…"

Pleasepleaseplease…

"…in stable condition and expected to recover."

I close my eyes and exhale, and the ball of nails in my gut shrinks. Beside me, Talia sobs. Across from me, Wade drops his head into his hands and breathes deeply, in and out. I don't even try to hide the gush of tears that comes along with my relief.

Dr. Koch simply sits very still in his chair, face and body revealing nothing.

Adam puts up a hand.

"Before we get too excited, know she's still in serious condition. And we need to get to the bottom of what happened yesterday, starting with why we got separated. Although…" He gives me a hard, disappointed look that speaks volumes. "I already have a good idea how that happened."

Yep, this is why the ball of nails is still lodged in my stomach. I look at my hands and try to swallow the shame, but it's not going anywhere because I fucked up. I was selfish and stupid and I fucked up and the results were practically catastrophic.

All of that after I promised him no trouble. Doubtful

he's struggling with any further feelings for me now.

"Anyway. Once we have your drug tests back and get to the bottom of it all, there are going to be consequences. Uh"—he clears his throat again—"probably for me as well. But we need to talk about what happened—ideally with the rest of the group that was there yesterday, so we can all process it. Most of them don't even know yet what happened."

"Nor will they," Dr. Koch says, coming into the conversation like a hammer—a velvet-covered hammer, but a hammer nonetheless.

"Wha— P-pardon me?" Adam stammers.

"You heard me. I know what I need to know and so do all of you. Beyond the people in this room, no one is to discuss any of the details of yesterday. That is my decision."

"But—"

"Today is not about processing. It's about damage control. I have a public relations nightmare on my hands: photographs of my patients circulating on the internet, another patient in the hospital, Mr. Miller's management team hounding me, and a veritable horde of upset parents on their way here at this very moment, all of them threatening to take their children out of the program and some threatening legal action."

"Well, that's why we need to—"

"Quiet," Dr. Koch snaps, and then stands, walks to the desk, picks up a small pile of papers, and turns back to us. "Here are the results of the drug tests."

He looks each of us, minus Adam, in the eye.

"No one has seen them but me." He lifts something that

looks like a garbage bin onto the desk, flips a switch, and proceeds to shred the documents while we sit there with our mouths hanging open.

He's destroyed evidence of Talia's guilt, sure, but also of Wade's and my innocence—at least in the category of drugs. This means if it ever got out that there were documents and they were destroyed, we would look guilty. Even to Adam we might look guilty.

"And now," he continues in a soft, steely voice, "I will tell you how this is going to go. This afternoon we will be having a community meeting that will include all patients and staff, plus any parents or visitors who have braved the paparazzi outside the gates. In this meeting I will strive to allay everyone's fears and reassure them that our patients—you—remain absolutely safe in our care. At that time I will explain to them how Miss Montgomery—your friend Jade—collapsed from a combination of heatstroke and de-hydration."

"Dehydration?" I say.

"That is correct. Dehydration." Dr. Koch stares me down. "Combined with heatstroke. And I believe that is consistent with what you saw, Miss Carlyle. Is it not?"

"Um…"

"It is. And that is what Miss Montgomery's hospital files say as well."

"But what about those two guys? Ricky and Sam? And that paparazzo—he took pictures of Talia and me, and of Wade fighting. And the entire universe saw us all standing around *in handcuffs*."

"The photographs from the paparazzo who followed you into the woods...have been found and destroyed. Suffice it to say I have my ways. My own resources. And those two miscreants are going to be too busy trying to save their own skins to make accusations. Disney security has handed them over to the authorities. They were found with substantial amounts of drugs on them, they may or may not be legally in the country, and they know they're lucky we're not pressing charges for attempted rape of a minor. The remaining difficulty is the photographs of you three, unmistakably in handcuffs. But Mr. Miller's people have come up with a solution, even for this. Mr. Miller, would you like to tell them?"

"Publicity stunt," Wade says with an apologetic shrug. "We're just going to say it was a publicity stunt for an upcoming action film I'm starring in."

"You're starring in an upcoming action film?" I ask.

"My manager says I can be," Wade answers with a chuckle. "We had some scripts we were looking at already. He's working on it. And in the end if it doesn't pan out, it's easy to say the project got scuttled."

Adam looks like he just ate goose turds, but he keeps his mouth shut.

It's ridiculous, of course. And potentially no one will believe it. But that's the thing—on the one hand, you can't hide anything from anyone in Hollywood these days, but on the other hand, you can have your people say almost anything to cover your ass and even if no one believes it, as long as there's no proof, it can still get you off the hook. So it may be ridiculous, but it'll probably work.

"Okay," I say. "But what do we say when someone asks how we got separated? Because it's more than just the people in this room who know about that."

A moment of awkward silence ensues.

"I mean, I know I did it," I say, careful not to look at Wade. "I instigated it. We were just…joking around but then it kind of snowballed."

Wade stares at the floor, Adam looks at me with sorrowful eyes, and Dr. Koch considers.

"I don't believe we'll be needing any confessions from you, Miss Carlyle. Why don't you leave that part to me and trust that I will not hang you out to dry."

"But—"

"Trust me."

"All right," I say.

But of course, I don't.

CHAPTER THIRTY-ONE

Wade stays behind to talk to Dr. Koch.

Talia goes to breakfast.

I find myself in the lobby with Adam.

"I'm sorry," I say.

He looks at me for a long time and I just stand there, dying.

"Can we talk somewhere?" I say.

"Is it going to change the outcome of yesterday?" he asks.

"No," I say. It comes out in a whisper. "Not in terms of Jade or Talia or any of that…horrible mess. But maybe in terms of what you think I… Well, I don't know what you think happened."

He turns and stalks off.

I follow, not sure if this is an invitation or if he's trying to get away, but unable to let him go. He ends up at a door to the outside, slides his card in, and goes out. The door almost hits me as I go through after him.

He follows the path out to the long, grassy area before the beach and stops in the middle of it. We're far enough away that no one would be able to hear us, but in plain sight of anyone who might look out a back window of the main building.

"Look, Lola," he says, still standing, legs wide, sending the clear message that this is not a cozy meeting and not a friendly one, either. "I'm angry and I'm other things, too. But whatever you have to say, whatever excuses you're going to make, the take-home point for me in all this is that I am at fault for my own lack of judgment. About leaving the group alone, about you, about my ability to be objective about you. Because probably you shouldn't have been there yesterday. But I vouched for you because I knew you wanted to go. And because I wanted you to be there. Obviously it was a mistake."

"Adam—"

"The worst and most obvious cost of that is one of our patients is in the hospital with an overdose," he says, running right over me and almost shouting. "But on a personal level…" He stops, takes a deep, shaking breath. "To have had to spend the day watching you and that fucking guy together, and then to find out you'd actually taken off with him—"

"But—"

"Don't lie to me, I know you did. My point is that every

single part of what happened yesterday is a lesson in poor judgment—my own poor judgment—that I'm not likely to forget."

I do my best to take it, stand there and let him get it out, even though it hurts. Regardless that he's got some of it wrong, I deserve this. Good intentions, I finally realize, do not excuse shitty results.

"Is there more you want to say?" I ask quietly when he stops talking.

"Not at the moment."

"All right. May I speak now?"

"My saying yes or no never stopped you before," he says, but not in the funny, rueful way he used to. "I'll tell you right now, I'm not interested in excuses and justifications or even really in apologies. But go ahead."

I want to ask him to sit down with me or maybe take a walk, but it's clear he's not going to do any of that. It's also clear he's not in the frame of mind to even hear anything I say. Still, I look at him, emotionally bruised, and ragged and raw from lack of sleep, and it seems like I can feel all of it— all the pain and anger and fear from the past twenty-four hours. I want to reach out and pull him close, run my hands over all the invisible wounds and make them better. I want him to do the same for me. But I can't. I can't lighten the effects or fix any of it, but I also can't turn away from him, can't help wanting to at least try.

"I'm not going to make excuses," I say, forcing myself to keep my distance, forcing myself not to beg or wheedle or try to be cute. "I was stupid and irresponsible and weak."

He nods.

"I've learned lessons I'm never going to forget, either, about poor judgment. I would say this qualifies as learning the hard way, and for the record, I don't think the learning is worth the price of what could have happened, or even what did happen."

He nods, but in agreement, not to let me off the hook.

"I did take off with Wade and it did cause a chain reaction, and I'm responsible for that. There's nothing I can do to make that untrue, Adam. Jade, Talia, the massive scandal we're dealing with—that's on me."

"And him," Adam points out.

"Sure, him. Both of us."

He crosses his arms over his chest and waits, watching me, and I have to steel myself because all of a sudden I want to cry.

"There are just a couple of things," I say, gutting it out, "that…maybe aren't going to matter to you, but…" I swallow. "Number one: we only left the group for a couple of minutes. It wasn't my intention to take off—we just went up over the hill."

Adam starts to talk but I hold up my hand.

"I know that doesn't excuse it. I just want to tell you that I came back and everyone was gone."

"*You* came back? What about him?"

"Well…" I squirm inside, uncomfortable with the idea of trying to pin anything on Wade, but also needing to tell the truth. "He was upset. So…I came back by myself, and then I made him come back, and we waited there for half an hour, hoping someone would return and find us. And then we were on our way to an information booth and we ran into Talia and Jade, and they were high and with those guys, and Talia took off and it all just…went to hell from there, basically, and we were trying to catch her the entire time from then on, until you found us. Again, it's not an excuse, but you need to know we weren't, like, partying or running around the park having fun."

"Do you have any idea how fucking scared I was, Lola?"

"Yes."

"Or how hurt?"

"I'm not with Wade, Adam."

"I don't mean that."

"No?"

"No," he says, not quite meeting my eyes. Then, "It's way bigger than that, than him."

"Him" comes out with a particular violence of tone, but I decide not to press.

"Fine, even if you don't care about him, I'm going to tell you: I'm not with him. I don't want to be with him. He somehow got the impression—okay, early on in the program I gave him the impression—that I liked him. I thought I did. And he came on like a tornado yesterday and I was…taken off guard and didn't want to be mean and okay, maybe I was feeling a little hurt still, and rejected by you. Even though I now fully understand—*fully*—why I'm not supposed to be falling for my mentor, and vice versa. So I didn't discourage him as much as I should have at first, and I didn't get how… sort of crazy he can be, and not taking no for an answer, and not believing when someone says she's not into him, which I finally had to just tell him, straight up."

Adam's posture shifts, just slightly, and I can tell he's at least listening.

"It took more than once for it to get through, and he didn't respond well, Adam."

"Is that why you took off with him?"

"It doesn't matter, I still did it. But…I was trying to be gentle with him because I finally got how fragile his ego is and how… Well, he's an addict and he's at a crossroads, right? I mean, I knew him as a kid, and he was a good kid. He was my friend. I didn't want to mess him up."

"Part of growing up is realizing you can't always have everything you want," Adam says. "He has to learn it."

"And so do I," I say, finding I need to look away… because I want Adam. Adam is really all I want right now, all I'm going to want for a long time. But the damage is too great, the trust is broken, and he was right that we shouldn't have been getting involved. "Anyway, I am sorry. I'm about as sorry as I can be. That's it."

He doesn't say anything. I gather my courage and look back up at him. He's less furious, but that's about all I can read from his expression.

"Are you… I guess you really are going to try to get reassigned now. From me."

A bark of laughter.

"What?"

"Reassigned? You think Koch is going to reassign me? You're hilarious."

"I…I don't get it."

"Oh, I think Dr. Koch has bigger plans for me than that."

"Wha—"

"Put it this way, Lola: I'm not going to be asking for any favors. I did this for the experience, for the money, sure, because I need to pay tuition, but also for the ability to put it on my résumé and have a good reference. I'll be lucky to get through the day with the job, much less the rest of it."

And with that, he heads back to the main building, lets me inside, and, feeling like a miserable, steaming pile of crap, I head upstairs to the dorm.

Chapter Thirty-Two

The community meeting starts two hours later, in the chapel.

Inside, they've set up a zillion chairs in a kind of stacked semicircle and the place is packed with staff, patients, and visitors. The room is buzzing with worry, anger, supposition, and a thick tension.

My eyes find Adam up front, facing forward in a chair like the rest of the staff. He's showered and shaved and even put on chinos and a button-down shirt, not to mention his game face. It's such a switch from his normal, casual uniform of jeans and T-shirt that I almost humiliate myself by gaping. He could be cast as a hot young lawyer (with a secret, gritty past he's brooding about) on a legal drama, or as a cocky young surgeon on a hospital show. My mouth is dry and my increased heart rate is totally inappropriate for the situation, inappropriate for all the situations I'll ever be in with him again, which is to say none. But still...

He is delicious—painfully so.

Wade is there, too, sitting in front with the other kids from yesterday. Like Adam and Talia and me, he's obviously showered and put on clean clothes. Unlike all of us, he looks miraculously fresh, unworried, and clear of conscience. There are two empty chairs beside him, but I pull Talia toward the back row. Unfortunately Dr. Koch sees us and zooms up the center aisle.

"Up front, ladies," he says. "We need everyone to see you hearty and whole."

Talia gets there first and leaves the seat next to Wade open.

I probably should have told her I'm off him, but there hasn't exactly been a good time for conversations about boys lately.

I sit down without looking at him. I will admit that once we were on Talia's trail yesterday, he stepped up, stopped being a jerk. But I can't help but remember the other side I saw, and I hate how he wants to go along with Koch now, and overall it's hard to feel friendly toward him.

"Carlyle," he says in a low tone, keeping his face forward.

"Yes?"

"I meant to say, I'm sorry about yesterday. I was kind of a tool, you know, about—"

"It's fine," I say, cutting him off before he can say more.

"I just...I'm pretty stressed out. And tired. All that stuff. I know you are, too. But you being my friend is the only good thing I have going right now."

I close my eyes.

"I just want us to get through this, okay?" he says, and reaches out to gently squeeze my hand. "And later, whenever we can, we'll talk. We'll have a big talk. I want to stay friends. Okay?"

"Okay," I say.

Moments later, Dr. Koch goes to stand at a lectern he's had set up at the front, and the room quickly goes silent.

He launches into the spiel: "As you are all aware, an incident occurred during one of our sober outings yesterday" — yada yada — "internet is a place of unfiltered information... Cannot be taken at face value" — blah blah — "set the facts straight and more importantly to reassure you" — and so on — "Miss Jade Montgomery...unfortunate accident...DE-HYDRATION...RECOVERING WELL... Because of our numerous high-profile patients...misinterpreted...used by the media...LIES...OUTRAGEOUS LIES..."

Ding, ding, ding. Clearly Dr. Koch does not suffer from any kind of internal bullshit bell. Meanwhile I'm hearing it and I'm not even the one talking.

Next comes the stuff about Wade and the handcuffs and the supposed movie, which apparently Talia and I are also cast in.

"The man has no shame," I murmur.

"No kidding," Talia whispers back.

"Can you act?" I ask her.

"Not well," she says.

Then he has Wade stand up and everyone *cheers* and Dr. Koch gestures toward Wade's management team — three of them sitting together looking very shiny and Hollywood next to two slightly frumpy and extremely wholesome-looking people who I realize, with a shock, must be Wade's parents—and all of it is suddenly like we're at freaking Comic-Con or the Sundance Festival, instead of in rehab.

Two weeks ago that would have made me happy.

Wade sits down just as Dr. Koch is saying, "And I'm guessing if we're very lucky, Mr. Miller would sign some autographs after the meeting for those of you who may be fans…"

"Are you kidding me?" I mutter.

"Better than being kicked out," he whispers back, but his face is taking on a pinkish hue.

"Uh, you shouldn't have to sign autographs in rehab, Wade."

"This is one of those real-life things, Lola," he says, his voice taking on an edge. "Play the game. Or it plays you."

"Those your parents back there?"

He nods grimly.

I turn for another peek.

His mom is tiny and trim and put together in what I imagine is a going-to-church-in-Ohio kind of ensemble—a long flowered skirt and matching ivory sweater set. His dad is lean and broad-shouldered in a checked navy-and-white shirt and khakis.

"They're cute," I whisper.

"Thanks. Yours, too."

"What?"

"Shh. Right behind them."

"No." But I do a subtle check and proceed to have a minor coronary because Wade is correct—my mom is sitting just behind and to the left of Wade's parents, and directly beside her is my dad.

"Holy shit," I whisper.

"Merry Christmas," Wade says.

The people I would normally most want to see, on the day I least want to see them, not to mention in the place I least want to see them, and sitting together, no less. Nothing like a scandal to bring on the supposedly concerned parents. They both look like they'd rather snort wasabi than acknowledge each other, which means Dr. Koch probably strong-armed them into it.

For the first time since this morning, I'm happy I agreed to go along with Dr. Koch's cover-up, because what I do not need is my mom and dad to know I am the person whose reckless actions nearly killed someone less than twenty-four hours ago.

Of course, there's another problem. If my parents stick around after this meeting, anyone who spends more than a minute in the same room as us will know how full of shit I've been about them. They'll all see how "Daddy's Girl" is a term that could only be applied ironically. God help me, we might even get dragged into group family therapy, and then both my parents will either be lying their asses off or it'll be obvious to everyone that they don't know anything about me and basically don't give a shit.

This thought shoots through me like a downward-facing space shuttle, scorching my insides, and all of a sudden it's clear to me that this knowledge/fear that my parents don't care about me, and the fear that everyone will find out, and under that fear the very deepest fear that *they're right not to and I am essentially worthless,* is at the root of almost every crazy, stupid thing I've ever done.

It is my deeper why.

I sit in the midst of the meeting, floored, and glance at Adam. I wish I could talk to him about this, because it's sort of huge and he would get it. And Dr. Owens. She would be very excited for me right now. I wonder if she has another bell, one she could ring for truth, because I can practically hear it.

"And now I'll open up the floor to questions, in case any of you have lingering concerns," Dr. Koch says, his voice breaking into my thoughts as he winds up his speech.

Of course the panic and anger in the room have subsided, what with the reassurances and Dr. Koch's nauseating charm combined with the prospect of a celebrity autographing session. Nevertheless, several hands shoot up, and the doctor starts fielding questions.

Simultaneously reeling from my little epiphany and trying to figure out how to deal with the upcoming face-to-face with Mom and Dad, I tune back out.

But a few minutes later, there's a shift in the energy of the room and Dr. Koch is wearing his gravest face and saying something about consequences for the staff member responsible for the patients at the time we became separated.

Adam has gone pale and is unnaturally still. He seems to know what's coming. I didn't believe him earlier, but now I do.

Trust me…

Yeah, right.

He's about to fire Adam—and in the most humiliating, public way possible.

He's stringing him up, essentially.

For something *I* did.

My insides, ringing with bells of truth and clarity and freaking rainbows just a few minutes ago, now twist and clench and boil.

I swallow, remembering how this morning I vowed to become something better if only Jade would live.

And she's alive.

Time seems to stretch, giving me a sudden, strange, quiet space in my mind. (Holy cow, it's the quiet place.) All this time I've been pretending to be something better than I am, all the while feeling worse, and yet hoping that pretending will somehow make it real and I can go back to feeling wanted and loved and all that crap that seemed to disappear when my family blew up. I would get it from my parents or I would get it from Wade. Or I would get it from my parents because they would see I had Wade and suddenly think me worthy. Or I would get it from Wade, which would make me care less about not having it from them. Or something.

Even with Adam, even though my attraction to him feels different from all that, still I might have used him just to fill the hole. Except he knew it somehow, and he wouldn't let me.

The point is, I keep doing things to make people love me…being bad, being good, pretending not to care, faking and bullshitting my way through everything...

It wasn't supposed to hurt anyone, but here's Adam about to get fired and possibly have his education and future jeopardized, on top of everything else.

Telling the truth wouldn't make them love me any better. And Wade would be furious and I'd probably get kicked out and Adam would probably still get fired.

Better to stay out of it, right?

Exactly.

Except I appear to be on my feet all of a sudden, saying, "You can't fire Adam."

"Indeed I can," says Dr. Koch with a lift of his eyebrow.

"Well, you can, but you shouldn't. Because it's my fault."

Dr. Koch levels an icy look at me.

Wade tugs at my arm.

"Sit the hell down," he says under his breath.

I yank my arm away.

Fuck it. *I* have to love me better.

And so I stay on my feet and tell the truth.

Well, most of it.

Some of it.

That is, I tell the part that should keep Adam from being fired—that Adam had no choice but to leave us alone, trusting us as a group, and then I was the one who stupidly instigated everyone taking off. I skip the stuff about Wade and me because it's private, and I leave out Jade and Talia taking drugs and Talia running around naked because I don't want to cause either of them any more problems and I figure if they feel the need to confess, that's up to them.

Plus I'm very aware that Dr. Koch is looking more wound up with every word I speak and it doesn't take him long to weigh in. "This young lady has proven herself to be unstable. She has been disruptive and disingenuous."

"Yes, I have, Dr. Koch. You're right. And I'm very sorry."

This stops him, at least temporarily.

"I realize now that I took this whole experience too lightly. I didn't understand addiction or the crazy things it can make you do. I wasn't even sure I had anything wrong with me—I actually kind of thought I was coming to a spa. Funny, right?"

A few people—fellow patients—actually laugh.

"Turns out I have my share of issues, though, and I'm coming around to believing when things go wrong we should admit it and talk about it, not hide it and cover it up and bury it inside. That doesn't work, especially not for addicts. I mean, what good does it do me to let someone else get fired for my actions?"

I turn to look at Adam, whose stunned, fixed stare makes me dizzy for a moment. I continue, looking right back at him. "Why would I do that to someone who has been awesome to me even when I've been a total pain in the ass, and gone out of his way for me, and taught me—taught me by example— some of the most important things I'll ever learn about trust and…love…and…" I clear my throat, freaking out inside that I just said "love," while looking straight at him. "And… putting other people's needs before your own? Why would I let that happen to someone I care about? I won't."

"You are poisonous," Dr. Koch says, practically sputtering. No doubt he can already taste the shit he's going to be in once someone thinks to ask why Adam was left to chaperone ten teenage addicts all by himself. "You are a master manipulator and a nuisance."

"Excuse me, that is my daughter you are speaking to."

I stop breathing entirely as people around me gasp.

Because Ben-freaking-Carlyle, my *dad*, is on his feet, and he is pissed.

"This is a gong show," he continues in his booming, perfectly enunciated, Yale-trained voice, his sheer presence dwarfing almost everyone in the room. "It is an outrage. And you, Dr. Koch, are a most despicable little weasel. A cockroach."

"Ben, don't," my mother murmurs into the silence. "You're not helping."

"Mr. Carlyle," Dr. Koch intones, then clears his throat, "you know how pleased I am that you're here, but perhaps we can discuss your daughter in private, once this meeting is over."

"Don't you try to handle me," Dad roars. "And don't you insult my daughter simply because you're too weak and stupid to handle *her*. She is worth a hundred of you."

My throat is tight and I'm shaking. It's beautiful and also terrible because once Dad gets into this zone, no one is safe from his temper—not Dr. Koch, not the staff and patients, not the strangely familiar-looking guy sitting right beside Dad.

Well, my mom can stop him. Sometimes. And now she's on her feet, a picture of blazing righteousness. "Can it, Ben," she says.

"I will not," he thunders.

As my parents start to have it out in front of practically the entire universe, I put my hands over my ears. *LA LA LAAA...*

But it doesn't stop me from hearing the next thing, which is Mom saying, "Don't come in here pretending you give a shit when you have been a total asshole and an absentee father. You're the one who froze Lola out more than a year ago. I'm sure you're the reason she started drinking in the first place."

No, no, nooooo...

"Mom," I manage to choke out, "I never said—"

"You didn't have to. I know what he's like."

"Jules," Dad says, and then turns his tone from fire to ice, "we do not discuss our problems in public. And regardless, I am here now, am I not?"

"Oh my God, stop," I say, voice breaking. "Please stop."

They stop. Too late, but they do stop.

I'm back to having serious doubts about the benefits of honesty, especially when it causes this kind of snowball effect.

On the other hand, I'm still standing here.

I've been exposed, unmasked, and totally mortified. And it didn't kill me.

Become something better.

I sigh. "Look: I never *started* drinking. Okay? I didn't just exaggerate, and I wasn't confused. I faked it. I lied. I lied because I actually wanted to come here, crazy as that seems now. And yeah, since it's out there—thanks, Mom—my dad and I don't have such an amazing relationship. I lied about that, too—to everyone. I didn't want to be the daughter someone would dump and just…walk away from because of a stupid fight." I meet my dad's eyes. "And I didn't want you to be the kind of person who would do it, who wouldn't try harder instead of bailing. So I lied, told people what I wanted to be true, and hoped at some point reality would line up. But…it didn't exactly pan out."

Dad holds my gaze for a moment and then breaks it, looks down. Obviously he's not thinking I'm worth a hundred of Dr. Koch now, and my mom looks mad enough to spit.

I have to get the hell out of here.

"So," I say, "I'm a fake and a liar. Sorry, everyone. I guess there are worse things to be, but it feels pretty shitty. What I am not lying about is my part in yesterday's fiasco, though, and that's what I stood up to talk about. If none of you trusts my word—I guess I can't blame you if you don't—there are others here who can back it up. I'm really sorry, Adam. Don't worry, Dr. Koch, I'm going. Again. I hope your paparazzo friend"—I point at the guy sitting next to my dad—"the same guy who followed us around all day yesterday, I believe, gets all the details right. Including the fact that you have him, or his agency, on speed dial."

Everyone turns to look at the guy, whose guilty expression gives him away instantly, and then to Dr. Koch, who is, for once, caught off guard, and also looking guilty as hell.

Suffice it to say I have my ways…

"See you later, Dr. Koch," I murmur, delighted and simultaneously nauseated that my hunch about this was correct. "Suffice it to say I have my ways, too."

Chapter Thirty-Three

Adam finds me at the beach where I am standing arms out, eyes closed, pressing myself against the wind.

"The beach is closed, Lola," he says, coming to a stop a few feet away from me.

"I know."

"Should I even ask how you got down here?"

"Celebu-spawn superpowers," I say, risking a sideways glance at him. "Should I even ask how you found me?"

He cocks his head. "Mentor superpowers."

I'm doing my best to act normal, to pretend I didn't just practically declare my love for him in front of everyone, and then admit I'm a huge liar and a fake about everything else. Another thing I have to live with.

"I came to say thank you," he says, rather formally. "And wow. You left Koch in such hot water he forgot all about firing me. You probably saved my job…"

"Yeah, but then there's Jade in the hospital, Talia relapsing, Wade bullshitting when recovery is all about being honest."

"They made their choices. It's not all about you."

I choke back a laugh.

"What?"

"I just hear that a lot."

"Maybe I should have said 'on'—it's not all *on* you," he says. "It's a pretty wild swing—you've gone from never taking any responsibility to taking all of it. By the way, your parents are up at the mansion waiting to talk to you."

"Oh God."

"No, I think it's good. They seem… I don't know them, but they seem okay."

"Keep in mind, my mother's an actor and my dad's a very charming guy when he feels like it."

"But they seem subdued. Kind of the opposite of all that. And they weren't fighting. Don't be scared."

I roll my eyes.

"Don't try to tell me you're not," he says.

"Don't make me say I am."

I turn back out to face the water, and he does the same.

The silence is awkward and full of all the things we've said, all the things there's no point saying. I'm under no illusions—this is good-bye. I'm grateful, at least, that I'll get to say it. Hopefully I'll manage not to cry my face off.

"Why'd you do it, Lola?" he asks after a couple of minutes.

"Which part?" I say, still not looking at him. "I seem to have done a lot."

"Why'd you come here? I mean, why would you want to if you're really not an addict?"

"You saying you believe me now?" At this, I can't help turning to study him.

"Can you just answer the question?" he says in his bran muffin voice.

"I came to make life miserable for my mentor, apparently."

"In that case, you succeeded." He crosses his arms over his chest to show me he's still waiting for my real answer.

"And I wanted a tighter ass."

His eyes narrow.

"And a better tan."

"You could get both of those at home. Don't you live on the beach?"

"Okay, honestly, Adam? It's so fucking stupid, I'm not going to tell you."

"*More* stupid than a tight ass and a tan?"

"Much more. Okay, let me put it this way: I was trying to recover something I lost. Something I thought I lost. But I couldn't really get it back because it wasn't what I thought it was. And maybe I never had it in the first place. Deep, huh?"

"Not to mention cryptic."

I laugh.

"But not stupid," he says, eyes finally softening a little. "It doesn't sound stupid at all."

"Oh, believe me, I gave you the positive spin. I have changed, though. Learned a few things. Kind of an uphill battle, but still."

"Well, you've *grown*. I don't know about changed. You're

still very much…you."

"Yeah," I say, flushing and looking down at the sand.

"What's wrong?"

I shake my head, refusing to look up at him because I might start sobbing. And that would suck.

"Lola," he says, coming closer, which is torture. "What?"

"Just…I'm guessing I'm about to be kicked out, so this might be the last time I see you." I stop, swallow hard, stare at the sand. "I would have liked it to be more…I would like not to have fucked everything up so thoroughly."

"Ah, that," he says. "You know what the thing is about you, though?"

"Mm?"

"Look at me, Lola."

I look up.

"As thoroughly as you tend to fuck things up, you have a pretty extravagant way of…fixing them, or making up for them, anyway."

I allow myself a tiny smile and blink back the tears.

"So I have good news and bad news," he says.

"Go ahead," I say, bracing myself. "Tell me."

"You are being kicked out, and your parents are going to take you home."

"Is that the good or the bad?"

"Both," he says.

"And that's because…?"

He comes closer, holding my eyes captive with his superpower gaze.

"Because you're so kicked out that you're not even

going to have outpatient privileges."

"And that's good news because...?"

"Because I am only going to be your mentor for about... five more minutes."

The circus starts up again in my stomach.

"And?" I say. "Last I checked, you considered it kind of a lifetime position."

"I did, yes." He nods, then reaches out and takes my hands in his. "But I'm allowed to change my mind."

"You *don't* want to be my lifetime mentor, then?" I'm staring at him, searching his face for confirmation of what I think, hope, he's saying.

"I want a lot of things," he says, voice husky. "But no, I don't want that."

"All right then, Adam." I grip his hands, feeling like I might burst, feeling like I could go up in smoke at any moment. "In that case I'm totally firing you. I'm firing you right now. Because five minutes seems like a really long time to wait for—"

I don't get to say anything else because all of a sudden Adam is kissing me. One second we're standing there holding hands and talking, and the next he's swooped me up into his arms and his mouth is on mine, hot, deliberate, and full of a million pent up emotions.

If I thought my clothes were going to melt off last time, this is a whole other level of melting—melting and melding, drowning and flying, my entire sense of reality dropping away so there is only this moment, and there is only him, me, us.

We kiss until we are gasping and I think I might be crying and really it feels like we both might fall down if we didn't have the other person to hold us up because we are dizzy, drunk, on fire.

He holds my face to his so we are forehead to forehead.

"We have to stop," he says, clearly no more ready to than I am,

"Not again," I almost wail.

"No, no. So you can go up there and make this official."

"Oh. Official, huh," I say, trying to get my brain back online and pull myself together.

"Officially not professionally connected," he says, still holding me. "Not to mention, you'll be free to invite me to your house for lasagna from New York City."

"I'm inviting you to my house to lock you in my bedroom," I say. "I may or may not feed you first."

He gives me a boiling-hot look, pulls me even tighter up against him again, gives me a hard kiss, then steps away with obvious reluctance, keeping his eyes on me.

"Real world," he says, his back to the ocean and jerking his thumb toward the stairs.

"Give me a minute," I say, coming back to him, sliding my hands up his (very chiseled) abs, up to his shoulders, and slowly walking him backward as I kiss his lips, his cheeks, his neck.

"A minute…for what?" he says, trying to focus but not succeeding.

I slip my hands up under his shirt, around to his bare back, holding onto him and kissing him deeply, hoping to keep him distracted as our feet enter the water.

"Lola?" he mumbles, his mouth against mine. "What are you doing?"

And that's when I use my body weight against his to tumble him backward, with me on top of him, into the ocean.

"What the hell...?" He's roaring and laughing and trying to pin me in the sand. "Now you're really in trouble."

I kiss him fast, then escape, grinning like a fool. "I told you I'd do this when you didn't expect it."

"You're right, I did not expect that."

"If you're going to be scandalized you should close your eyes," I say, and then I pull my T-shirt over my head and throw it onto the sand.

He almost chokes, then covers his eyes with his hands. "I'm not scandalized," he says. "That's not at all a description of what I am right now. But what exactly are you doing?"

"If I'm getting kicked out anyway, I'm going skinny-dipping first."

"I don't suppose you'd listen if I forbid you to—"

"Forbid me?" I howl with laughter, then go deeper into the water so I can wriggle out of the rest of my clothes discreetly. "Good luck with that, Cupcake. And by the way, I am going to mock you so hard every time you use that voice. I fired you, remember?"

"Oh, I remember. I think it's pretty much seared onto my brain matter," he says, peeking out of one eye, then opening them both when he realizes I'm underwater from the neck down.

"Plus, I don't want you to think I've stopped being me."

And with that, I toss the rest of my clothing onto the beach and swim out into the deep water.

On the shore, Adam gets to his knees and watches me, seeming to know I need a minute alone.

The wind has dropped, leaving the water calm, smooth, and cool while above me the sun is hot, and for this moment in time, everything feels amazing.

Yes, I'm still sick about Jade, embarrassed about being unmasked, and I feel stupid about holding a four-year torch for a guy I never really knew. But I'm happy to have met Talia, and even Jade, because they both helped me learn a few things—about myself and about life. And at least in the end I managed to stand up and do one decent thing.

Plus, out of it all came Adam, who's real, and loves me for real, even if he hasn't said so yet.

I breathe deeply, swimming in wide circles, feeling my muscles flex and extend.

Yes, the rehab project turned out to be an epic freaking disaster.

But I wouldn't trade it.

And come to think of it, once we're away from here, I could probably get Adam to bounce a quarter off my butt cheeks—if only to humor me.

Acknowledgments

It takes many dedicated people, besides the writer, to get a book out into the world. I am tremendously grateful to have had wonderful, smart, talented, and hardworking people on my team, from conception to publication of this book. Among my friends, family, and the greater writing community I'm so lucky to be a part of, there are too many people to name. To all of you: thank you. It would be very lonely, and so much harder, without you.

There are some specific people who need to be thanked. My deepest gratitude and appreciation go out to:

-my agent, Emmanuelle Morgen, for her hard work, sharp eye, and patience, as she worked with me on every stage of this book;

-my Entangled editor Stacy Abrams, for giving the book such detailed and intuitive attention, for helping me to make it better and better, and for being gentle when she had to tell me some of my references were out-of-date or slightly less than cool;

-Bev Katz Rosenbaum for connecting me with Stacy, and Entangled, in the first place;

-the fabulous team at Entangled, including Alexandra Shostak for the fabulous cover art, Erin Crum for her meticulous copyediting, Heather Riccio and Debbie Suzuki for publicity, Meredith Johnson for production, and the rest of the team, including marketing and sales people at both Macmillan and Raincoast…at the time of this writing I don't yet know them all by name, but I know it's a stupendous group of talented and hardworking people;

-my early readers and critique partners: Bev Katz Rosenbaum, Maureen McGowan, Joanne Levy, Keith Cronin, Shelley Saville, Michael Wacholtz and Nicole Muyres;

-Stephanie Saville, another of my beta readers, and my very generous go-to for general psychology research and more specifically, information about rehabilitation programs, treatment methods, and teen addiction;

-Veronica Canfield for specifics on the legal details and practices of rehabilitation centers from state to state;

-Lainey Lui, for the intelligent and thought-provoking assessment and coverage of Hollywood Gossip on her blog, www.laineygossip.com, which influenced my own thoughts on celebrity and its effects on character;

-Kimberley Stevens, for helping me push through the first draft of this by setting a timer and making me work while she sweated it out on the elliptical machine right behind me;

-in addition to those listed above as beta readers, fellow authors Adrienne Kress, Caitlin Sweet, Tish Cohen, Lesley Livingston, Eileen Cook, Jon Clinch, Jessica Keener, Renee Rosen, Sachin Waikar, Karen Dionne, Lauren Baratz-Logsted, Elizabeth Letts, all of whom have offered encouragement and inspiration over the years;

-my family—my incredibly supportive husband, Michael, and our two sweet girls, who all pitch in to help when I have a deadline; Cindy and Gary Ullman, Beatrice and Jim Wacholtz, Brian Younge, and the larger circle of family, encompassing Saville, Ullman, Wacholtz, and Younge, all of whom have been immeasurably supportive and awesome;

-and finally, my readers—it would be pointless without you!

From the bottom of my heart, thank you.

LIFE UNAWARE

by Cole Gibsen

Regan Flay is following her control-freak mother's "plan" for high school success, until everything goes horribly wrong. Every bitchy text or email is printed out and taped to every locker in the school. Now Regan's gone from popular princess to total pariah. The only person who speaks to to her is former best-friend's hot-but-socially-miscreant brother, Nolan Letner. And the consequences of Regan's fall from grace are only just beginning. Once the chain reaction starts, no one will remain untouched...

WHATEVER LIFE THROWS AT YOU

by Julie Cross

When seventeen-year-old track star Annie Lucas's dad starts mentoring nineteen-year-old baseball rookie phenom, Jason Brody, Annie's convinced she knows his type—arrogant, bossy, and most likely not into high school girls. But as Brody and her father grow closer, Annie starts to see through his façade to the lonely boy in over his head. When opening day comes around and her dad—and Brody's—job is on the line, she's reminded why he's off-limits. But Brody needs her, and staying away isn't an option.

PAPER OR PLASTIC

by Vivi Barnes

Busted. Lexie Dubois just got caught shoplifting a cheap tube of lipstick at the SmartMart. And her punishment is spending her summer working at the weird cheap-o store, where the only thing stranger than customers are the staff. Coupon cutters, jerk customers, and learning exactly what a "Code B" really is (ew). And for added awkwardness, her new supervisor is the very cute—and least popular guy in school— Noah Grayson. And this summer, she'll learn there's a whole lot more to SmartMart than she ever imagined...

My Not So Super Sweet Life

by Rachel Harris

The daughter of Hollywood royalty, Cat Crawford just wants to be normal. But when her prodigal mother reveals that she has something important to tell her daughter…causing a media frenzy, normal goes out the window. Lucas Capelli knows his fate is to be with Cat Unfortunately, a scandal could take him away from the first place he's truly belonged. As secrets are revealed, rumors explode, and the world watches, Cat and Lucas discover it's not fate they have to fight if they want to stay together, it's their own insecurities. Well, and the stalkerazzi.

Photo Credit: Jirg Kao-Beserve

Danielle Younge-Ullman is a novelist, playwright, and freelance writer. She studied English and theater at McGill University, then returned to her hometown of Toronto to work as a professional actor for ten years. Danielle's short story, *Reconciliation*, was published in *Modern Morsels*—a McGraw-Hill anthology for young adults—in 2012; her one-act play, *7 Acts of Intercourse*, debuted at Toronto's SummerWorks Festival in 2005; and her adult novel, *Falling Under*, was published by Penguin in 2008. Danielle lives in Toronto with her husband and two daughters.

www.danielleyoungeullman.com

Lola Carlyle is lonely, out of sorts, and in for a boring summer. So when her best friend, Sydney, calls to rave about her stay at a posh Malibu rehab and reveals that the love of Lola's life, Wade Miller, is being admitted, she knows what she has to do. Never mind that her worst addiction is decaf cappuccino; Lola is going to rehab.

Lola arrives at Sunrise Rehab intent on finding Wade, saving him from himself, and—naturally—making him fall in love with her...only to discover she's actually expected to be an addict. And get treatment. And talk about her issues—the ones she refuses to admit, even to herself. Plus she has insane roommates, and an irritatingly attractive mentor, Adam, who's determined to thwart her at every turn.

Oh, and Sydney? She's gone.

In a place full of fragile, damaged people, L̶o̶l̶a̶ ̶i̶s̶ ̶a̶b̶l̶e̶. But like it or not, she will be rehabilitated. And along t̶h̶e̶ ̶w̶a̶y̶ ̶d̶ herself, and love...if she can open her heart l̶o̶n̶g̶ ̶e̶n̶o̶u̶g̶h̶ ̶t̶o̶ pen.

"An intoxicating blend of romance, humor, and honest emotion that will keep readers turning pages."
—Eileen Cook, author of *Remember*

a Stacy Cantor Abrams Collection book

entangled TEEN

an imprint of Entangled Publishing, LLC

Simply thrilling.   Entangled Publishing, LLC

US $9.99 | CAN $11.50
ISBN 978-1-62266-785-7
5 0 9 9 9 >

9 781622 667857

www.entangledpublishing.com